"[Diana's] inexorable descent into mania, narrated by her brother Dave, is as gripping as the mystery itself. A–."

—*Entertainment Weekly*

"Cook is one of the most literary of psychological-suspense authors. . . . The narrative [of *The Cloud of Unknowing*] is sustained by its thematic richness and the subtlety of its psychological portraits of tormented characters. . . . [Cook] writes eloquently about the fears that lead people to equate intelligence with madness, suppressing the imagination and taking refuge in mediocrity."

—Marilyn Stasio, *The New York Times*

"A chilling thriller wrapped in a study of insanity . . . in this well-crafted story, Cook explores the tragic consequences of a life where there is plenty of knowledge, but love is in desperately short supply."

—*Calgary Herald* (Canada)

"Cook writes piercing thrillers that often have a haunting quality, and that is certainly the case with *The Cloud of Unknowing*. . . . The brilliant structure . . . makes for consuming suspense almost too concentrated to bear."

—*New York Daily News*

"An eerie, unsettling, beautifully composed and suspenseful novel quite unlike anything Cook has written before. So spare and precise, it feels as if it has been chiseled in stone with something like a surgical instrument."

—Joyce Carol Oates

"Cook is a consistently fine author of psychological novels, the kind that leave a nasty chill at the end. *The Cloud of Unknowing* is one of his best, an intriguing study of madness and murder, with surprising depth of characterization. . . . Cook is masterful when he takes us into the sad, unhappy worlds of the Sears family. . . . There's also a twist at the end that will leave you really stunned."   —*The Globe and Mail* (Toronto)

"A superbly structured tale written in an elegant, literary style."
—Associated Press

"Cook smartly goes against genre expectations. . . . What's at stake isn't so much the resolution of a mystery as the integrity of a family."   —*Time Out New York*

"A new novel by Thomas Cook is one of those little treasures in life. He is undoubtedly one of the finest fiction writers putting pen to paper these days. And each offering is suitably different from the last to leave readers in awe. *The Cloud of Unknowing* doesn't fail his fans. . . . Fascinating . . . Once again, Thomas Cook has produced a novel which begs to be read in one sitting."
—*Calgary Sun* (Canada)

"Unusual, chilling . . . Cook reveals all the pieces of the shocking story with an absolutely steady hand. It's a bravura performance."
—*Publishers Weekly* (starred review)

"In crisp, chilling prose, Cook deftly juxtaposes the maddeningly complex Sears family and a straight-shooting detective 'rooted in a world where crimes leap like fish from crystal streams of motivation.'"   —*Booklist* (starred review)

"This is not a mystery in any typical sense. Rather, it is a deeply compelling literary exploration of the effects of madness through several generations."   —*Library Journal*

THE CLOUD OF UNKNOWING

ALSO BY THOMAS H. COOK

FICTION

Blood Innocents
The Orchids
Tabernacle
Elena
Sacrificial Ground
Flesh and Blood
Streets of Fire
Night Secrets
The City When It Rains
Evidence of Blood
Mortal Memory
Breakheart Hill
The Chatham School Affair
Instruments of Night
Places in the Dark
Interrogation
Taken (based on the teleplay by Leslie Boehm)
Moon over Manhattan (with Larry King)
Peril
Into the Web
Red Leaves

NONFICTION

Early Graves
Blood Echoes
A Father's Story (as told by Lionel Dahmer)
Best American Crime Writing: 2002, 2003, 2004, 2005, 2006 editions
(ed. with Otto Penzler)

THOMAS H. COOK

THE
CLOUD
OF
UNKNOWING

An Otto Penzler Book

A Harvest Book • Harcourt, Inc.

Orlando   Austin   New York   San Diego   London

www.HarcourtBooks.com

The Library of Congress has cataloged the hardcover edition as follows:
Cook, Thomas H.
The cloud of unknowing/Thomas H. Cook.—1st ed.
p. cm.
"An Otto Penzler book."
1. Brothers and sisters—Fiction.   2. Schizophrenia—Fiction.
3. Family—Fiction.   4. Psychological fiction.   I.Title.
PS3553.O55465C57   2007
813'.54—dc22   2006013951
ISBN 978-0-15-101260-2
ISBN 978-0-15-603280-3 (pbk.)

Text set in AGaramond
Designed by Cathy Riggs

Printed in the United States of America

First Harvest edition 2007
A C E G I K J H F D B

For Julian and Lillian Ritter,

second parents

The patient search and vigil long
Of him who treasures up a wrong.
—LORD BYRON

You thought you were a crystal stream, cleansed of debris, especially the vast store of facts and quotations you'd early acquired and later suppressed, so that you'd finally become exactly what the Old Man had so contemptuously called you, a "movie fan."

But in truth you were a river of fear, clogged and murky, with your own dark undertow.

You know how deep this river ran by what has been dislodged from its silt-covered bottom, a whole world of buried reading.

You suddenly recall Tolstoy's "Three Deaths." You remember following the story through the first death, then the second, growing anxious as it nears its end and still there is no third death, nor even any character who seems destined to suffer it. Then a workman appears, an ax balanced on his shoulder, trudging across a cemetery toward a large tree. With the first blow of the ax you feel the great tree shudder. Its outspread limbs tremble in panic. You sense the tree's terror in every quaking leaf. With each blow, it weakens, a life force

I

ebbing until the murdered tree finally groans, falls, becomes the tale's third death.

Now four deaths swirl around you like the splintered remnants of a stricken ship. You feel a hint of unexpected moisture on your fingertip, rising water at your ankles, a span of rain-drenched black wrought iron, a heavy limb.

A guard appears, his badge muted by the dull gray light. Still, for a moment, you can focus on nothing but the badge. Then it flashes brightly, like a photographer's bulb, and you wonder if that is how she saw it, blinding, and in some way unforgiving.

The guard draws open the cell's steel door.

"Detective Petrie is ready for you now," he says.

You rise from the cot, move across the concrete floor, then down the corridor and into a room where you expect to find Petrie waiting to hear your version of what happened. You have waived your rights, and will, according to your own counsel, tell your tale.

But Detective Petrie is not yet in the room, so you take a moment to survey it, get your bearings as best you can. There is a card table with a coffee machine, its glass urn already full of coffee. A stack of Styrofoam cups rests next to the machine. There is a clock on the wall, and a calendar.

You walk to the window, and peer out at the small portion of the world that has held your little life like a pebble in its palm. You have become a student of reenacted murders. You recall a TV movie about the Hillside Strangler, how the prosecutor took the jury to a hill, then had the light from a police helicopter move first to this spot, then that one, then that one over there, each where a body had been found. The last light illuminated the killer's house, the grim geometric center of this carnage. Now you stare out the window and move your gaze like a spotlight from Victor Hugo Street to Dolphin Pond, to Carey Towers, to Salzburg Garden. You imagine long bands of yellow tape running from site to site, connecting supposed scenes of crime.

"Mr. Sears."

You turn.

Petrie steps into the room and closes the door behind him. "Have a seat."

He nods toward a table and two chairs. You notice a tape recorder, a notepad, a blue pen. You recognize these things as the usual instruments of interrogation, though you know you are surely not the usual suspect.

You walk to the table and sit down.

Petrie sits down in the chair across from you, turns on the tape recorder, recites his name, your name, the date, time, location. He is dressed very neatly, everything in place, jacket buttoned, the knot of his tie pulled tight and straightened, a cool professional, convinced he has heard it all, will not be jarred by what you have to tell him.

"Ready?" he asks.

You don't know where to begin. There is so much to tell, so many currents in the river.

"Ready?" Petrie repeats.

A woman's voice chants in your mind.

> *Father/Sister*
>
> *Twister.*
>
> *Father/Daughter*
>
> *Slaughter.*

You are a river of fear, with bodies circling in the still-churning water. You are at the tragic terminus of this river and must now return to its origin.

"Where do you want me to begin?" you ask.

Petrie appears as solid and impenetrable as unweathered stone. "Choose your own starting point," he says.

And so you do.

ONE

We lived on Victor Hugo Street in a rambling, dilapidated house that was the family's last remaining asset. For years the Old Man had strung a living together in pale bits and pieces, like popcorn on a string, freelance editing, book reviews, a little fact-checking here and there, the table droppings of the literary profession. Sometimes, when his ever-fluctuating mood allowed it, he'd even worked as a substitute teacher at the local high school. He called this "educational day labor," and despised it. His students were beneath him, as were the lowly, salaried teachers who, he said, pursued their modest pensions like scraps of holy writ. His contempt was bottomless, and it erupted in fits of spiraling rage.

In the midst of such seizures, he used the telephone like a whip. In the room where I was made to study, a tiny thing beneath its towering bookshelves, I could hear him leafing through the ever-expanding pages of the "enemies list" he kept in plain view on his desk, each entry made up of the enemy name and occupation, along with the Old Man's one-word judgment: *James Elton, professor, lackey; Carolyn Bender, editor, coward; Stephen Horowitz, headmaster, charlatan;* and the like. At some point he would inevitably select certain names from this roll of the damned. Then the calls would begin.

I remembered a particular afternoon when I'd suddenly paused outside the door of his study, then glanced through its slightly open door. He was sitting behind his desk, screaming into the phone: *You are a fake, you hear me! You are a plagiarist!* I listened as he steamed on, citing the crimes and misdemeanors of whomever he'd called. He'd gone on and on, then abruptly stopped, so that I'd heard the voice at the other end, metallic and inexpressive, *The time allotted for this message has expired. Please call again to continue.*

It was pathetic, I thought at the time, all that mighty rage futilely expended into the insensate ear of an answering machine. King Lear had thundered against our earthly plight. In comparison, the Old Man's fury seemed little more than sour grapes monstrously inflated. When he died, I felt that a dark, devouring force had been stilled at last. I wore his death like wings.

At the gravesite, I told my sister exactly that, then added, "You can go on with your life, Diana. You don't have to take care of him anymore."

She nodded silently, then tossed a single rose into his grave.

And I thought, *At last she's free of him. At last she can be happy.*

But then came Death, as the Old Man might have put it in his stilted and archaic dictum, an untimely death that came like that fabled highwayman whose poetic exploits Diana had so often recited for his pleasure, *Riding, riding, riding,* as I can hear her even now, *up to the old inn door.*

It was a Friday afternoon when the court pronounced its judgment that no one was to blame for Jason's death and that no one would be held accountable for it. Since Diana had already separated from her husband, Mark, by then, I'd come to the courthouse with her instead, the two of us seated at the front of an almost empty courtroom, listening silently as the judge declared Jason a "victim of misadventure."

"Shallow," Diana whispered. Then she stared directly at the judge, watching as he rose and left the room.

"Shallow," she repeated in a tone exactly like the Old Man's when he closed a book and with a word pronounced his verdict.

I started to get up, and expected Diana to do the same, but she didn't move.

"Not yet," she said, and gently tugged me back down onto the bench beside her.

She remained seated for a long time, her hand resting on mine, both of us now waiting as Mark rose and left the courtroom. He was dressed in a white shirt and dark blue trousers, his usual attire. As he left, his eyes briefly darted toward Diana, then no less quickly skirted away.

For her part, Diana never glanced toward Mark, but instead held her gaze on the mythical representation of blind justice that hung from the wood-paneled wall behind the judge's bench. She breathed slowly, rhythmically, and her hands remained steady, with no hint of trembling. She kept her back straight, her head erect, and seemed determined to stay that way, not to grow faint or swoon. In such an attitude, she looked more like a warrior than a grieving mother, as if grief itself had become a lifted sword. Her eyes were dry and her lips were pressed together tightly, like someone sealing in a scream, though other than the few words she'd already uttered, she made no sound at all. After a moment, she closed her eyes and for those few seconds she actually looked resigned to the court's decision, ready to accept it and move on.

"Diana," I said softly. "We should go now."

She nodded but her eyes remained closed, her body eerily still.

After a moment, people began to trickle back into the courtroom, Bill Carnegie among them, looking suitably solemn in his neat gray suit. He'd represented Mark in the divorce, though there'd been little for him to do beyond making the offer Diana had immediately accepted.

"Hello, Dave," he said as he passed on his way to the defense table.

Diana opened her eyes and stared at him.

"Hello, Mrs. Regan," Carnegie said.

"I'm Miss Sears now," Diana told him, though without

any hint of bitterness, merely a fact-checker making a small correction.

"Ah yes, of course," Carnegie said.

"The court has determined that my son died by misadventure," Diana added.

Bill glanced at me warily then turned back to Diana. "Anyway, nice seeing you," he said, and quickly continued down the aisle.

We rose, walked out of the courtroom and into a radiant late September afternoon, its light so bright it seemed to sparkle. Diana drew her hair into a bun and pinned it, exposing her long white neck in such a way that she looked oddly sacrificial, like a woman to be killed in exchange for rain.

We reached my car, and without a word Diana took her place on the passenger side and waited for me to get in behind the wheel. She said nothing as I put the key in the ignition, turned it, and began to back out of the shady space where I'd parked. We were already at the main road before she spoke.

"Truth matters, doesn't it, Davey?" she asked.

Her question abruptly returned me to the dinner-table inquisitions I'd endured from the Old Man, philosophical questions to which he'd demanded quotation-studded responses. His intimidating voice crackled in the air: *What say you, my young Daedalus?*

"You sound like the Old Man," I told her.

"I didn't mean to remind you of Dad," Diana said.

I shrugged, as if wholly indifferent to the mention of his name, though I continued to recall the nightly interrogations at the dinner table, the Old Man firing questions or demanding that I recite whatever passage he'd assigned me. I'd always responded haltingly, stammering and faltering, forgetting lines, going blank. Which was when Diana had always cut in, lifting her small white hand into the air, saving me from any further ridicule or humiliation.

"*Bleak House,*" Diana murmured.

Before the Old Man's death it had been typical of Diana to encapsulate everything in a book title, as if her mind worked in a high-velocity shorthand. But the practice had abruptly disappeared at his gravesite, and it surprised me that she'd suddenly returned to it.

"Not bleak for you," I said. "You were his shining star."

Again I found myself returned to the house on Victor Hugo Street, watching Diana from the shadowy corner where I stood like a poor relation, listening as she recited passage after passage, the Old Man erect in a chair before her, breathing softly, his shining black eyes fixed upon her. These recitations had been the way she'd found to quench the fires that burned inside him, the rage he felt for the world's indifference to his genius, its corruption and mediocrity, what he called, quoting the *Rubáiyát,* "the sorry Scheme of Things entire."

"He could be cruel," Diana said. "What he said to you that last day."

I saw him turn as Diana led me into his study, the cold glint in his eyes, that twitching mouth, the dreadful words they formed. *You are dust to me.*

"But he was crazy," Diana said. "He didn't know what he was doing."

Her mood was clearly darkening. I moved to stop its descent.

"Why don't you have dinner with us tonight," I said. "We can all relax. It's been a long day."

She nodded silently.

"Good," I said, then hit the small button on the console and locked all the doors.

Her eyes shot over to me. "I'm not going to jump out of the car, Davey," she said. "I know what I'm doing." She seemed suddenly seized by a grim recollection. "Don't ever think that I'm like Dad."

S o you saw nothing particularly alarming?" Petrie asks.

You know that in an old noir detective movie, Petrie would be slouched in his chair, with a rumpled shirt, perhaps wearing suspenders, certainly smoking. He would speak in a hard, tough-guy vernacular, refer to you as "pal" or "fella," as he urges you to "spill your guts." But the modern version is neat and well-groomed, Petrie a college graduate, a degree in criminology from John Jay, a student of profiles, astute at defining human behavior.

"No early warning signs?" Petrie adds.

You search your memory for such signs. Was there something wild in Diana's eyes that day? Did you see some spark of madness in them? These questions direct your mind to a deeper one: In any long journey of error, where is the first erroneous turn?

With the posing of this question, you are a little boy, sitting on a darkened staircase, facing the front door, squeezing a red rubber ball. You see the door open, Diana standing in the light, backlit by the sun. Is that where it began?

Petrie's gaze does not waver. "Nothing . . . suspicious?"

"No."

"So what was your first inkling?"

You're not sure. Was it the reference to *Bleak House*? Or was it the way her mood darkened when you first mentioned the Old Man?

"Mr. Sears?"

It is Petrie's polite use of formal direct address that pulls you back to the room, the table, the soft purr of the recording device. Mr. Sears. As if you are a client or a patient. Mr. Sears. As if you could rise and leave. Mr. Sears. As if there is no blood on your hands.

"Inkling," Petrie repeats in order to return you to the question at hand, the well-trod path of murder, a crooked road, perhaps, but one usually navigated quite easily, marked with road signs that say SEX or MONEY.

"Your sister," Petrie adds. "An inkling."

You know you have to give him something.

So you do.

"Maybe at my house later that night," you answer. "That business of the apes."

TWO

I lived in a subdivision, with one house quite close to the next, all of them laid out on a clean, uncomplicated grid, everything, all wilder routes, in forfeiture to order. Had I been able to find a walled city, I probably would have chosen it, aware, as I was, that the Old Man had often wandered the undefended streets of our town. We'd gone in search of him many times, but as I drove Diana toward my house that afternoon, a particular episode returned to me. Diana had been old enough to have a driver's license by then, so I must have been around thirteen years old at the time, too young to rebel, and so still under the Old Man's stern instruction to read and read and read.

We'd spotted him on the outskirts of the college campus where he'd later made such a horrendous spectacle of himself, been arrested by campus police, and subsequently transferred to Brigham Psychiatric Hospital.

"There he is," I said when I saw him shambling across an open field, a huge figure with massive shoulders, coatless and bareheaded, dressed only in baggy corduroy pants and a soiled gray sweatshirt despite the cold wind and icy rain that hurried other people past him so quickly they probably heard not a word of whatever he was muttering.

Diana pulled over to the curb and we got out of the car and headed toward him, Diana calling, "Dad, Dad."

He turned when he heard her, then stood in place and waited until we reached him.

"You have to come home now," Diana told him.

I touched his arm, but added nothing.

He felt my touch and drew his arm away.

"You are Checkers," he said to me. His eyes swept over to Diana. "You are Chess."

It was the first time he'd made such an overtly invidious comparison, and all through the following night I'd turned it over in my mind, an upheaval Diana had later noticed and tried to soothe with kind words: *You're the best brother in the world, Davey.*

Now it seemed up to me to do the soothing.

"You should think about moving into this part of town," I told her. "Maybe a house just down the block."

"Mark wanted to live outside of town," Diana said as if she were reconsidering the matter. "Way outside," she added. "Isolated."

And so they'd rented an old stone house several miles from town, remote and surrounded by forest, with a large pond only a short walk away.

"He said it was better for Jason," Diana said.

And it probably had been better for him, I thought, since its seclusion had presented fewer of the distractions that would have otherwise bedeviled him, traffic and the sounds of other children, ordinary in themselves, but which would have filled Jason with foreboding.

"Are you going to stay in the house?" I asked.

She shook her head. "Not without Jason."

I saw her son in my mind, a little boy with blond hair and pale complexion like his mother, but with his father's darkly glittering eyes. Then I thought of my daughter Patty, the life that stretched before her, then again of Jason, how little of life's bounty he had known, not only because his years had been cut short, but because even those years had been blighted, his world so filled with invading shadows he'd probably glimpsed no light at all.

Abby was sitting on the porch when Diana and I arrived. She is a tall woman, thin, with brown hair and large green eyes. We'd met in Old Salsbury, where I'd briefly worked at a law firm. She'd been a paralegal in the law office, and I'd found her quiet and self-effacing, not at all prone to challenge. We'd married a year later, and since then built a life based on smoothing the edges, avoiding conflict, a world where father knew best, or someone did, where no line ever blurred or skirted out into infinity.

Abby rose and came down the walkway as Diana and I got out of the car.

"Nice to see you, Diana," Abby said cheerily.

"The judge declared Jason's death accidental," I told her in order to get the subject out of the way.

Abby nodded softly. "Well, I guess it's nice to have closure," she said.

"Closure," Diana repeated, as if she were going through the word's various definitions, trying to decide if any of them were relevant to her state of mind.

"Diana's staying for dinner," I added quickly. "I thought we'd cook out. It's certainly warm enough."

We all went into the kitchen. I poured each of us a glass of wine, then walked out onto the deck to light the grill. A glass door separated the deck from the grill, and through it I could see Abby preparing a salad while Diana sat on a wooden stool a few feet away. Abby was talking in that animated way of hers. Diana listened, but said nothing, her fingers wrapped loosely around the glass, as if such sustaining refreshment, the actual food and drink of life, were no more than an afterthought.

Our daughter Patty had gotten home by the time the table was set. She was fifteen and could not have been more typical, a member of her high school band, with rows of Bs on her report card, attired in clothes from the Gap or Old Navy, exactly the opposite of Nina, my partner Charlie's daughter, a teenaged girl who dressed in Gothic black and continually changed the luminescent colors of her hair, and whose sudden presence at the office had never failed to set my mind wondering what she might have tucked in the pocket of her long black coat.

"Hi, Aunt Diana," Patty said politely as she lowered herself into a chair.

Diana looked at her in a way that appeared oddly penetrating, like one stripping plaster from a wall to view the structure beneath.

"How are you, Patty?" she asked in a tone that was unexpectedly solemn and which appeared to take Patty somewhat off guard.

"I'm fine," Patty answered.

Diana took a sip of wine, but her eyes never left Patty's.

"Did you know that apes can never speak?" she asked.

Patty shook her head.

"I read about it last night," Diana continued. "Even if an ape had the same intelligence as a human, it wouldn't be able to speak."

"Why not?" Patty asked, her curiosity sparked in a way that surprised me.

"Because the tube that goes from the vocal cords to the mouth and nose is too short," Diana answered. "There's not enough room for the air to vibrate, and so it can't make words." She appeared to retreat to some distant place, remain there a moment, then return, her gaze once again directed toward Patty. "Do you read much?" she asked.

Patty looked at me quizzically, then turned back to Diana. "Just what they assign."

"Dad made us read all the time," I said.

Diana looked at me. "Schiller," she said. "Remember Schiller?"

I did, but shook my head, claiming that I didn't, knowing that no matter what I recalled of him, Diana would remember vastly more.

"He said that before love, we would not have felt the deaths of others," Diana said. "Not even our own children. We would have been numb." She shifted her gaze to Patty and raised her glass. "Let's hope your life is anything but that," she said.

Shortly after dinner, I drove Diana back to her house on Old Farmhouse Road. It was a cool, clear night, full of stars, and I recalled the look on Diana's face the first time she saw Van Gogh's famous painting of a starry night. The Old Man had taken us to the Modern, one of his "scholarly trips," as he called them, and which often included nearby battlefields and historic villages. It was our first trip to New York. Diana was twelve years old, clothed in a dark blue dress with black shoes and white socks, beautiful as girls can sometimes be on the brink of adolescence. She kept her hand tucked in the Old Man's arm, as if to anchor him, though for the last few weeks he'd seemed almost normal, making meals at actual mealtimes and combing the paper for various jobs.

"The brushstrokes are very deep," Diana said as she stood before the painting.

My father nodded. "Van Gogh died very young," he said quietly.

Diana gazed at the deep furrows of circling blue. "Maybe he always knew that," she said.

I glanced over at her now, and saw her face almost as it had been that afternoon in the museum, grave and strangely probing, eyes that held you dangling, like hooks.

"Do you ever talk to Mark?" she asked. "I thought he might have called."

"No, he hasn't called me."

She nodded briskly, then got out of the car and waited for me to join her at the end of the walkway.

When I reached her, she turned and we headed toward the house together.

"Why did you think Mark might have called me?" I asked.

"I thought he might have questions."

"About what?"

"About me," she answered. "The fact that I scare him." She looked at me. "That's the word he used. Like I might pull a knife on him."

I laughed at this vision of my sister's violence, how exaggerated it seemed, no less impossible than her suddenly taking flight.

"He said my eyes scare him," she added. "The look in my eyes."

Her gaze grew very intent, like someone peering at something either very large or very small. I couldn't tell which. "Don't call me for a while, okay?" she said. "I know you want to check on me, but please don't. I want to think a few things through." She smiled. "I'll be okay. I really will. I just want some time alone."

"All right," I said.

"I'll call you," she assured me. "Don't worry. I'll call you when I'm ready."

When I'm ready.

In the coming days, I often thought of those words, of what they actually meant. At first I supposed no hidden meaning at all, that Diana was simply saying that she was ready to walk the rest of the way to the house, ready to open the door and step inside. She did all those things only a few seconds later. But later I came to believe that she had been declaring a different readiness that night, a readiness to let slip the lines that had bound her for so long, the trusty moorings of her life, and thus set sail toward that place whose dangers the ancient cartographers could not guess, nor act against, save by issuing the dark and futile warning they inscribed upon their maps: *Here there be dragons.*

S o she said strange things?" Petrie asks.

He wants it to be simple, this Q&A, simple questions and simple answers. A constricted inquiry: the color of the car, the caliber of the bullet. You see that his life in rooted in the sturdy matter-of-factness of evidence. He wants identifications that are positive and fingerprints that match. How will you ever be able to show him the cloud and the mist, the view blurred by rain, bad lighting, distance, prints whose whorls spin into the unknowable void?

You look at the notepad he balances on his lap, the small blue pen with which he has been scribbling notes. One of them says "Bleak House."

"Is mentioning a book title strange?" you ask.

"You seem to think it is."

"Perhaps I do," you admit. "Did."

"Why would you think that?" Petrie asks.

"I don't know," you answer. "It's just that it was strange, the way

Diana was doing it again. Talking in that way. She hadn't done it since the Old Man died."

Petrie appears briefly to return to that rainy day ten years earlier, a young detective then, thinner, but only slightly, everything else the same, the self-confidence, trusting his eyes and ears, the testimony of voices that come from moving lips.

"The weather was dreary," you add softly. "That day. And cold. We had trouble with the fire."

You wonder to what extent Petrie recalls the room's stark details, the Old Man dead in his chair, eyes closed, mouth open, Diana beside him, cradling him softly, you on the tattered brocade sofa, peering out into the backyard where a mound of ashes still smoldered, the remains of what had once been a bathrobe, a pair of tattered house shoes, a large green pillow.

"So this manner of speech struck you as some kind of reversion?" Petrie asks.

Reversion. A technical word. The sort Petrie clearly prefers and may have encountered in one of his criminal psychology classes: *Prior to psychotic breaks, certain reversions in behavior may present themselves. These include bed-wetting, infantile speech, and various forms of obsessive nostalgia.*

"Like someone who suddenly starts using an old accent," Petrie explains, "from the place he'd lived as a child, returning to the past. Did Diana do much of that?"

"Just using literary references," you tell him. "No other... reversion."

Petrie is obviously disappointed by your answer, would have preferred designated signposts.

"All right," he says. "Did you notice any other changes in Diana?"

There were so many, you think now, and they had seemed so large. But were they? Were they really?

"Yes," you answer. "There were other changes."

"Like what?"

The list is long. You pick one randomly.

"Her music. She'd always listened to a wide range of music. Classical. Folk. Rock. You name it. But a wide range. After Jason's death it became very narrow, repetitive. Only one singer."

"Who?"

You see the CD pass from Diana's hand to Patty's, and in that vision, now so fraught with tragic error, you wonder that you have not made those same hands tremble.

Petrie's pen comes to attention. "Who?"

You feel the name in your mouth like bits of bone in an evil potion.

"Kinsetta Tabu."

THREE

Following Diana's wishes, I made no effort to contact her after that night. And so two weeks passed before I heard from her again. Then it was her voice over the phone. "I'm moving out of the house," she said.

"When?"

"In a few days. I found an apartment in Carey Towers. It's small, but that's okay. I don't need much room."

It was good that she was moving, I thought. The house on Old Farmhouse Road was no doubt clogged with loss and grief and pain, a gloomy, mournful place she'd be well served to abandon.

"I'm having a yard sale on Saturday," she added. "Mark's already taken whatever he wanted from the house. I'm selling the rest."

"Want some help?"

"Sure. Come early. We can have breakfast."

Abby came with me on that bright Saturday morning, which, of course, I'd fully expected her to do. The surprise was that Patty decided to come along, too.

"Are you sure you want to spend a whole Saturday pid-dling around a yard sale?" I asked as she came down the walk-way to the car.

"I don't have anything else to do," she answered. "No band practice, and I've finished Mr. Donovan's paper."

As we rounded the bend near Diana's house a few minutes later, I noticed Patty press her face against the window and stare out at the large number of items Diana had spread across the lawn.

"It's like she's purging," Patty said. She kept her eyes on the lawn. "Vomiting everything out. Like Nina does. In the bathroom after lunch."

"Nina purges?" I asked.

"Sure," Patty said. She appeared surprised that this was news to me. "Lots of girls do it. It's a mental thing."

I glanced toward Diana's house, and wondered if Diana had been struck by a similarly weird convulsion, a "mental thing" that had resulted in her spewing the yard with her possessions.

The evidence seemed to mount as I pulled into Diana's driveway. She'd spread blankets across the lawn, then covered them with the varied contents of shelves and drawers. She'd dragged out a few bulky items as well, a wooden chest, several spindly bookshelves, and a couple of CD racks, the CDs themselves arranged for easy identification, labels out, in old shoe boxes.

But she'd gone beyond simply scaling down from a house to an apartment. She'd brought out her entire library, for example, along with all her kitchen pots and pans and utensils. There were boxes filled with canned goods, salt, pepper, various spices, some of which had not yet been opened. She'd piled her towels and linens onto one blanket, and all but one pair of shoes on another. Sweaters and skirts and blouses hung from a long gray rope she'd stretched between two trees. All of Jason's toys were for sale, along with his childhood clothing. Every lamp. Every chair. Every piece of art, whether painting or sculpture. There was an entire table piled high with empty picture frames, another with games and videos and even a couple of audiobooks.

I glanced from blanket to blanket, all neatly squared on the front lawn, very well ordered, so that it suddenly no longer looked like "purging" at all.

"She's starting over," I said. "Good for her."

We walked to the front door and Diana immediately opened it. "There's not much left to do," she said.

Which was true. Because inside, the heavier items—television, stereo, beds, tables, a sofa—had already been tagged with prices so low there was little doubt that by the end of the day my sister would have nothing. In fact, only my father's clanking old Royal typewriter was marked "Not For Sale," along with a trio of obviously recent purchases, all three still in their boxes, a laptop computer, a small laser printer, and a fax machine.

Abby glanced about, then offered her best smile. "Well, you've certainly been busy."

Diana gave her a look I'd seen before, partly in wonder at my wife's effort to put a shine on things, partly in admiration for the enormous energy it required, the heavy weight of seeming light.

"There's still a place to sit in the kitchen," she said. She looked at Patty. "You can have anything you want." She smiled. "Anything at all, Patty."

"Thanks," Patty said. "I'll look around." She turned and headed across the lawn, moving from blanket to blanket, before she stopped at the one covered with shoe boxes filled with CDs.

"I made coffee and bought a box of donuts," Diana said.

Abby and I followed her into the house, back to the kitchen, where we sat down at the only table left in the house.

"I noticed you're keeping the Old Man's typewriter," I said.

Diana nodded.

"Many a false, paranoid accusation came burning out of that thing," I added.

Diana took a short sip of coffee, her eyes peering just above the white rim of the cup. "Paranoid, yes," she said as she drew the cup from her lips. "But one or two were true."

By late that afternoon almost everything was gone. A few picture frames lay on an otherwise empty table, and a scattering of clothes still hung from the gray rope between the trees. But the yard was otherwise bare and the house empty.

"You priced things very low," Patty said in a voice that suggested more inquiry than statement of fact, a gentle probing.

"I didn't want anything left," Diana said. "Did you find something for yourself?"

"No," Patty answered lightly.

"You can't leave without something," Diana said. She walked over to a dark green backpack, unzipped one of its small pouches, and plucked out a CD. "Take this," she said.

The CD had a purple cover and Gothic letters I couldn't quite make out.

"Kinsetta Tabu," Diana said.

"I've never heard of her," Patty said.

"She uses ancient instruments," Diana told her. "Her songs are about the world before people like us came along."

"Like us?" Patty asked.

"Before our brains fused."

Patty looked at her silently, but clearly in search of further explanation.

"It's possible that before the brain fused, one part of it actually spoke to the other," Diana told her. "So these people, the ones before us, they would have heard their own thoughts as voices outside themselves." She looked to the right, where Dolphin Pond glimmered softly under the lowering sun. "Like Jason."

I imagined those voices coming out of nowhere, invisible mouths floating in the air. How threatening they must have seemed to Jason, issuing bizarre commands, warning him against other children, painting his world in nightmarish hues.

I wondered if in the end one of those voices had spoken as he'd stood by the storm fence, peering out toward the pond, the large stone that rested heavily, like a gatepost, at the edge of the water. *Go there.*

"That must have been very frightening," Patty said.

"Yes, frightening," Diana said. She looked at me. "By the way, I'll be working at the library."

I thought of the cluttered rooms of the house on Victor Hugo Street. "Surrounded by books," I said. "Just like old times." I glanced about. "What are you going to do with the rest of this stuff?"

"I'll take it to the dump," Diana answered. She looked at her now empty house, then turned her attention toward Abby, and, to my surprise, walked over and drew my wife into her arms. "Davey's very lucky," she said.

Abby peered at me quizzically, her head over Diana's shoulder. She was clearly surprised by Diana's unexpected gesture of affection. Even so, she smiled brightly and hugged Diana back.

Diana released Abby, then turned and drew Patty into a similarly affectionate embrace. "Let's talk sometime," she said.

"I'd like that," Patty replied.

Diana took Patty's hands in hers. "So be it then," she said.

It was one of the Old Man's arch constructions, and he'd always delivered it sonorously, as if he were handing down an ultimatum from the floor of the Roman Senate.

"I haven't heard that in a while," I said.

"Heard what?" Diana asked.

"The Old Man talking."

She seemed genuinely surprised. "Really, Davey?" she said. "I hear him all the time."

"What was that all about?" Abby asked as she climbed into bed later that night. She propped a pillow behind her back and plucked a small jar of face cream from the nightstand beside the bed. "Giving Patty that weird CD." She unscrewed the cap from the jar, dipped her finger in, and scooped a small amount of cream into her other hand. "Telling her they should talk sometime." She rubbed her hands together then began applying the cream to her face. "Do you think she's lonely, Dave?"

"Well, she's lost her son, her husband, too, so—"

"I mean Patty," Abby interrupted.

"What makes you think Patty's lonely?" I asked.

Rather than answer, she laughed lightly. "Remember that name your father wanted for her?" she asked. "Hypatia. I don't remember who she was, but something terrible happened to her."

"Hypatia was the last pagan astronomer in Alexandria," I told her, recalling the details of one of the Old Man's evening lectures. "A Christian mob scraped her to death with oyster shells."

Abby shook her head. "Imagine wanting your granddaughter named for a woman who was killed that way." She shivered melodramatically. "Your father had such awful things in his mind, Dave. That's who Diana got it from, I guess."

"Got what?"

Abby drew herself beneath the covers. "Those dark thoughts she has."

"What makes you think she has dark thoughts?" I asked. "Dark thoughts about what?"

"About Jason," Abby answered. "I noticed it the day she came back from the courthouse, the way she looked when you told me what the judge decided. Like she didn't believe it was an accident."

"How could she not believe it was an accident?" I laughed. "I think you're the one with dark thoughts."

Abby made no further argument, but I felt a peculiar need to strengthen the case.

"She had a weird childhood, Abby," I said. "All that reading. Reciting for the Old Man all the time, trying to calm him down. I never thought she'd have a normal life."

I went on to talk about my relief that after the Old Man's death, Diana had married, gotten pregnant, given birth, been a good mother, and in doing all these things managed to come out from under the skewed and nutty course of her upbringing, escaped, as I thought I had, the consequences of our father's madness.

"Diana is a triumph," I said. "A survivor."

Abby reached for the lamp. "Whatever you say, Dave."

Within seconds she was fast asleep, but I was still going over the whole matter in my mind an hour later when the phone rang. It struck me as strangely coincidental that it was Diana.

"I'm reading about Cheddar Man," she said. "The skeleton that was found in Cheddar Gorge, England."

"What about him?" I asked.

"There were animal bones in the cave with him, and they had the same marks on them," Diana answered. "Scraping marks. So he was eaten. By other people. Using tools." She paused briefly, then added, "I'm sorry, Davey. I didn't notice the time. Did I wake you?"

"No," I said. "I was still up. Why are you reading about this . . . Cheddar Man?"

"Because Kinsetta Tabu has a song about him. Wait. Listen."

Another brief pause, then a woman's voice came on the line chanting to a primitive accompaniment that sounded vaguely like a blade scraping ice or stone, repeating a single eerie phrase, *World of whirl is whorl of world.*

Diana came on the line again. "It's on the CD I gave Patty. I bought another one for myself. I thought she might have questions after she listened to it, so that took me to Cheddar Man."

I recalled all the other CDs, boxes of them for sale.

"Why did you keep that particular CD?" I asked.

"Because Jason was listening to it," Diana answered. "While I was gone."

"The day he died?"

"Yes."

There was another brief silence, and I could almost feel my sister thinking, hear the minute firings of her brain.

"So it was the last voice he heard," I said. "Kinsetta Tabu's."

Her answer had the effect of a tiny point of steel pressed into my flesh, worrisome but not life threatening.

"Maybe," she said.

Maybe,'" Petrie repeats. "That's all she said?"

You nod, watch his eyes, looking for any sign that he is not entirely familiar with the terrain into which you are leading him, has the slightest sense that here there be dragons.

"So you saw no real change in Diana's behavior?" Petrie asks.

You realize that Petrie remains in his element, holds to the clipped, no-nonsense pace of movie script interrogations.

"But I saw a change in mine," you tell him.

"What kind of change?"

"A hint of fear."

"What were you afraid of?"

"Delving any deeper."

Petrie nods, and you know that you share this with him, this hesitance to look. You wonder how many shower curtains he has stood before, silent, frozen, not wanting to see what he knows must lay in bloody sprawl behind them.

"It's a common failing in people like us," you add.

"People like us?"

"People who gather evidence, rely on evidence."

You watch as he flips back a page and peers at his notes.

"But to be precise, it was your wife who first brought it up, isn't that right?" he asks. "That something was going on in Diana's mind."

Abby's voice sounds in your head. *Like she didn't believe it was an accident.*

"Suspicion," Petrie adds, as if to return to that same earlier moment in his notes. "About Jason's death."

You are suddenly standing by the pond. A little blond-haired boy pauses at the water's edge. He is dressed in a white T-shirt and dark blue shorts, arms at his sides, unblinking eyes peering out over the water that laps at his toes, one tiny, shoeless foot rising to step in.

"That it might not have been an accident," Petrie adds.

What is Petrie seeing now, you wonder, this neat, well-dressed detective. Which suspect in a lineup of faces is the object of his true suspicion? Which crime? Which death? What name will he mention next?

You wait for him to make his choice.

You study his eyes and make a guess.

But you are wrong.

"Cheddar Man," he says.

FOUR

Abby was already preparing breakfast when I came into the kitchen the next morning. She always slept deeply and awoke refreshed, whereas I always had trouble dropping off, and thus awakened like a man who'd been chased all night by wild animals, my face each morning a scary reminder of the Old Man's, with the same oddly ravaged eyes.

"Did somebody call last night?" she asked.

I glanced out the window to where Patty waited for her bus. The twin white cords of her iPod slithered up from the pocket of her jacket to the tiny speakers nestled in her ears.

"Yes," I answered.

Abby brought over a cup of coffee and set it down on the table in front of me. "Who was it?"

"Diana. She was telling me about Cheddar Man, this . . .

fossil, I guess." I took a quick sip of coffee. "She said the bones showed that he'd been eaten by other people."

Abby looked puzzled. "Why would she be reading about something like that?"

"Because this singer, the one on that CD she gave Patty, there's a song on it about this Cheddar Man character. She mentioned that Jason was listening to this same CD before he left the house that morning."

I wondered in what way Diana might now be going back over the painful facts of Jason's death, perhaps even her last glimpse of him, which must have been in the family room where the audio equipment rested on metal shelves, perhaps as he sat on the dark red sofa, his back to the window, Dolphin Pond shimmering in the late-morning sunlight beyond it, the voice of Kinsetta Tabu circling in the air around him, his head cocked slightly to the right, listening.

Abby took a nip of toast and washed it down with coffee. "Well, maybe the new job will help her get over it."

I imagined Diana in the library, curled over a table and peering down at a book. I had seen her in just this pose many times when she was a child, legs tucked under her, long hair hanging in a curtain of pure gold.

"The bus is coming," Abby said.

I glanced out to where Patty stood at the road. There were others around her now, clumped together in small knots of animated conversation. Patty stood apart from them, as I noticed, facing the bus as it closed in upon her, head cocked slightly to the right at just the angle I'd previously imagined for Jason on the day he died, like him alone, like him listening.

I got to my office a few minutes later. Dorothy, the reception-ist, greeted me with her usual smile. "Lily's out today."

Lily was my secretary.

"And Charlie's waiting for you," Dorothy added.

Charlie was my partner in the firm, father of Nina, whom I suddenly imagined in a thicket of shadows, a girl who clearly had much to hide.

"Thanks," I said, then headed down the corridor to where Charlie stood at my office door.

"Morning, Charlie."

He held a photograph in his right hand. "This came in as a fax with your name on it," he said as he lifted it toward me. "Got any idea who sent it?"

I looked at the photograph, and the answer was obvious. "My sister," I told him.

He looked at me oddly. "Your sister?"

"A new interest of hers," I explained, then walked into my office, sat down at my desk, and looked at the picture.

In the photograph, Cheddar Man lay on his back, with legs folded under him. There was a large wound on the skull, one that might have been associated with a violent death, though such a gash could just as easily have been the result of any number of less malevolent causes. The empty sockets were large and round and I could almost feel Cheddar Man peering back at me from the dark well of his missing eyes.

Kinsetta Tabu's whispery chant filtered through my mind, *World of whirl is whorl of world,* and for no clear reason, I recalled Jason on the day he was born, delivered by C-section and placed in an incubator. He lay naked under the glass, on his back, with one shoulder slightly raised and his legs drawn up beneath him, a position that eerily seemed to mirror Cheddar Man's. Mark had stepped up to the window beside me, and at that precise moment, as I remembered now, a loud announcement had blasted over the hospital intercom. In response to it, Jason had started fiercely, kicking his legs, jerking his arms, crying out so loudly and with such helpless panic, I could hear his scream through the glass. How frightened he must be, I'd thought at that moment, alone in the dark, unable to interpret the sound that had startled him or even guess the direction from which it had come, life itself scary and unknowable, with its weird lights and noises, everything from outside, everything threatening, *World of whirl is whorl of world.* I'd looked at Mark, knowing that he must feel the same as I did, seized with an urge to rush in, comfort his newborn son, hold him in his arms and assure him that in the end he would become familiar with all these strange, frightening sensations. But Mark gave no sense of having such an impulse. Instead, his face broke into a broad smile.

"Did you see how quick his reflexes are?" he asked proudly.

I looked at the small naked infant behind the glass. He had a great mass of curly hair, but that was less noticeable than the expression on his tiny face, how frozen in dread it seemed to be, dread and a strange sadness, as if he already knew that he was damaged goods, incapable of meeting his father's exalted expectations.

Now, as I glanced back down at the photograph of Cheddar Man, his awful nakedness, the testimony of his bare bones, I wondered if, even in his primitiveness, this ancient creature might have felt embarrassment at not having been quick enough to outrun those who pursued him, or smart enough to have eluded them in some other way. Had he felt the sting of his own inadequacy, the brutal disappointment of his relatives and peers, painfully understood the fatal consequences of his own terrible failure to comprehend the danger before it was too late?

I opened my desk drawer, put the photograph inside, and closed it with an unsettling sense of our distant but still common heritage, how naked to the elements we remained, how helpless before chance, a weird sense of entrapment and powerlessness passing through me as I pressed Cheddar Man back into a darkness he would never leave.

A few minutes later Dorothy announced that my first appointment of the day had arrived.

"Send him in," I told her.

Ed Leary came into my office a few seconds later. He was fifty-five, the owner of our town's only monument business, and he was currently ensnarled in a bitter wrangle over his modest worldly goods, mostly the stock of granite tombstones upon which he carved the names and dates of the dead, along with the final sentiments of those who'd either loved or claimed to love them.

His wife had filed for divorce three months before, and Ed had come to me for representation. "Ethel wants everything," he cried at our first conference. "Everything I've worked for all my life. And what's she done? Nothing."

"Domestic duties count," I reminded him gently.

"What domestic duties?" Ed yelped, this time with a lifted fist. "She never kept a clean house. She never had a meal on the table when I got home at night."

He had raged on in a similar manner in all our subsequent meetings, the process of discovery, offers and counteroffers, moving toward the dissolution of his twenty-nine-year marriage like a great lumbering beast, dazed, furious, weary, but more than anything profoundly puzzled by the sheer vindictiveness of his wife. "I wouldn't hate a snake the way she hates me," he once said disconsolately, "and what did I ever do to her but marry her?"

"Maybe that's it," I told him. "Maybe she thinks that marrying you wasn't just a mistake, but *the* mistake of her life. I see that all the time. It's not the husband the woman hates, it's the life she ended up with because she married him."

Ed pondered this a moment, then said, "Well, why didn't she divorce me sooner then? I mean, how does a woman live with the man she thinks ruined her life, turned the whole thing into a waste?"

"I don't know how they do it, Ed," I admitted. "I just know they do."

He shook his large head despairingly. "She wants me homeless. So that I got to start over. Build everything up again from scratch. But who has time for that? I'm not a young man, Dave."

On this particular morning, he was wearing gray khaki pants and a flannel shirt that was vaguely olive. There were small crescents of sweat beneath his arms, and he drew his breath in short spurts, like a runner. Fifty-five and counting, I thought. Fifty-five, with the wolf at the door.

"So, no change, I guess?" he asked as he sank into the chair before my desk. "She still won't settle." He shifted uncomfortably. "All she wants to leave me with is a little tombstone with my own name on it. She wants to see me on welfare. Ruin me. But tell me this, what does anyone get out of ruining somebody else?" He eased backward and released a weary sigh. "Hell of a thing we got here, Dave."

There was no direct point to argue, so I added nothing to Ed's remark.

Ed got to his feet. "Hell of a thing we got here," he repeated as he turned toward the door.

I had no idea what Ed meant, or any real wish to know. There was business to attend to. I opened my drawer and reached for yet another case. Ed turned back to me, as if he'd been called by some voice I couldn't hear, and as he turned, he glanced toward my desk, and I saw his eyes register the photograph he glimpsed there, Cheddar Man with his cracked skull, the empty sockets of his eyes.

"What's that?" Ed asked.

"Nothing," I said with a shrug. "Just a picture my sister sent me."

"Your sister," Ed repeated. "I read about her."

"You read about Diana?"

His tone turned melancholy. "Lost her son."

So that was what he'd read, one of the local news items about Jason's death.

"Yes, she did," I told him.

He shook his head. "Hell of a thing we got here, Dave," he said.

I nodded.

"This world," he added softly. He gazed at the photograph a moment longer, then lifted his large careworn eyes back up to me. "She knows," he added, "your sister." Then he turned and walked out of my office, down the corridor, and across the parking lot. From my office window, I watched him climb into his truck and drive away. *She knows,* I heard him say again, as if he and Diana shared a secret, sorrowful and arcane, a map not of treasures hidden but of unknown tragic shores.

At noon I met Charlie for lunch at Sara's Diner on Main Street. We'd been partners for fifteen years in what Charlie jokingly called "our distinguished firm of two." He was an easygoing man who'd always been pleasantly lacking in ambition. We'd attended the same mediocre college, graduated from the same mediocre law school. Like me, Charlie had never tortured his mind with grave issues. He was personable and competent, but he'd long ago quenched whatever small fire, if any, had ever burned in his now substantial belly.

As usual, Charlie ordered the burger deluxe with a large Pepsi. I settled for a salad and a cup of coffee.

"So, you have it out with Ed?" he asked.

"I brought him up to date."

Charlie laughed. "Funny, I was sure as hell he sent you that skeleton."

"Why would you think that?"

Charlie took a bite of the burger and chewed it slowly. "Figured it was our turn. A couple days ago, Bill Carnegie got a rock in a shoe box."

"A rock?"

"With weird scratches on it, he said. It shook him up a little. Like it was a threat. Like, next time this will come through your window. There are weird people out there, you know."

I thought of Nina, his daughter, dressed in Gothic black, her hair an iridescent blue or green or pink, bent over a toilet, purging, and wondered if he ever feared some deeper weirdness, this same pale girl slinking down a dark corridor, moving toward his bedroom with a knife.

"Bill figured it might be Ed who sent it to him," Charlie added. He dabbed a red spill of ketchup from the side of his mouth. "You know, because he's representing Ethel." He shrugged, then added absently, "Of course, he might just as easily have suspected your sister."

"Diana?" I held my fork motionlessly in the air. "Why on earth would he suspect her of something like that?"

"Oh, he wouldn't really," Charlie said, dismissing the idea. "It's just that Bill mentioned that they'd had a bit of a disagreement." He took another bite of his burger. "Over lawyer-client privilege, I'd guess you could say."

"Lawyer-client privilege? How would that come up?"

"Because she wanted Bill to tell her what Mark said to him."

"About what?"

"About Jason."

"You mean his death?"

"Yeah," Charlie said. He took a sip of Pepsi. "He's some kind of egghead, isn't he? Mark?"

"He's a biochemist. A brilliant one, evidently. Close to a breakthrough, he says."

"Breakthrough." Charlie laughed. "Eggheads," he said derisively. "I wouldn't have one for a client. That whole field, intellectual property. What a headache. Some egghead comes up with some theory and right away he thinks the whole world's out to steal it. Paranoid as hell, those guys."

I leaned forward. "So tell me, what exactly was Diana after?"

Charlie forked a french fried potato into his mouth. "It wouldn't have mattered. You know Bill, strictly by the book. He wouldn't tell Diana. That's what made him think maybe she sent him that rock. Mad at him because he wouldn't tell her anything."

"Diana would never do anything like that," I told him.

Charlie took a final sip of soda. "Anyway, Bill got it all off his hands. Told Mark to see Stewart Grace."

"Stewart Grace?" I asked.

Charlie wiped his mouth. "Yep."

"But Grace handles criminal cases," I said quietly. "Serious stuff."

Charlie glanced out the window, toward the little town whose people we knew all too well, the countless petty dissolutions that afflicted them. "Yeah, he doesn't bother with the little shit we handle." His eyes swept over to me. "With Stewart, it's usually murder."

Murder.

You see the word register in Petrie's eyes, the deaths it is now his duty to explore, each of which you suddenly envision in fundamental images of cloth, water, iron, wood. You have no doubt that entirely different images of violence swirl about in Petrie's mind—guns, knives, rope, the grim stage props of slaughter.

"What did you think when you heard that Bill Carnegie had referred Mark to Stewart Grace?" Petrie asks.

You recall Grace the day you went to him, how open his face was, how little veiled in treachery. You remember how small you'd felt as you stood before him, how stained by mediocrity, the dreadful and ineradicable blotch the Old Man had always called "the true mark of Cain."

The Old Man's voice flares in your mind. *So tell me, my young Daedalus, what divides Hades from the world of the Living?*

A river.

Only one?

No . . . four . . . two . . . no . . . five.

Name them.

Acheron.

Which is?

The river of woe.

Next?

Cocytus . . . the river of . . . lamentation.

Next?

Phlegethon. The river of . . . fire?

Is or is not Phlegethon the river of fire?

I think . . . it is . . . but . . .

Uncertainty is death.

Yes . . . yes, it is.

Next?

Lethe.

Which is?

The river of forgetfulness.

And last?

"Mr. Sears?"

You return to the room, look at Petrie, and wonder if he now sees them glimmering in your eyes, the little fires that flicker on the far side of the Styx, the river of hate.

You remember Petrie's original question and quickly answer it.

"I wasn't really thinking about Stewart Grace at the time," you tell him.

"Who then?"

"Bill Carnegie. I wanted to know why Diana had gone to him in the first place. I was trying to sort things through."

You remember Diana in the courthouse, the odd look in her eyes as she'd spotted Bill Carnegie. Or was it odd? You can no longer be sure, and in that uncertainty you are suddenly standing in the terrible space where she labored, staring at the medieval quotation she'd printed in bold black letters and hung like an anthem on the wall behind her desk: *Send out a beam of ghostly light, and pierce this cloud of unknowing.*

"I didn't know what any of it meant," you tell Petrie. "So I went to see him. Bill. I'm sure you already know that."

Petrie nods softly. "Yes."

In your mind you see Bill Carnegie come through the door of the courthouse, reaching for a pack of cigarettes as he trots down the stairs toward you. His first words had surprised and strangely alarmed you. *You look a little tense, Dave.*

You imagine that you looked exactly that, tense, unsure, perhaps even at that early stage already fearful of the road ahead, that first step that leads from twist to twist, until, at last, you reach the precipice.

FIVE

Over the phone, Bill Carnegie made no bones about his professional obligations. "I can't talk about Mark," he warned. "Only your sister."

"Diana is all I want to talk about," I assured him.

We met outside the courthouse early in the afternoon, standing together as a troubled stream of litigants flowed up and down the long cement steps.

"You look a little tense, Dave," Bill said.

"I do?"

"Troubled, maybe that's a better word," Bill said. He lit a cigarette with a silver lighter, flipped the top into place, and returned it to the jacket pocket of his suit. "Nasty habit, I know," he said. "You should see the looks I get. You'd think I was a child molester." He took a long draw and blew out a thin column of smoke. "So, Diana."

"Like I said on the phone, I was surprised to hear that she came to see you."

"Me, too."

"I'd just like to know why she did that."

Rather than answer, Bill took his customarily cautious approach. "If you don't mind, what exactly is your reason for asking, Dave?"

"I'm worried about her."

"Why?"

I realized that until that moment, the actual posing of the question, I hadn't clearly known the reason myself. Then, in an instant, it was all too clear.

"My father," I answered. "He had a problem."

Bill took another draw on the cigarette and waited.

"A mental problem," I added. "He was paranoid. A paranoid schizophrenic."

All the terrors of my boyhood flashed through my mind for a moment, the Old Man storming from room to room, throwing books, yelling for Diana while I cowered in some dark corner of my own vast upheaval.

Bill dropped the cigarette and crushed it with the toe of his shoe. "Just a few quick puffs, that's all I allow myself," he explained. "So, you think Diana may have this problem, too?"

"I'm just trying to figure out what's on her mind," I said. "What she's thinking."

"She's thinking about Jason."

"What about him?"

Carnegie glanced to the right, nodded to a passing attorney. "I don't have a lot to tell you. It was a short meeting."

"Anything might help."

"She wanted to know what Mark had said about that morning," Bill told me.

That morning.

I went back over its few events, Mark home from work, Diana out shopping, Jason in the family room, listening to a CD, then rising, walking to the door, then through it and across the lawn to where a storm fence stopped him for a time, then didn't.

"She seemed to be after facts," Bill added.

"What kind of facts?"

"Where he was at any point."

"Who?"

"Mark."

"You mean, like a timeline?"

"That sort of thing, yes," Bill said. "She asked if I'd recorded any of our conversations. I told her no, but it wouldn't matter anyway, because they were private. Attorney-client privilege. She argued with me about it a little, but I didn't get the idea that she meant it. It was more like a show, like she knew from the beginning that I wouldn't tell her anything Mark had said to me."

"So why did she ask you about it?"

Bill shrugged. "Who knows. Maybe she wanted to know if there was some kind of record of our conversation. Notes. Tapes. Whatever. Other people have tried that one on me."

"Why would that matter to Diana?"

"It wouldn't unless she planned to break into my office." He laughed at so absurd a prospect, a woman with a burglar's tool kit, jimmying the lock to his office door then taking a crowbar to the cabinet in which he stored his most secret information. "But even if there was a full record of my conversations with Mark, it wouldn't help her."

"Why not?"

"Because Mark never mentioned Jason, or anything about what happened to him."

"Not at all?"

"Not once in all our conversations," Bill said. "We talked about the divorce, the settlement. That was it."

"Did you tell Diana that?"

"Sure. Why not?"

"How did she react?"

Something in Bill's eyes shrank inward. "That was the weird thing," he said. "She didn't seem surprised. As a matter of fact, I got the idea this was what she'd come to find out, maybe even confirm what she already suspected—not something Mark might have said about Jason, but the fact that he hadn't said anything at all."

"Patty won't be home for dinner," Abby told me when I arrived home later that evening. "She's working on some sort of project."

"How's she getting home?"

"Nina's driving her," Abby answered.

"I didn't know she was friends with Nina."

"I don't think she is," Abby said. "They just happened to be working on this project together, and Nina has a license."

I didn't like the idea of Nina driving Patty home, but kept it to myself since I knew it was based not on any sense that Nina was a bad driver, for which I had no evidence, but that she was an unstable person, immature for someone on the verge of womanhood, not at all a healthy influence. Charlie, himself, often referred to her as "the freak," and seemed anxious for her to graduate from high school and go to college. "Believe me, Dave," he'd said. "I won't feel a twinge of empty-nest syndrome."

"When did Patty say she'd be in?" I asked.

"Later," Abby answered casually.

"Where is she, exactly?"

"The library."

"The school library?"

"I don't know, Dave," Abby answered. She looked at me quizzically. "What's the matter?"

"I don't know." I shrugged, and changed the subject. "Diana went to see Bill Carnegie a couple of days ago. She wanted to know if Mark had said anything about Jason."

I saw that this did not strike Abby as news.

"She's been acting a little weird," she said. She gazed at me indulgently, as if to say, *I'm sorry to tell you this.* "People talk, Dave," she said. "I met Leonora Gault in the grocery store. She lives just across from that little apartment complex where Diana moved. She's seen her walking around at night. Really early. Two, three in the morning."

I recalled the Old Man's late-night wandering, the sound of the door as he left, then later, that same sound, more quiet, and which alerted me that Diana had set off in search of him.

But because we survive as much by denying a thing as by confronting it, I said, "I wouldn't call that 'weird.' She has a lot on her mind. Her whole future. Not long ago she had a family. Husband. Son. Now all she has is me."

None of this changed Abby's opinion, or more than briefly interrupted her narrative.

"Leonora went over, knocked on the door," she continued. "Diana came to the door but she didn't invite Leonora in. She came out instead. Closed the door behind her."

"So?"

"It just seemed strange, that's all," Abby said. "Like Diana didn't want Leonora to get a peek inside her apartment. Leonora thought it was spooky."

"Spooky?"

I thought of Diana's visit to Bill Carnegie. "If you were Mark, would you be spooked by Diana?" I asked.

I saw one of Abby's thousand little lights go out. "Yes," she said, as if acknowledging it for the first time, "I would."

After dinner I went to my small study to review a few of the cases that were approaching the calendar. I was still at work when Patty came home. She peeped in, smiling.

"Hi, Dad."

"Hi."

She said nothing else, but only drew back out of the doorway and headed down the corridor to her room.

Normally I would have continued with my work, and later gone to bed, with no need to see Patty again before morning. But after a few moments, I found myself returning to my childhood, the long hours I'd spent in my room, fearing to go out, listening to the Old Man's movements, knowing that when they became frantic, Diana's voice would accompany them, soft, soothing, reciting the verses and passages that slowed him down and finally settled him into sleep. It was that long-ago fear I felt now, deep and pure, and which seemed to return to me like a chronic ache whose severity time had masked, but which was now emerging again.

And so I rose from my desk, walked down the hallway, and knocked on Patty's door.

After a brief flurry of activity, the door opened and she looked at me with an uncharacteristically wary expression.

"I just thought I'd check in," I said.

She peered at me like a creature whose shape had slightly altered. "Check in?" She squinted. "What's going on, Dad?"

I nodded toward the inside of the room. "May I come in?"

She was clearly surprised by my request.

"My room?" she asked.

"If you don't mind."

She shrugged, then stepped back into a room that struck me as vaguely more disordered than it had been in the past, with her iPod balanced at the corner of her desk, its thin cords dangling like small white vines toward a short stack of books that leaned unsteadily to the right.

"Is there anything in particular you're looking for?" Patty asked.

"I'm not looking for anything," I told her. My tone

struck me as strangely defensive. "I mean, what would I be looking for?"

"Drugs, maybe," Patty answered crisply. "Nina's dad is always searching her room for drugs."

"You're not Nina," I said. "And besides, I'm sure if Nina had drugs, they'd be well hidden from her dad." I glanced to the right where, to my surprise, Patty had placed an old photograph of Diana.

"Where did you get that?" I asked.

"I found it in some stuff I was going through," Patty answered.

I walked over to the desk for a closer look. In the photograph, Diana sat in the park near the old house on Victor Hugo Street, her legs drawn under her, Indian style. With the long hair and flowery skirt, she might have been a sixties hippie, one of those girls at Woodstock, sliding in the mud or swimming naked in the nearby river. Films of all that—the dancing in circles, the peasant dresses, even the wildly idealistic slogans, *All You Need Is Love, Give Peace a Chance*—had always struck me as sad, almost heartrending, not a snapshot of some moment in our social history, but of that instant within each life when making something happen seems within our grasp.

Suddenly I remembered Diana the year she'd left for college. She'd been only seventeen, on full scholarship at Yale, and, as always, relentlessly inquisitive. She'd never had a boyfriend before then, but on visits home she sometimes mentioned this or that boy from Yale, or some equally Ivy

League fellow blown in from Boston or New York. None had ever made much of an impression, which made it all the more remarkable that she'd later been taken with Mark so suddenly and with such force. I guessed that it was his brilliance that had attracted her. On the night of our first meeting, he'd talked about the cleansing of the gene pool, the possibility that one day there might be almost wholly engineered human beings, genetically bred for maximum physical, intellectual, and even emotional strength. "At some point we may actually be able to take the bad stuff out," he'd said emphatically, "like debris from a stream."

It had all sounded very Jules Verne to me, along with a hint of something more sinister, people designed to be perfect in every conceivable way, each man an *Übermensch*. As far as I was concerned, the shadow of *Frankenstein* always hung over such grandiose schemes. And yet no one had ever spoken with more conviction than Mark about such a miraculous possibility, and I'd left our first meeting quite impressed with him, even hopeful that Diana had found her match.

"Do you have a boyfriend?" I blurted before I could stop myself.

Patty was clearly surprised by the question. "Why would you ask me that?"

"I guess I just want you to have a normal life," I said. "Husband. Kids."

Her answer was not at all what I expected.

"That's only normal for you, Dad," she said. "It might not be normal for someone else."

"Okay," I said. "Maybe I should have said that I want you to be happy."

Rather than respond directly, Patty drew the picture of Diana from my hand.

"What was she like?" she asked. "I mean, when she was my age. You've never really told me about that. Just that she read all the time. Could recite all this stuff. But what was she like . . . as a person?"

"She was always standing off somewhere by herself," I answered, remembering just how isolated she'd been even as a little girl, how often she'd stood apart from the other children. Time and again I'd urged her back into some kind of group play, my impulse always to make her less—the word hit me without warning—freakish. But it had rarely worked. She'd always retreated back to her solitude.

Patty appeared to see all this. "So, she didn't have any friends?"

"No, she didn't," I answered.

"She e-mailed me," Patty said. "About Kinsetta Tabu. Which songs I like. What I think they mean." She shrugged. "And other things."

"Other things?" I asked.

Patty's gaze suddenly turned wary. "I shouldn't have told you about them," she said. Her tone was unmistakably guarded. "It's between Aunt Diana and me, anyway."

"Okay," I said. "It's just that . . ." I stopped, unable to put my finger on what I found vaguely alarming about the correspondence.

"You don't like it," Patty said. "That we're talking."

I started to respond, but Patty abruptly stepped over to her desk. "It's nothing to worry about, Dad," she said. "I guess I can show you." She reached into one of its drawers and pulled out a short stack of e-mails she'd printed. "She gives me things to think about, that's all," she said. "Questions for me to think about. It's nothing terrible, so you don't have to get all weird about it." She drew the first e-mail from the stack and handed it to me. "Here, see for yourself."

I read the note, and as I read, heard Diana's voice pronounce the words, *What if the world were itself alive?*

What if the world were itself alive?

Petrie studies the words he has written in his notes and you see the world he wishes to ensure. It is one in which clarity never dissolves and control never falters and we never find ourselves in a deep wood, alone.

"Odd," Petrie says, like one slowly opening a forbidden door just a crack before soundly closing it. "Questions like that. But would you call them dangerous?"

You know that the end of the rope is not where Petrie grasps, the far spaces not where he looks.

"No, not dangerous," you agree. "If you can dismiss them."

"But they bother you?" Petrie asks. "Questions like that?"

You are surprised that you have revealed this, the context in which you heard Diana's question, the alarm it sounded deep within you, like a buried bell.

"I didn't want Patty exposed to them," you tell Petrie. "Questions like that. I didn't want her exposed to them the way Diana was . . . by her father."

"The professor."

"He was never a professor," you correct him. "Except in his own mind. But he ran a school where he was the headmaster and Diana and I were the students. He ran it in our house on Victor Hugo Street. I stopped attending classes. I never graduated. You can think of it like that. But Diana kept going. She kept going, and it shaped her mind."

The nature of that mind returns to you, the way Diana's initial ideas always became more focused as she closed in on whatever she was "researching" at the moment.

"Or misshaped it," you add.

Petrie looks at you wonderingly.

"She was full of quotations," you explain. "Hundreds of them. It was easy for her to remember them, recall them. Some kind of photographic memory."

You know this is not enough, that it was more than Diana's prodigious memory that had impressed and finally awed the Old Man.

"Phrases were like whips on her back," you add. "The psychology of fire. The heart of darkness. The shock of recognition. The power of blackness."

Petrie stares at you a moment, then, very slowly, slips down the knot of his tie.

"It was passion," you add fiercely. "It was intellectual passion that . . ." You feel the ground open up beneath you, a breath sucks you in, as if the earth really were a living thing, you the tiny creature it is devouring, ". . . that she couldn't escape."

"But that didn't make her dangerous," Petrie says cautiously. "And certainly not murderous."

You think of the movie murderesses you've seen, *Play Misty for Me, Fatal Attraction,* the chill they send down every male spine. Petrie is right, you admit. These are crazed women, stalkers, with murder on their minds, rejected women who in their rejection sought a terrible vengeance.

"That's true," you tell Petrie. "Not a woman scorned. Not some horror-movie psycho."

"What then?"

"Lonely," you answer. "It made her lonely."

You see a shadow pass over Petrie's face and realize just how powerful it is, the notion of loneliness, the deep ravine it carves.

"I thought she had escaped it," you add. "By having Jason. By loving him so much. And if he'd been normal . . ." You stop, amazed that for a moment, against all sense, you feel yourself blame a poor, dead child for being born, and being sick, and finally for drowning in a clear blue pond. "If he had lived . . ."

"Yes?" Petrie asks.

You think, *Three deaths. Four deaths? Will it ever truly end?* "If he had lived, I wouldn't be telling you this story."

The blue pen holds as motionlessly as Petrie's eyes. For a trembling instant, the world goes silent. Then he says, "Go on."

And so you do.

SIX

It was hard for me to imagine that Mark, during all his conversations with Bill Carnegie, hadn't so much as mentioned Jason, and as I drove to work the morning after speaking with him, I went over the preceding years, how happy Diana had been when she'd gotten pregnant, and later given birth.

But that first joy had faded as the weeks passed and she watched Jason ever more closely, sometimes writing her observations in a small notebook.

Meticulously, she'd recorded a variety of common infant illnesses, earaches and colic, two bouts of pneumonia. By the time he was two, these illnesses appeared to have taken a toll on his overall stamina. He had a tendency to lie still for a long time, or slouch silently in his high chair, his hands in his lap, his dark eyes blinking slowly as if he were dropping off to sleep.

"I'm worried, Davey," Diana said to me one afternoon as we sat in the town park. "About Jason."

He was almost three years old that afternoon, sitting no more than ten feet away from us, his bare legs nestled in green summer grass. Other children were frolicking all about, but Jason paid them little mind. Instead, he kept his body rigid, facing the same direction, his attention focused, or so it seemed, on some point in the distance, a blinking light no one else could see.

Diana continued to peer at Jason. "He doesn't smile, Davey. He hardly ever cries."

I could see how troubled she was, and tried to ease her anxiety. "Diana, look, Jason's probably just a little odd." I smiled. "Maybe he's a genius. Who knows? Einstein was odd, remember?"

"Mark cares about that, but I don't," Diana said.

"Cares about what?"

"Whether Jason's some kind of genius or not," Diana said. "He's like Dad in that way. That line from Schopenhauer, remember? The one he was always quoting." Her voice suddenly sounded eerily like the Old Man's: "'Talent hits a target no one else can reach. Genius hits a target no one else can see.'"

I looked at her, stunned. It was the first and only time Diana had ever betrayed the slightest sense that she regarded the Old Man's furious intellectualism with anything but total admiration.

She saw the shock on my face, noted the mute silence of my slightly parted lips, and looked away from me as if I'd suddenly flashed a bright light in her eyes.

"Anyway, I hope you're right about Jason," she said.

But I was wrong.

Diana told me on a snowy December day. We were in the village square, amid the holiday whirl of lights and people hawking Christmas trees. She was buying presents for Mark and Jason, while I was looking for a video game for Patty. Jason had just turned four, his hand in Diana's, though with little grip, as if he were merely a wooden toy dangling from his mother's hand.

We stopped in front of a particularly festive window. I remembered Diana's face in the glass, her features superimposed over stacks of colorfully wrapped packages. Jason tugged his hand from hers and then, as if called by a voice, strolled over to a nearby parking meter.

"Jason's not okay," Diana said very quietly.

I glanced over to where Jason now stood beside the meter, his eyes fixed on its arc of numbers.

"Mark thinks he's schizophrenic," Diana said.

"But he's only four," I said.

"It's rare, but it happens," Diana said. She fixed her eyes on the shop window. "It's in the family, after all." She looked at me. Her eyes were glistening. "We both know that, don't we, Davey?"

"Yes, we do."

She brushed at her eyes. "Mark will want to put him away," she said in a sudden, vehement whisper. "I know that's what he'll want to do. But he can't do it if I don't sign the papers. And I won't do that. Not ever."

"Then what are you going to do?"

She straightened her shoulders. "I'm going to take care of him." She looked back into the brightly colored window. "As long as he lives," she added. Her eyes flared visibly with the same quick and oddly violent flames that Mark had probably seen as well, the deep and scary part of my sister. "No one is going to take Jason. No one is going to get rid of him."

From that day until his death, Diana had never left Jason's side, save for that one summer morning when Mark had decided to work at home rather than make his usual pilgrimage to the research center.

I imagined the instant Diana must have first discovered that her son was missing. Moment to moment, like the separate frames of a film, I saw her pull into the driveway, remove the groceries from the back of the car, walk into the house, through the foyer and down the corridor to the kitchen with its large bay window. The sun was high, I knew that much, and so the pond must have been glittering brightly in the distance. At that point, I had no doubt that she would have put down her groceries and then, almost reflexively, begun to look for Jason. Living room. Den. One bedroom. Then another. Calling to him as she made her way through the ground-floor rooms and then up the stairs, listening to the tap of the keyboard as Mark worked in his small office at the far end of the corridor, wondering if Jason might be there with his father as she closed in upon that closed door, increasing her pace as she neared it, catching her breath as she turned the knob, the flickering movement of her eyes as they searched the tiny office where Mark sat, his gaze fixed on the monitor, until she said, "Jason."

What had she been thinking, I wondered now, as she stood in that door, faced that tiny room, with nothing but Mark in it, Jason's name on her lips? Was it that she had failed, that for all her mighty effort, the purity and care of her motherhood, her son had, in fact, been gotten rid of?

And how, sunk in the darkness of such a grave suspicion, could she ever be happy again?

And yet, for all that, Diana didn't seem unhappy when I ran into her a few days later. It was just after six and I was driving home when I saw her walking down Lancaster Street, her eyes cast downward as if following invisible tracks. She'd cut her hair so that it now fell just below her ears, and the blouse she wore had a distinctly military look, green, with dull metal buttons, something she'd no doubt purchased at the army-navy store a few blocks away.

I guided the car over to the curb beside her and honked. She stopped, turned toward me, then walked over.

"Need a ride?" I asked.

"No, I'm headed back to the library," Diana answered.

I smiled. "Do you like working there?"

"Very much."

I thought of Cheddar Man. "Still reading anthropology?"

"Not exactly."

She appeared reluctant to tell me more about her reading or anything else, and so I didn't press the issue. There had always been an intensely private aspect to her character, but on other occasions her secretiveness had been purely selfless, simply a way of protecting me from some hardship she felt no immediate need to share. She'd never told me why the Old Man had been suddenly seized and whisked off to Brigham when I was five. She'd also kept the Old Man's final breakdown from me as long as she could before placing him, however briefly, in Brigham once again. She'd never spoken of her marriage, or of what she did with Jason all day, or the lonely nights she'd spent in the old stone farmhouse, waiting for Mark to come home from the lab.

"So, how's the new apartment working out?" I asked.

Just fine, she told me, and for the next few minutes, she offered one of her customarily shaved-down descriptions. Her place wasn't fancy, she said, but it was "functional." Best of all, she added, it was set on a hill, and even though she had a ground-floor apartment, she could go up to the building's rooftop terrace and from that height catch a distant glimpse of Dolphin Pond.

Dolphin Pond . . . where Jason had drowned.

"And way in the distance, I can see the rim of Dover Gorge," she added.

Dover Gorge was the place we'd explored as children, she gathering specimens for her botany collection, I merely strolling along beside her.

"We should go there sometime, Davey," she said now. "We could take a walk the way we used to."

There was hardly anything in my youth that I remembered more vividly than the walks Diana and I had taken together. I remembered the ones at Dover Gorge well enough, but it was the ones through our town that most often returned to me. By eight in the evening the Old Man was either immersed in a book or snoozing in his library chair. We would look in on him, assure ourselves that, in one way or another, he was out for the night, then quietly tiptoe down the short corridor, through the small, square living room, and then out into the night. Everything seemed better in the cool of evening, with just the two of us alone beneath the great overhanging oaks, sometimes walking hand in hand through the nearly deserted streets, then over to the campus quadrangle and up into the bell tower where we stood and looked out over the town.

"There's an overgrown path that leads to an interesting formation," she added now. "Inside Dover Gorge, I mean."

"You've been there lately?"

"Not exactly."

"What does that mean?"

"I read about it," Diana answered. "This formation. We must have passed by it many times, but never noticed it." She smiled. "We should go there again. Like old times."

"Anytime you say," I assured her.

She said nothing in response to this, and so an interval of silence followed, one I found uncomfortable and which gave a sense that she had embarked upon a secret mission she was unwilling to reveal. For a moment I envisioned her quite romantically as a movie spy, trotting down a rain-swept street, her body wrapped in a trench coat, the enemy's invasion plans tucked beneath her arm, beachheads marked with red x's.

"You look . . ." I stopped because I had no words for the way she looked, the hair that now hung boyishly at her ears, the urban guerrilla blouse. "Different," I said finally.

She made no response to this, but I sensed that my description had put her on alert in some indefinable way, and felt that the distance between us had widened, that we were like two astronauts, linked by a heavy cord that was now fraying, fiber by infinitely tenuous fiber, and that if it broke, we would drift out and out until we were finally no longer in the same universe. I was seized by an urgent need to reconnect to her, draw her back within the circle of our old intimacy.

"You haven't sent me anything else," I said. "Like that picture you faxed me. Cheddar Man. It made quite a stir at my office."

She looked at me quizzically.

"Charlie took it for a threat," I added. "People do that sometimes. Like in the *Godfather*. That horse's head in the guy's bed. A little message. 'Be careful. I know where you live.' That sort of thing."

Diana peered at me intently. "What does that have to do with me?"

"Nothing really," I said. I could see that something in what I'd just said had raised a dark antenna. "It was all in context," I explained. "He mentioned that Bill Carnegie had gotten this weird rock in the mail."

Diana looked unsettled, her manner now curiously edged in fear.

"And, well, you'd talked to Bill, right?"

"Yes."

Her fear seemed to be building, as if, step by step, I was pressing her toward the edge of a precipice.

"Bill didn't accuse you of anything, Diana," I said quickly.

Her gaze took on a piercing clarity, pure as death rays. "I have to go," she told me.

"Yeah, sure," I said. "I'll be in touch."

She turned immediately and headed off toward the library. Within a moment she was gone, but as I made my way toward home, I realized that the arid look in her eyes remained with me, dry and floating, like dust motes in the air.

W hat were you afraid of at that moment?" Petrie asks.

"I'm not sure," you answer. "I guess fear is like . . ." You surprise yourself with a literary image. ". . . Medusa's head. All those flapping tentacles. Maybe love is like that, too. Hatred. Maybe all the really big emotions are."

"Are what?"

"Shifting. Entangling. They wrap around each other."

Petrie looks like a man unexpectedly adrift in a river of unmapped twists and turns, depths and shallows he cannot fathom, or even know whether it is Acheron or Lethe that bears him away, Phlegethon, Cocytus, Styx, or the yet murkier stream they form when they meet in some mythical lake and begin to flow together.

You sense that he will now paddle furiously to shore, return to solid ground.

And you are right. He does.

"Of course, you weren't the only one who was beginning to fear Diana," he says.

He means Mark, the fact that I'd already learned that he'd been referred to Stewart Grace. This is the terra firma Petrie relies upon, the hard rock of the case. Or is it the cases? He has deaths to explain, perhaps murders to solve. But how many? One? Two? Three? Four?

"No, not the only one," you confess.

"All right," Petrie says. "Let me ask you this: At this point, precisely at this point, what were you thinking?"

"Only about Diana."

Petrie is clearly relieved to be back on track, rooted in a world where crimes leap like fish from crystal streams of motivation. He is himself the streamlined creature of this world, efficient, exact, focused on the evidence.

"All right. Fine," Petrie continues. "What about Diana?"

"I was thinking that she'd taken a second step," you answer. "First she'd refused to accept Jason's death as an accident. Now she was thinking about that morning, about what happened that morning. Things were coming to her." You see a flash of light in high grass. "Things no one else knew about, or would have ever known."

"Like what?"

"The fact that Mark stayed home that day," you answer. "Because he wanted to give Diana a break." You see Diana pause at the door before leaving. She looks back to where Jason sits on the sofa, his back to the large bay window, Dolphin Pond in the distance.

"Why would that have aroused her suspicion?" Petrie asks.

"Because he'd never done it before."

"Stayed home from work?"

"Not in the last five years."

"That's not real evidence," Petrie says.

"What is?"

"Something admissible," Petrie answers. "A footprint. A weapon."

"A witness?"

"Yes," Petrie says softly.

You know he is thinking about it now, the closing circle of your fate, what you took for "evidence," how much, in the end, you may be "like Dad."

"I'm not crazy," you tell him. Then you quote Diana, " 'You're only crazy when you don't know what you do.' "

Petrie falls silent for a moment, as if to regroup, put everything he's learned so far in order.

"All right," he begins again. "Let's get back to your meeting with Diana. The one outside the library." He sits back. "The things you'd learned so far. The things Bill Carnegie had told you. The things Diana had told you. Had they aroused your own suspicion?"

"Yes," you answer.

Aroused it easily, as you know now, because the threat had not yet moved to you.

"What did you do about it?" Petrie asks.

"I began to . . . investigate."

Petrie is clearly pleased by your answer.

"How?" he asks.

"I started where you would, I guess."

This pleases him even more. "And where is that?" he asks.

"The scene of the crime," you answer, though you know now that there was more than one scene, more than one crime.

But Petrie doesn't ask which crime, and so you lead him along the path you took yourself, the one you still cannot imagine has led you to this place.

SEVEN

I reached my office at the usual time the next morning, but I didn't turn into its small gravel parking lot as I had every other weekday morning for over fifteen years. Instead, I continued down Main Street, and on out of town until I reached Old Farmhouse Road. Then I turned and followed it until the pavement gave way to reddish clay.

As I continued down the road it struck me in an unexpectedly disturbing way just how remote my sister's house really had been. The nearest neighbor was several miles away and the surrounding area was densely forested, a thick wood of towering trees and thick undergrowth that broke only when I reached the narrow dirt driveway of the house itself. It also occurred to me just how easy it would be to read something terribly sinister into the place itself, to find even the choice of it, which had been Mark's, darkly premeditated, the trees, the pond, even the large gray stone at the water's edge, all of them pieces of a plot whose true design could only be seen after it had been carried out.

There was a FOR RENT sign on the front lawn, otherwise the place looked empty and so I pulled directly into the driveway. The flower garden where Diana had spent hours with Jason contained nothing but a few arid stalks, and the surrounding yard had grown high and weedy, both of which gave the place a look of immemorial abandonment. The whole place appeared strangely dead, the structure no more than the desiccated bones of a house, its gray windows as empty and unlighted, it seemed to me suddenly, as the eyes of Cheddar Man.

I got out of my car and walked around to the back of the house, moving slowly along the high storm fence that bordered the yard. Beyond the fence, the high grass rippled in a slight breeze, then immediately came to rest, as if an invisible hand had first roused then abruptly stilled it. Nothing remained of the people who'd lived here only a few short months before. Everything had been completely cleared away; no sign of Jason's toys, Mark's elaborately geared mountain bike, or even the wooden picnic table where we'd often gathered for a summer cookout, Mark at the grill, flipping burgers, Diana pacing about with Jason in her arms, I strolling along beside her while Abby led Patty through the gate and toward the pond.

The pond.

I turned and followed the narrow trail I thought Jason might have taken on the day of his death. It led through a cove of trees, then passed the large stone that stood like a centurion at the edge of the pond. For a moment I paused on the bank and looked out over the pond's shimmering surface, listening as tiny waves beat softly, rhythmically, like a watery heart.

I'd been en route to a distant part of the county the day Jason drowned, so that by the time I got to the house, the police had already arrived, searched the surrounding area, then hauled a boat to the water's edge. Divers were in gear, and the boat was being carried toward the center of the pond where it suddenly deepened at a distance of perhaps fifty yards from shore.

Diana stood at the edge of the water, cradled under Mark's arm, the two of them staring out over the pond, watching the divers as they climbed into the boat and paddled out to deeper water. Mark tightened his arm around her when he saw me, his eyes very dark and sad, at least so they'd seemed at the time. Diana's eyes were wet and red, and there was an animal terror in them, as if she, herself, were being drawn underwater.

"Jason," she said softly when I reached her.

"He must have undone the latch," Mark told me. "At the back gate."

"They've searched the woods," Diana added. Her eyes drifted over to me. "He's in the water, Davey."

"Let's go inside, Diana," Mark said quietly. He drew her back toward the house. "Just wait here, will you, Dave?"

I did as he asked, remained there at the edge of the pond while the divers did their work. I don't know how long I stood in that terrible silence until a voice broke it.

"Mind if I get your name?"

I turned toward a tall man dressed in a navy blue suit with a white shirt and red tie. It was mid-June, very hot, but he'd not taken off his jacket, and so held an air of unassailable professionalism.

"My name is Dave Sears," I told him.

He gave me a close look. "Diana's brother."

Then I recognized him. I'd never known his name, but he'd come to the house the day the Old Man died, a young detective then, but with the same coolly knowing air.

"I remember you, too," I told him. "Not your name, but—"

"My name is Petrie," he said. "Samuel Petrie. Do you still live around here?"

"Still in the area, yes," I answered. "I guess you do, too."

"A couple towns over," Petrie said. He reached inside his jacket and pulled out his ID. "I still work for the county. And you?"

"Lawyer," I said.

"You must not do criminal work," Petrie said. "Otherwise we'd have run into each other."

"No, it's all civil litigation," I said. "Divorces, mostly."

He fell silent for a moment, but his eyes remained on me with an unsettling stillness. "I remember that day. Your father was some . . . person of note."

"He'd done a little writing, if that's what you mean," I said. "Poems."

Petrie glanced out over the pond, then brought his attention back to me.

"I'd like to ask you a few questions about Jason."

I expected him to take out a notebook as cops did in movies, but he didn't.

81

"Did he ever wander off or run away?"

"No."

"In general, what can you tell me about him?"

I suddenly felt a piercing sense of failure. For the terrible truth was that I had very little to tell Detective Petrie. I didn't know Jason. I had been present at the hour of his birth, watched him grow over the years, but who he was, what he felt, and, least of all, what might have led him into the pond, were all part of an inner world I knew no way to explore, the habitat of dragons.

"He was . . . is . . ." I shook my head. "I . . ."

Petrie appeared to understand my dilemma, and in that understanding he struck me as quite sturdy and experienced, a man who'd been in such situations many times before, dealt with other people through the long, heartrending ambiguity of missing persons.

"Mr. Regan says that Jason has a few problems," Petrie said. "How would you describe them?"

"Mark didn't tell you?"

"I prefer to approach certain matters from different angles," Petrie said. "Would you say that Jason is retarded?"

"No," I said. "Well, not exactly. I think there've been a few different diagnoses since it was first noticed."

"Since what was first noticed?"

"His behavior."

"Which is?"

"Well, when he's in a room with other kids, he doesn't really interact with them."

Now Petrie did what I'd originally expected him to do. He

drew a small notebook from his jacket pocket, along with a plain blue pen.

"Has he always been this way?" he asked.

"Yes."

"So this condition wasn't something that just came upon him at some point?"

I wondered if Petrie were looking for abuse, for some cruel damage that had been inflicted upon Jason, a kind so serious it had unhinged him, cut him off from others. I had no doubt that Petrie had seen such cases in his career because I could see the afterimage of that long record briefly mirrored in his gaze.

"It happens, you know," he said. "People suddenly—"

"Not Jason," I assured him. "Jason was born with this problem."

"You said there have been different diagnoses? Like what?"

I rattled them off in the order they'd been made. "Autism. Asperger's syndrome. The last one was schizophrenia."

"That word casts a wide net."

"It was what his father first suspected."

"Why?"

I heard myself repeat Diana's earlier words. "Because it is in us. Schizophrenia. In our family."

Petrie's pen whispered across the page. "But about Jason. Was he on any drugs?"

"I don't know," I admitted quietly. "He was at one time, I think."

"Do you know when?"

It was at that moment I realized that these were all questions Petrie had surely already asked Mark or Diana, and that he was not actually seeking information, but contradiction. He was looking for a lie.

"Where do you think Jason is?" I asked flatly.

Petrie looked up from the pad. "I . . ." he began softly, then stopped as if at an unspoken, but formal command. "I only know things when I know them, Mr. Sears," he said. "It's dangerous country, beyond the facts."

Diana and Mark had still been in the house, and I still beside the pond, when one of the divers surfaced and pointed toward the bottom of the lake. He'd nodded slowly, and in the heaviness of that gesture, the weight of the discovery it acknowledged, I knew that Jason had been found.

Petrie saw the same signal, and walked back over to me from where he'd been standing with a couple of other officials.

"Do you want me to tell them?" he asked.

"No, I will."

To my surprise he accompanied me back into the house. Diana and Mark were in the small living room, Mark seated beside the empty fireplace, Diana at the front window, her back to me as we came into the room. She didn't turn until she heard my voice.

"Jason was . . ." I began quietly. "He was."

"In the pond," Diana said flatly.

I expected her to break down, perhaps even drop to her knees, wail like women in movies, their faces lifted toward the sky, demanding another result or railing against one that cannot be changed. But instead, her body stiffened, then she turned smoothly, as if on a slowly revolving wheel, and walked silently up the stairs.

Mark got to his feet wearily, a man weighted down, so that he appeared to sink even as he rose.

"Thank you," he said to Detective Petrie. "Please thank your people for all they've done." He offered his hand, and for an odd moment the detective appeared reluctant to take it. Then he did, and shook it slowly.

"We'll need a positive identification," he said.

"I can do that," I told Mark. "I mean, if you prefer."

"Would you, Dave? Thank you."

"And there'll have to be an autopsy," Petrie added.

"I understand," Mark told him.

Then Petrie left, so that only Mark and I were in the room.

"I don't know what to say, Mark," I told him.

Mark returned to his chair. "There's nothing to say."

I glanced toward the stairs. "You think you should check in on Diana?"

He shook his head. "She'll respond in her own way."

It was almost at that instant that an awesome groan came from the upstairs bedroom, a long primitive wail that finally resolved into a low, animal moan.

"Now she has," Mark said.

Diana's final moan seemed to hang in the trees as I stood once again beside the pond, peering out to where, as exactly as I could recall, the diver had surfaced, then pointed straight down. They'd brought up Jason's body right away, then hustled it off to a nearby funeral parlor, where it would later undergo autopsy, a report duly generated, one the judge had later relied upon in determining that Jason had died by "misadventure."

I remembered the way Diana's body had gone rigid the instant the judge handed down his ruling, and it struck me as the same sudden tightening that had followed the news of Jason's death, as if her flesh had abruptly hardened, holding everything inside, steeling her long enough to make it up the stairs, where, in what must have seemed to her an absolute solitude, she'd released her wail.

I heard it again now, only instead of coming from a few feet above me, it seemed to drift down from the sky itself, sound as substance, cold and wet, falling forever in a dark eternal rain.

The chair across from you is empty now. Petrie stands at the window, his back to you. You know that he is recalling the day you have just described, the two of you on the banks of Dolphin Pond, talking quietly as the divers do their work, watching as they lift themselves over the gunwale of the boat and sink into the water, remembering, as you remembered the day you returned to the pond, that the boat had been near the center of the lake, where the water abruptly deepened, how far it was before this happened, and thus how far Jason would have had to walk before it reached his waist, then his shoulders.

"Shallow," you say quietly.

You watch as Petrie's shoulders tighten almost imperceptibly, as if in response to a tiny pinch of pain.

"So you realized what Diana had meant," he says. "In the courtroom that day."

"Shallow," you say again, quoting Diana. "She said it twice."

Petrie continues to peer out the window. "But at the time, what did you think she meant?"

"I had no idea at the time," you answer. "But I suppose I would have thought that she meant the proceedings, or maybe the final decision. That it was all . . . shallow."

Petrie's shoulders lift with a long breath.

You know that he feels this new current in the story's flow. He is like a skater on a familiar lake, one whose familiarity begins to fade even as he skates, a tree over there, and in the distance a small shed, neither in their old positions, a shift in the landscape.

"A very long way," Petrie says, a clear reference to the distance between the edge of the pond and where Jason's body had been found. You know what he is thinking. That Dolphin Pond is a placid lake. Without currents. A body would not have drifted.

"Why would he have walked so far out?" you ask. "I think that was Diana's question. Because he'd never been taken into the water."

"Why not?" Petrie asks.

"Because he was afraid of the water." You see Jason's eyes, how easily they jumped at sudden movements, sudden sounds. "Jason lived in fear."

Petrie turns to face you. "Is that what you were thinking when you left the pond?" he asks. "That this was evidence?"

"Not exactly, no."

Petrie is clearly surprised by your answer. "What then?"

"How easy it was."

Petrie looks at you quizzically. "Easy?"

You remember the games. So many of them. Find Me. Treasure chest. Was it a house of games, Victor Hugo Street? Chess, not checkers, with the Old Man as king, Diana his knight, you, forever, a lowly, lowly pawn?

"What was easy, Mr. Sears?"

You are standing by the pond again. You turn back toward the house, thinking, *So isolated.* Then you face the pond again, peer out over the still water, thinking, *Shallow, shallow.*

"To be drawn in to Diana's . . . way of thinking," you answer. Patty's voice sounds in your mind, *Diana says I'm very imaginative.* "How easy it is to be seduced." You feel a wave of pain pass over you and marvel at how physical it is, as physical as heat or intense pressure. "Diana," you whisper, and at the mention of her name you see the little red ball move from hand to hand, the dark sparkle in her eyes, feel the touch of her hand as she takes yours, then leads you down the stairs.

"Diana," you begin again, then stop, unable to go on.

You shake your head. "Shifting," you murmur finally. "Entangled."

Petrie gazes at you intently, with a deep scrutiny that seems natural, unlearned, no longer a textbook inquisitiveness.

"Everything is shifting," you tell him.

Petrie's eyes glitter with small disturbances. "All right, Mr. Sears," he says cautiously, returning you to solid ground. "What did you do when you left the pond?"

You know he is drawing you back to the case.

You follow willingly, and feel again the sweet pull of gravity, the familiar earth. "After I left the pond . . ."

EIGHT

After I left the pond, I returned to my office and tried to distract myself with work. Lily had returned to her post, and I dictated the usual legal correspondence. Later, I went over various papers, made a few phone calls. Later still, I reviewed my correspondence on Ed Leary's behalf, the offers he'd made, Ethel's refusals to accept any of them. The final letter had come only the day before. It bore Bill Carnegie's distinctive letterhead, complete with a somewhat overlarge illustration of blind justice. The message was succinct: "It is my duty to inform you that my client cannot accept Mr. Leary's offer and will therefore press her demand in court."

I'd duly informed Ed that his wife had rejected his last offer. I'd also assured him that in my opinion he'd done everything he could to reach a just settlement, and that, also in my opinion, no subsequent offer, no matter how generous, would ever be accepted.

It was the last line of my letter to Ed that grabbed my attention now. It came only after several paragraphs of my characteristically correct and lawyerly language, a sentence that suddenly took a turn, one might even call it a dive, into the intransigent, irreconcilable, and profoundly unreasoning nature of the situation, and which even then struck me as oddly prophetic: *As in ancient times, it would appear that some settlements require blood.*

And then, as if on cue, it came.

The envelope was addressed to me, but with no return address, and yet from the tiny, fractured script, I knew it was from Diana.

There was no accompanying letter inside the envelope, no explanatory note, but only the photograph of what appeared to be a teenaged girl, perhaps fourteen or fifteen, with smooth pinkish skin and a great curly mass of radiant red hair. In bold black letters the heading declared YDE GIRL. Below the heading there was a single question: *Was She Murdered?*

The girl's face looked completely contemporary, with the healthy flush of a Midwestern farm girl, a far cry from the naked bones of Cheddar Man, and so for a moment I reasoned that Diana's "research" had unaccountably shifted forward to some more recent crime, the murder of a teenaged girl from "Yde," perhaps, though it was not a place I'd ever heard of.

I looked at the face again, the calm expression, the small,

sweet smile. The girl's eyes were open, but she didn't appear focused on anything in particular, like a person listening to music, but with nothing more than vague interest. The photograph gave no hint of violence or even the fear of violence. So why the question about murder?

I remembered a game Diana and I had played when we were children. She'd called it "Find Me," and in the game we'd taken turns giving each other one fact at a time. On Diana's side, it was more often a fate, usually tragic or macabre. For Charles Francis Hall, the doomed arctic explorer, her first clue had been *icy end*. For Marat, it had been *bloody bath*.

I wondered if Diana were playing some version of that childhood game with me now. Of course times had changed since we'd first played it, at least in terms of retrieving information. There was no need for me to rush to the library for a reference book. I simply went online and typed the words "Yde Girl" in the search engine.

And there she was, the same photograph Diana had sent me, only this time the colors were more vivid, the flesh tones more varied, highlights in her hair. Beneath the face there was a line of text that said simply, "Medical Reconstruction."

So the picture Diana had sent me was not the actual face of Yde Girl at all, but a model created on the basis of no doubt far less pristine remains. The accompanying text told me more. Yde Girl had been found in a peat bog in Yde, the Netherlands. A woolen cord had been wound around her neck and fitted with a slipknot. The cord had been pulled so tightly that it had left a visible pattern in the dead girl's throat. The question then was not whether Yde Girl had died violently, but whether she had been executed, sacrificed, or simply murdered. There would be no answer to this question, for Yde Girl had died nearly two thousand years before.

I held the photograph Diana had sent me up to the light and stared intently at the carefully molded face with its glass eyes and clean, shiny hair. Now it looked like the head of a doll rather than a human being, and I could see a jagged line of script that ran across the undamaged forehead, two words Diana had written, and which I recognized as just the sort of subtle hint she'd often given me when we'd played Find Me years before, clues that had never failed to draw me ever more helplessly into the pursuit. I flipped over the photograph with the same childlike eagerness I'd done as a little boy and read what Diana had written there.

Original sin.

"Original sin," I repeated softly, now recalling the specific way Diana had played the game in the past, how her clues had tended to be oblique combinations of references, sometimes comic, sometimes ironic. For example, her opening clue for Roscoe Arbuckle had been *fat chance,* a hint that pointed both to the actor's obesity and the fact that by sheer accident he'd been accused of rape and murder.

Original sin, I thought. By the word sin, she could only mean the murder. But what was original about murder? Nothing, of course. So what could possibly be "original" about Yde Girl? The answer came to me the way it often had when we'd played the game as children, simply out of the blue, as if it had been whispered wordlessly into my mind. The only thing original I might find about Yde Girl would be her corpse, the remains from which the decidedly unoriginal reconstruction had been made. These remains surely would be the "original" evidence of the "sin" that had been her murder.

I turned back to the article on my computer screen, ran the cursor down to the bottom of the Web page, and found a lighted reference entitled "Initial Discovery."

I clicked on it and once again she was there.

Yde Girl.

Hardly anything of the grotesque image that immediately flashed onto the screen gave any sense of that lovely, painted face. The abundant red hair now sprouted in a hideously frazzled ponytail from an otherwise bald skull. The rosy cheeks were gone, along with the little doll eyes. In fact, the "original" remains of Yde Girl revealed almost no face at all, or at least not one with discernible features. Her "skin," if it could be called that, was ash gray. Her nose was entirely flattened, and her cheek and cheekbones looked as if they'd been beaten into a featureless mass, so that the "face" of Yde Girl appeared more or less melted, her eyes mere drooping slits, her mouth little more than a hole gouged into a lump of clay.

Find me.

It was Diana's voice. She wasn't there, of course, but the vacant space where I imagined her lips at my ear seemed oddly electrified, as if some presence had briefly taken form, then vanished, leaving only its tingling imprint in the empty air. I got to my feet, as if yanked by an invisible hand, then walked to the window, steadied myself, and looked out onto a brilliant, and profoundly ordinary, autumn day.

Find me.

Suddenly it was no longer what actually existed beyond the window that I saw, but a narrow trail through a field of tall, gently swaying reeds, my gaze moving like an invisible camera, following a teenaged girl as she closes in upon the bog, catching her only in glimpses of her flaming red hair as she swims in and out of an early morning mist. Then, in a no less sudden shift, it was Jason I trailed behind, moving with him toward the pond, his shadow drifting over the summer grass, into the darkness visible, as I abruptly saw it, of his approaching death.

And I instantly knew that this had been Diana's design all along, to bring me back to Jason, a murder she clearly thought no less painfully unresolved.

As if summoned by some weird telepathy, Diana was waiting beside my car when I left work that evening, leaning against the rear bumper, eating an apple. She was wearing a dark red shirt, with the collar lifted, so that its tips gave the appearance of small wings at her throat. I half expected them to flutter.

"Hi, Davey," she said. "Did you get what I sent you?"

"You mean, Yde Girl?" I answered. "Yes, I got it." I gave no hint that I felt certain that I'd uncovered the design. "What interests you about that . . . murder?"

"I don't know," Diana answered. "It's just something Dad used to do. Read about old crimes."

"I don't remember him doing that."

"Oh, yes," Diana said. "William Roughead, for example. Thomas de Quincey's 'On Murder.' He said reading about old crimes taught him something about justice."

"And what was that?" I asked pointedly.

"That it was hard to achieve . . . but worth it."

I chuckled dryly. "I could have told him that."

"He loved a particular thought of De Quincey's," Diana added with a sense of studied nostalgia, as if she were researching her past rather than simply recalling it. "That a man doesn't need to keep his eyes in his breeches when he confronts murder."

"What does that mean?" I asked.

"That faced with a murderer, you know what you know," Diana answered.

I smiled. "Opinion is not admissible in court."

"If it's only that," Diana said.

She added nothing more about the Old Man or De Quincey or murder or her vague concept of knowing "what you know," but instead reached far back and gave the apple a hard throw, sending it arching across the driveway and into the wooded area at the other side.

"Let's go for a ride," she said.

"Where to?" I asked.

"Dover Gorge," she answered.

"Why there?"

"Because that's where Dad and I had our last good talk, Davey," Diana said. "And I want to have another one, but this time with you."

We drove toward Dover Gorge through a landscape that was, to say the least, multicolored, and on the way I recalled the trips we'd taken there as children, the Old Man at the wheel, windows down in all weather, wind whipping through his wildly disheveled hair. We'd had a small car, and he'd never liked being physically crowded. Because of that I'd been relegated to the backseat, Diana up front, the two of them talking about whatever Great Idea the Old Man had chosen for the day's subject, death, the afterlife, the lessons of history, conversations to which I no longer attempted to contribute.

"Lascaux," Diana said after a moment. "Have you heard of it?"

"It's a cave, isn't it?" I asked, reaching back to some reference I remembered from a travel magazine.

"In France," Diana said with a nod. "It has around fifteen hundred prehistoric drawings. Some are beautifully colored. They used vegetable pigments and ocher, the first painters."

She smiled and I recalled all the many times we'd sat in the Old Man's library, she beneath the light, explaining this new interest or that one, transforming the most ordinary things, a bird's nest, a pinecone, into objects of unearthly fascination.

"They drew animals, mostly," she added. "No human beings, but that's not unusual in prehistoric art." She faced ahead, as if searching for the first glimpse of Dover Gorge. "The unusual thing about Lascaux is that the cave floor was covered with thousands of reindeer bones." She paused, as she often had in her younger days, to intensify interest, create dramatic emphasis, add a beat of intellectual suspense.

"But there's not a single drawing of a reindeer in Lascaux," Diana said. "Why do you suppose that is, Davey?"

"I have no idea," I answered.

For a moment I thought she was going to attempt an answer to her own question, but instead, she shrugged. "Neither do I," she said. "But it's something to think about."

"And you've been thinking about it, I suppose?" I asked cautiously.

"Yes."

"About Lascaux in particular?"

"No," Diana answered. "But that whole business of no reindeer bones."

"And concluded what?"

"No conclusion," Diana said. "Just a notion that maybe they didn't paint the animals they ate because they had to separate themselves from them."

"Why would they need to do that?"

Her eyes sparkled oddly, like one caught in dark conjecture. "Because you have to separate yourself from something before you can kill it," she said.

We reached Dover Gorge in a bluish twilight that gave the whole area a ghostly feel, or if not that, then the timelessness of unfeeling things. The granite walls were very high and appeared to lean forward like great stone giants looking down at the tiny, frightened creatures over whom they asserted a terrible dominion.

We parked in a nearly deserted lot, got out of the car, and stood facing the nearest of the cliffs.

"There's a crevice over there," Diana said with certainty, so that it was clear that she had a map of the gorge in her mind.

She raised her arm and indicated a path that led into the woods. "That little trail goes to it," she added. "The crevice is very narrow, barely big enough for a human being to get through."

"How do you know all this?" I asked.

"From something I read," Diana answered.

With that we moved across the lot and into the woods, walking together down a path that grew increasingly narrow as we approached the stone wall. At the wall, Diana glanced left and right, then with a quick nod, led me to a second trail, this one unused and untended, so that we walked more slowly, plowing through the thickening undergrowth until we reached a jagged breach that ran upward from the base to the full height of the wall.

"Here," she said. "Here is where he heard it."

"Heard what?" I asked.

For a moment she seemed unsure of an answer. Then she said, "A murmur of stones." She took a small square pamphlet from the pocket of her blouse. It was very old, with yellow pages, and looked as if, at any moment, it might turn to dust.

"Douglas Price," she added. "He came here in 1947." She opened the pamphlet and delicately began turning the pages. "He'd been an airman in the war. Thirty-seven sorties."

I'd seen enough war movies to know what that meant, thirty-seven takeoffs, the skyward thrust, then the leveling out, the long flight over lakes and farmland, to where the target waited with its network of defending guns.

"He had trouble with loud noises after that," Diana added. "He found them 'alarming.'"

I imagined Price as a young man in a wildly shaking plane, the fuselage rattling so loudly in midair he must have thought it would surely tear apart, the noise of exploding shells finally drowning out the inhuman shuddering of the plane, so that the world must have become in those few moments he soared above the target little more than an unbearably deafening roar.

"He got a job at Brigham," Diana said.

Brigham, I thought, where the Old Man had twice been taken, first when I was five, then a second time, years later, so that he might have died there had Diana not left college and brought him home.

"There were quite a few soldiers in Brigham in 1947," Diana added. She appeared to retreat to that era just after the war, when the debris had come floating back in waves of wounded bodies and damaged minds. "Price listened to their stories." She glanced down at the pamphlet, turned to a page she'd already marked, studied what was written there a moment, then looked up at me. "One day he went for a walk and ended up here at Dover Gorge."

Now she was with him, as I could clearly see, walking along beside him as he drifted up the steadily narrowing trail to where the great stone split.

"It was a bright summer day," she said. "Green, dotted with white flowers."

This sounded like a quotation, so it didn't surprise me when she lifted the pamphlet slightly. "His writing is pretty bad, actually," she said. "Very mannered, I mean."

Then she read:

The simple lushness of the scene served to avert my thoughts from life's pervasive acrimonies, so that I felt myself transported into a fantastical world of sweetness and harmony, before the first branch had been in anger lifted, the first stone hurled.

She looked up and smiled. "See what I mean about the writing?"

Then she resumed reading, and as she read I felt her wizardry again, how easily she could pull you into the deep water of whatever subject commanded her attention.

Now I joined her at Price's side, the three of us moving "along a dense, verdant path with rivulets of white flowers on both sides." Together we drifted deeper and deeper into the woods, then along the side of the cliff until we reached a jagged fissure that Price somehow saw as "tragic, a broken heart of stone."

"This is where he stopped," Diana said. "Right at this spot where we're standing." She lowered the pamphlet and let her eyes drift up the cruelly jagged rift in the granite wall. "This is where he heard them. Voices."

She had memorized Price's words, and now recited them. "'A rustling in the undergrowth, along with numerous faint cries.'" She drew her gaze back to me and continued her recitation in the same soft voice she'd used as a child, and which once again, after all these years, I found utterly mesmerizing:

I cannot describe the sensation that settled upon me, save as a visitation, a haunting. And yet, I saw no floating appari-

tion, heard no wailing, as of a child in the wood or at the end of a corridor. The ghostliness gave no visual clue as to its nature or identity. It spoke only, and this in soft cries and a low, unbroken wail which translated to me a feeling of abandonment, of helplessness in the face of grave affliction, of ancient wounds unhealed and ancient wrongs unavenged and thus condemned forever to cry out from the hard eternal grit of immemorial stone.

She closed the pamphlet slowly, like a priest at the end of a homily. "Douglas Price is still alive, you know," she said. "I'm going to talk to him."

"Why?"

She turned toward the granite wall we stood beside and with a strange, impossible grace, reached out and raked her fingers down the jagged fissure in exactly the way I'd seen her touch the side of Jason's face. "To find out what he knows," she said.

P etrie considers the trip to Dover Gorge, and I can see that something in the walk disturbs him.

"So at that time, Diana said nothing about Mark or Jason?" he asks.

"No."

"Just Douglas Price, that pamphlet he wrote."

You nod because you have nothing to add.

"She didn't say anything about her having any suspicions concerning Jason's death?" Petrie asks.

"Nothing at all," you admit, now recalling a line the Old Man often quoted, Emily Dickinson's notion of telling the truth, but at a slant. Was that Diana's strategy, you wonder now, another of her gifts, a genius for evasion and misdirection?

"No hint of a plot?" Petrie asks.

You see just how determined Petrie is to keep to the plan he has established for this interrogation, to gather only admissible evidence.

"None at all," you tell him.

"So you knew no more about what Diana was doing after the walk than before it."

"That's right."

"Nothing gained."

"Nothing beyond a sense of something ominous," you tell him, an answer you know Petrie will not like.

It is odd, you think, how stories unfold, particularly this story, how you are about one-third through it now, but can already feel the downward slope, know that from here on the descent will be steady and grow ever more rapid. You sense that Petrie knows this, too, sees the pained crinkle of your eyes and recognizes the indisputable fact that for you it begins here, the true disaster.

"And a sense of failure," you add. "I felt a sense of failure on the drive back into town."

A silent drive, you recall, with Diana's gaze locked on the road ahead, the darkening air, saying nothing so that you suddenly felt that you had disappointed her in the way you'd all your life disappointed the Old Man, been inadequate to the task.

"Did she say anything more about Dover Gorge?" Petrie asks. "Why she'd taken you there?"

"No," you answer. And yet you'd detected something in her manner. It wasn't spoken. But it was in her eyes.

"Something made me think that this whole business at Dover Gorge had been a test," you tell Petrie.

"Of what?"

"Of me. Of whether I could be trusted. I felt a shift away from me." You see the Old Man and Diana together in his library, talking quietly as you linger at the door, checkers to her chess. "I'd felt it before. But that was with my father, the way he shifted his attention to Diana, focused all of it on her."

You shrug, as if to unload an invisible burden, and in that instant a truth declares itself, and you know that it isn't what we lose that haunts us, but what we lose by just a blink. A shudder passes through you, becomes physical, a trembling in your hands, so that you quickly draw them into your lap.

"After leaving Diana, I went home," you continue. "It was just like every other night." You see them in their usual seats. Abby at the opposite end of the oval table, Patty between the two of you, an ordinary dinner, meat loaf, green peas, mashed potatoes.

"At dinner I mentioned that I'd just left Diana," you tell Petrie. "That we'd gone to Dover Gorge. I told them what I told you, that she had this pamphlet some guy wrote after the war, that this man, Douglas Price, that he'd been at Brigham." You see Abby's gaze shoot over to you, see the question in her eyes. *Isn't that where your father was?* Then it is Patty who speaks, *I just got an interesting e-mail from Aunt Diana.*

"Patty told me that Diana had sent her something," you tell Petrie. "She must have sent it to her right after she got home that evening. It was an e-mail. A Web site."

"What Web site?"

"I asked Patty the same question."

Petrie's pen stands at the ready. "And her answer?" he asks.

NINE

W indeby Girl," Patty answered. "It's a Web site about Windeby Girl."

"Who's that?" I asked.

"I don't know exactly," Patty said. "Just something she's interested in."

"And wants to share with you," I said. "Like Kinsetta Tabu."

"I guess."

I couldn't tell if Patty was being completely open, or if some part of her remained guarded, the Web site Diana had sent her entirely innocent, or if something darker lay behind it.

"She sent me a Web site, too," I said. "Yde Girl."

Patty's eyes glimmered with what seemed to be recognition, but I made nothing of it.

"Ever heard of that?" I asked.

Patty shook her head.

And I thought, *She's lying,* and suddenly Patty appeared to me not as she was, sitting quietly at dinner, but as some variant of Nina, Charlie's vampirish daughter, the one I'd earlier envisioned drifting down a shadowy corridor with a knife in her hand.

"She was murdered," I said. "Yde Girl." I looked for a reaction in Patty, but she gave no hint of ever having heard of this ancient crime.

"What happened to Windeby Girl?" I asked.

Patty shrugged. "I don't know," she said. She took a bite of meat loaf and chewed it slowly before she added, "I haven't looked at the Web site yet. It was just a link."

To my astonishment, I had no idea if this were false or true, if Patty indeed knew nothing of Windeby Girl, or if, like Diana, she knew everything.

After dinner I went directly to my office, turned on my computer, and typed "Windeby Girl" into the search engine. Several Web sites appeared. I picked the first, and it was there, everything I needed to know, all of it written in an unusual script my computer identified as Monotype Corsiva 20:

The Landesmuseum of the Schloss Gottorf contains five bog bodies and one partially preserved head. One of these bodies, known as Windeby I, is that of a 14 year old girl. Windeby Girl's body was found in a peat bog in 1952. Although she drowned, her death was not an accident. She had been blind-folded, and her body had been weighted down with a stone and tree branches. Based on this evidence, scholars have determined that Windeby Girl's death, 2000 years ago, was a result not of misadventure, but of calculated murder.

Without in the least willing it, I took a deep breath and read the page again, now reliving the murder of Windeby Girl in each of its gruesome stages, a death done step by step, feeling each moment of her murder as it was carried out, first the soft texture of the blindfold, then the cool of the water as her face was pressed into it, and finally the terrible absence of air.

Certain words from the text now flashed up from the page in tiny explosions.

Not an accident. Drowned. Not of misadventure, but of calculated murder.

Those words had no doubt reminded Diana of Jason, I thought, though in what way I could not imagine.

"Dave?"

I looked up to find Abby standing at my door.

"What's wrong?" she asked worriedly.

I motioned her over to my desk. "This is the Web site Diana sent to Patty," I told her. Then I pointed out the words that had seemed to flash up from the text.

For a moment, Abby said nothing, but her face was veiled in worry. "You have to warn him, Dave," she said.

I had no idea what she was talking about. "Warn who?" I asked.

Her answer took me completely by surprise. "Mark," she said, and added nothing else.

I couldn't get Abby's warning out of my mind, how certain she was that Mark was somehow in danger. The lightness in her eyes had faded as she spoke, and her voice had drained of all cheer. It was as if she somehow sensed that a great stone had been dislodged and would soon be rolling toward us, inevitably gaining speed as it thundered down the unguarded slope.

But what was I supposed to warn Mark about? Was it the fact that Diana took early morning walks or seemed unwilling to have visitors at her apartment? Was he to be warned that she'd rid herself of everything from her past, or that she was sending e-mails and faxes about prehistoric and Iron Age murders?

For all of this, the fact remained that Diana hadn't so much as mentioned Mark while we'd been at Dover Gorge. Nor had she connected him to Cheddar Man or Yde Girl or Windeby Girl. As far as I knew, she'd made no accusation against him, to me or to anyone else.

When I got to work the next morning, I checked my fax machine for anything Diana might have sent during the night. I was relieved to find the tray empty, no eyeless skeletons, no leathery remains of murdered girls. There were no e-mails from Diana either.

At a little after ten Lily stepped into my office. "Ed Leary wants to see you," she said. "He's here now."

"Okay, send him in."

Ed appeared a few seconds later, looking a little less bedraggled than usual.

"I've had a change of heart," he announced as he lowered himself into the chair opposite my desk. "I want to make Ethel another offer. I want you to ask her what would put her mind at peace."

"Peace could get pretty expensive," I warned him. "She might come back with something quite drastic."

"I want to know what would put her at rest," Ed said, his tone a trifle more determined than before. "Peace, that's what people really want, don't you think?"

I didn't find it useful to ponder "what people really want." The range was too vast to contemplate. Unexpectedly I recalled one of the Old Man's sonorous pronouncements: *A king reduced, had wanted only a horse, while the whole known world was too little for Alexander.*

"Why this change of heart?" I asked.

"Your sister."

I felt a dark stirring, felt what I thought Abby had felt the night before, a sense of something malignant growing in our midst, a murky pool, eternally spinning, and into which, by misadventure, we fall and fall and fall.

"You've been talking to Diana?" I asked.

"Yeah," Ed answered brightly, and in an uncharacteristically cheerful tone, as if Diana had become a source of happiness or relief or inspiration, or perhaps all three, a ray of light that had managed to penetrate the gloom into which his life had settled.

I leaned forward. "Where did you meet Diana?"

"My shop is just down the street from the library," Ed explained. "She came in one evening. On her way home, I guess. She wanted to look at the stones."

"But Jason has a stone," I said, remembering the afternoon of the funeral, how silent Diana had remained all that day, uttering not a word at the gravesite, nor during the ride back to the farmhouse. Even then she'd spoken only a few words before she'd wandered out the back door, then through the storm fence that bordered it, farther and farther from the rest of us until she'd finally taken her place beside the large gray stone that stood on the banks of Dolphin Pond.

"Dave?"

Ed's summons brought me back to the little square office, the short gray filing cabinets and modest desk.

"Yes," I said. "Diana. You were saying?"

"She wasn't interested in looking at tombstones," Ed told

me. "The polished stuff, I mean. She was interested in raw stone."

"Why?"

"She had a picture of a drawing she was interested in. The picture looked like it was drawn on stone."

"What did the drawing show?" I asked.

"Just some lines drawn in blue. Sort of wavy lines. Running horizontal." He thought a moment, then added, "And there was a little splash of red in the middle of the blue part."

"Did she say where this drawing came from?" I asked.

"Nope, just that it was very old," Ed said. "Thousands of years back, she said." Then he repeated a phrase I knew he'd gotten from Diana. "That very dawn." He glanced out the window, then back at me. "Anyway, we got to talking. I knew about her son. I told her what I was going through, and so we talked about that, too. She could see how mad I was at Ethel. She said there were only two things a person could do to get rid of a rage like that. Pay Ethel off and forget it, that was one way."

"And the other?"

He laughed. "Kill her," he said.

I eased back slowly, as if pressed by the point of a blade.

Ed massaged his left shoulder, and winced slightly. "So I've made up my mind. I want you to make Ethel another offer." He winked. "Can't kill her, right?"

I stared at him silently as murder scene after murder scene flashed through my mind: Ethel sprawled across a frayed Oriental carpet, her head in a plastic bag tied at her throat; Ethel floating in a pool of bloody bathwater; Ethel slumped in a chair, a trickle of blood flowing down along the bridge of her nose from the single hole between her eyes; Ethel with a knife in her chest; Ethel bludgeoned, her face beaten into pulp like . . .

"Yde Girl," I whispered.

"What?" Ed asked.

"Nothing," I answered, returning to the matter at hand. But Ed didn't believe that it was nothing. He had seen something in my eyes. "She didn't mean it, Dave," he said. "She didn't mean I should kill my wife."

"Of course not," I told him, but even as I gave him this assurance, my mind raced on, now thinking of Diana, what she'd said to Ed, how extreme they were, the options she'd given him, and how profoundly limited, only two: peace through surrender or a terrible revenge.

Ed guessed none of this, of course. He rose lightly, as if a great burden had been lifted from him. "Just let me know what Ethel says."

I walked him to his truck, hoping to hear more, gather some detail about Diana that might bring things into clearer focus, give me some hint as to where exactly her mind was tending. For it was her mind that troubled me now, the building fear, one I could not suppress, that she was "like Dad."

"About Diana," I said after Ed had gotten into the truck and was about to pull away. "When you saw her last, did she seem okay?"

"Okay?" Ed asked. "What do you mean?"

The word leaped from my mouth. "Sane."

Ed laughed. "Sane? Diana?" He laughed again as he hit the ignition. "Nobody saner, Dave."

But for all Ed's assurance, the question continued to circle in my mind. And so, for the next few hours, as I worked at my desk, the meeting with Ed Leary kept returning to me, ominous as a vulture in a clear blue sky. I'd never heard Diana speak of killing someone, of murder being the solution to anything. In fact, I'd only seen true rage once in my life. It had suddenly exploded from the Old Man when he was in the midst of one of his paranoid delusions, and it had remained the most terrifying of all my childhood memories of him. It had happened the day before they'd taken him away. At just after noon, I'd opened the door of his study and found him on the floor, surrounded by stacks of books. He'd looked up at me, and at that instant, I'd seen the full face of his madness, a burning anger that lifted him to his feet. The look in his eyes still held me in a grip of terror, along with the words he'd said, *It's you.* Then, as if to cool whatever ire burned inside him, he'd marched up the stairs, where, seconds later, I'd heard him run a bath. What boiling rage must have seized him that day, I wondered now, one he'd rushed to cool in the waters of his bath. And did this rage, fierce and delusional, now burn in Diana, too?

If it did, I had no doubt that the subject of her ire was Mark.

And so I made the call.

"Dr. Regan," Mark answered.

"Mark, it's Dave."

Silence.

"I wonder if we could have a talk."

"About what?"

"Diana," I answered.

A second silence followed, brief, but undeniably charged, as if the very mention of my sister's name heated the atmosphere between us.

"I'm worried about her, Mark," I added in a tone that no doubt alerted him to danger. "She's seems a little . . . strange."

I t was a euphemism, of course," you tell Petrie. "I said 'strange' because I didn't want to say 'crazy.'"

Petrie writes this comment on his notepad, and you wonder if it will later show up in court, be offered as evidence against you.

"I was always afraid that it was in our blood," you add. "That one of us would be like Dad."

"One of you?" Petrie asks.

"Yes."

"So you were afraid for yourself, as well?"

"Always," you answer. "It's dangerous, this disease."

You feel the red rubber ball in your hand, see the front door open, Diana standing there, a little girl with long blond hair, fear in her voice when she speaks to you, *Where's Dad?*

"There are things a man is afraid to face," you tell Petrie, careful that he doesn't glimpse the exact nature of your fear, or any of the grave derangements that are its dreadful handiwork.

"Yes," Petrie says. His hand crawls up his already loosened neck-tie, pulls it down a little more. "What are you afraid of, Dave?"

Four deaths circle in your mind. Somehow, though different, they strike you as the same, mere strands in the web that holds you now.

"Afraid for," you answer. "That's a better question. Who was I afraid for?"

Petrie takes a long breath, like a diver before he heaves himself over the gunwale and sinks into the forbidding waters.

"All right," he says. "Who were you afraid for?"

Though you posed the question yourself, it's hard for you to give a correct answer. There are too many correct answers. Because you are a river of fear, with branching streams of warning.

"Who for, Dave?" Petrie asks.

"Mark," you answer, picking a stream. "I was afraid for Mark." You are standing in Diana's apartment now, staring from wall to wall. "Of what Diana might be thinking about him." The myths fly like bats through your mind, ancient names that should mean nothing, but for an instant, meant everything, Gaia, Uranus, Cronus. Horrid images swoop and dodge, a bloody knife, severed genitals. "And of what she might do to him," you add, almost coolly, holding back the icy shudder in your brain.

"And so you warned him," Petrie says. "I would have done the same."

"Would you?"

"Yes."

You smile quietly, then continue your tale, watching Petrie as he listens, thinking only how completely he has stepped into your cloud.

TEN

That night, as I drove toward the little restaurant where Mark and I were to meet, I thought of the movies again, *Play Misty for Me, Fatal Attraction,* and it seemed to me that they were only the most recent renderings of an old nightmare. For how long really, and from what ancient seat, had men dreaded and been awestruck by the passions that rock women and drive them to action? I wondered how many of the men I'd represented had warily turned away from their irate wives or girlfriends, hoping only to make it to the door without hearing the click of a pistol hammer or the rattle of knives in the nearby kitchen drawer, fearing a violence that also baffled them. *Can't you just accept it?* seemed forever the male question. *No,* the female answer men had never understood.

Mark arrived a little late, stopped just inside the door, peered about until he caught sight of me in the back booth, then made his way toward me in long, determined strides. At the table, he offered his hand, and I didn't hesitate to take it, though at the instant our hands touched, I wondered if Diana had imagined that same hand leading Jason into the water, then pressing him down and holding him below its surface, waiting while Jason thrust and wriggled and flapped his arms until the terrible stillness finally came.

"Good to see you again, Dave," Mark said. He pulled himself into the booth opposite me. "It's been a while since we talked."

"How are you doing, Mark?"

"As well as can be expected." He shrugged. "Mostly, I keep myself busy. I've rented a small apartment not far from the research center. Just a short drive, really. Very convenient." He smiled sadly. "But I miss the other house. The pond. Even that big rock at the edge of it." He allowed himself a small, oddly restrained laugh. "The ear of earth. That's what Diana called it. Jason used to like going there. With Diana, I mean. Then suddenly he didn't."

"Why the change?"

"Who knows?" Mark answered with a slight shrug. "Maybe he saw something that scared him. Something in the water. A fish. You know what he was like, always afraid." He appeared to revisit a particular episode in his life, and I wondered if it was the instant he'd glimpsed something scary in my sister's eyes. "Not a good thing, fear," he added.

The waitress stepped over and we each ordered a beer.

When she'd gone, Mark picked up the small, glass salt-shaker and rolled it between his open hands. "I read a study not long ago. About mentally ill people. They can be totally swamped with delusions of one kind or another. Totally crazy. But the last thing they lose, the last perception, is of danger." He returned the saltshaker to its place. "It's a brain mechanism, evidently. Very primitive. It explains why the crazy people you see on the streets, the ones who scream at women and kids, why these same people never scream at big guys. They're crazy, but the last vestiges of sanity remain, and because of that they see something and they say, 'bigger than I am, stronger,' and so they steer clear."

I nodded. "So fear is the last thing to go."

"Yeah," Mark said quietly. "I guess it reduces to that."

The beer came and he took a long pull, then set the glass down hard, like a hammer against the wood. "So, what's this about Diana?" he asked. "You said she's been acting strange?"

"Maybe I shouldn't have used that word."

"Well, you must have had a reason for using it, Dave."

Rather than give a direct answer, I said, "I heard you've retained Stewart Grace."

"That's right," Mark answered, though distantly, clearly reluctant to give any further detail.

"He's a criminal lawyer. Big time."

"Yes, he is."

"Expensive."

"It's just a retainer for now."

"Still not cheap, I'll bet."

"What are you getting at, Dave?"

"Just curious as to why you'd need a lawyer like that."

"I hired him as a precaution," Mark answered. "If I ever had to defend myself."

"You mean, against Diana?"

He looked shocked by such a notion. "Of course not," he said emphatically. "There's this fellow at the research center. Gillespie is his name. He's gotten more and more unstable. I'm sure the center will get rid of him eventually, but in the meantime I was afraid he might make accusations. That I stole his ideas, something like that. It could be anything. He's that unstable." He laughed dryly. "He sent a rock to Bill Carnegie. Can you imagine? With some kind of voodoo symbol on it. He's probably got a doll of me he sticks pins in." He shrugged. "Anyway, I decided to retain Stewart just in case." He laughed again. "You thought talking to Stewart had to do with Diana?"

"I thought it might, yes."

"Why would it?"

When I hesitated, Mark leaned forward. "Let me ask you something, Dave. Do you think Diana needs help? Professional, I mean?" He seemed to see the dark cloud that formed in my mind. "She had terrible dreams, you know. After Jason died. That's when I began to suspect that she might have a mental problem." He looked at me pointedly. "It's not like there's no history of this. In the family, I mean."

The whole grim chronicle of the Old Man's derangement unfolded in my mind, and as it did so, I knew precisely how Mark saw us, Diana, me, Jason, each a separate stream of DNA, but fouled by the same debris.

"Let me give you an example of what I'm talking about," Mark went on. "One night Diana walked all the way to the pond. She was in her nightclothes, just like an actress in a horror movie. She really looked like that, standing by that big rock. The 'ear of earth.' She was facing the pond, with her hair down over her shoulders and the moon on the water. I'm telling you, Dave, it was just like a scene in a movie. For a minute I thought I must be the one dreaming." He stopped, and I could tell that he was trying to find his next words. He looked for several seconds before he found them. "When I got to her, she was still in a daze."

"Did she say anything to you?"

"No," Mark answered. "She must have heard me come up behind her. She whirled around, and there was this look in her eyes. Scary."

"Why scary?" I asked.

"Because she looked like she hated me."

"Did she say that?" I asked like a lawyer questioning a witness.

"She didn't say anything," Mark answered. "Not one word. She walked back to the house, but she wouldn't come up to bed. She slept downstairs on the sofa. The next morning she told me to leave. So I did. I mean, the soul of wisdom is to know when something doesn't work, right?"

I'd never attempted to discover the "soul of wisdom," so I offered no answer to Mark's question.

"Why would Diana feel that way toward you?" I asked. "Hatred, I mean."

"I really didn't know at the time, but since then I figure it has to do with Jason," Mark answered. "She came to see Bill Carnegie. She wanted to know what I'd said about Jason." He shook his head. "Poor Jason. He used to stare at the wall for hours, Dave. Some little scratch on the wall, a smudge, anything." He drew in a slow breath. "I once asked Diana what she thought he was thinking about all that time. She said he wasn't thinking about anything, that he was just suffering, and that this suffering was pure. Like a drug at full strength." He released the glass and drew his hands under the counter. "So when he died I told her that maybe it was for the best." Even now, he looked vaguely addled by the violence of her reaction. "She just exploded, Dave. I really thought she was going to attack me."

"But she didn't," I said.

"No," Mark said. "Diana would wait. She would plot. Maybe even get someone else to do it for her."

"Someone else?"

"You know, murder for hire, that sort of thing."

"Do you really believe that?"

He shook his head. "Of course not," he said. "I only mean that Diana wouldn't let her emotions run away with her."

I remembered the day the Old Man died, how she'd not shed a single tear, but only quickly gathered up his things, the pajamas he'd been wearing, his house shoes, bathrobe, the shawl that had been draped around his shoulders. She'd handed me the green pillow that had propped up his head, said only, "Let's build a pyre, Davey. He'd like that." Then we'd gone into the backyard and despite the rain managed to burn all of it in a pile. The fire had still been smoldering when she'd finally called to report the Old Man's death to the authorities, after which we'd both gone back to his study and waited for them to arrive. I could still remember her eyes, how dry they were, though they'd been no drier than the words she'd said, *It was time for him to die.*

When I returned to the present, Mark seemed deep in thought.

"She's a loner," he said, as if in conclusion. "Always alone. In that little room she used at the house. Anytime she wasn't with Jason, that's where she was. Never at the neighbors. No friends, really. Just alone in that little room, tapping away at that old typewriter she got from her father."

I remembered the Old Man at work, hunched over his ancient black Royal, typing endless streams of notes and quotations, along with scores and scores of accusatory letters.

"Even at night, when sane people are in bed," Mark added. "Tap, tap, tap." He took a sip of beer and returned the glass to the table. "What's she up to, Dave?"

Rather than answer him directly, I asked a question of my own. "Have you gotten any communications from Diana?"

"What do you mean, 'communications'?"

"Faxes. E-mails."

He shook his head. "But you have, I take it?"

"Yes," I said. "Patty, too."

"Patty?" he asked. The mention of my daughter's name appeared to strike him in a way I couldn't quite decipher. "She's 'communicating' with Patty?"

I nodded. "She gave her a CD. Kinsetta Tabu."

Mark gave no indication that he'd ever heard the name.

"And stuff she seems to be studying. Prehistory. The Iron Age." I paused, then added, "Old murders."

Mark sat back slightly. "Old murders?"

It was the moment to ask him outright if Diana had ever mentioned that Jason's death might not be accidental, warn him about what I feared she might be thinking. But I was afraid that he might take Diana's suspicions as evidence that she was truly unhinged, scary, and that driven by his own fear, he might act against her in some way.

And so I simply watched silently as he slid his empty glass to the right, folded one hand in the other, then looked up and warned me instead.

"Be careful, Dave," he said. "Patty, too. She enlists aid, Diana. And she can be very seductive."

I recalled all the times she'd drawn me into games and plots, used secret signs and code words to create an insular and oddly unreal world, and wondered if she were doing it again.

"Yes," I said. "She can."

It was evidence enough of my growing dread that I waited outside the library until eight, when the lights flickered out.

A few seconds later Diana came out the rear entrance, her arms full of books. She didn't see me standing by her car at first, but when she did, she stopped dead, and I noticed an unmistakable tension claim her face, so that she briefly looked like a woman who'd been spotted not in the actual commission of a crime, but at some stage in the planning of it.

"Hello, Diana," I said as she came toward me.

"Hello," she said softly, and with the odd gesture of hugging the books more closely to her chest, like a child with a toy she feared some other child might take away.

As she drew near, I could see that she was studying each aspect of my face, gauging the set of my mouth, the squint of my eyes, trying to determine the reason I'd come, have an answer already prepared for any questions I might ask.

"Are you okay?" she asked. "Has something happened?"

"No," I said. "Nothing's happened. I just wanted to talk to you."

She motioned me over to a small wooden bench and placed the books like a wall between us. "What is it?" She eyed me closely, and under her gaze I felt like a specimen pinned to a cork, desperately squirming.

"Well, I just wanted to . . ."

"You've talked with Mark," she said suddenly.

She had always been this way, inhumanly prescient, able to read vast texts between the tiniest of lines.

"Yes," I admitted.

"And that's why you came here," Diana said softly. "To see if I'm making any 'progress.'"

I knew then that "progress" was a word Mark had used with Diana, that he'd no doubt measured it and found it wanting and lectured her on the very acceptance that seemed even further from her now.

"Did he come up with an analysis?" Diana asked. "Am I schizophrenic, too? Like Jason? Like Dad?"

I didn't answer, but my hesitation only made her more determined to find the answer I refused to give.

"Tell me, Davey," she said insistently. "What's the learned diagnosis?"

"I wouldn't call it a diagnosis," I told her.

She cocked her head. "I'm unstable then? Just generally unstable?" She looked at me pointedly. "Does he think I should be locked up? Like Dad, at Brigham?"

"Of course not."

Her gaze turned icy. "He wanted to lock Jason up, you know."

I'd never heard this before. Diana had earlier told me that she expected Mark to want Jason hospitalized, but she'd never indicated that he'd actually proposed such a thing.

"Put everyone away, that's his philosophy," Diana added. "Get rid of all life's inconveniences, the ones who cause us trouble, who demand attention, who block us from 'progress.'" She sat back, almost violently. "I know what Mark's doing, Davey. And I know why. It's because he knows I have questions about Jason."

I looked at her silently, waiting, but she said nothing else until I pressed her.

"Questions about his death?" I asked. "You think it wasn't an accident?"

Diana nodded, but very softly, reluctantly, like someone admitting to a thought that was not so much wrong in itself, as incomprehensible to others.

"And you think Mark had something to do with it?" I asked.

She answered with the same nod, only more reluctantly, but that didn't matter. Facts were facts, and even the most tenuous admission proved that Abby had been right all along about Diana's suspicions. In the face of that admission, I saw no other course but to put myself in the place of her interrogator.

"What evidence do you have, Diana?" I asked.

She seemed to find the question abrupt and unexpected, but knew she had to answer it. I could see her scrambling to find an answer, but at the same time fully aware that she didn't have a satisfactory one. She was like someone required to produce a diamond she did not possess, and so reached for a rhinestone and hoped that it would do.

"The badge," she said.

I had no idea what she meant.

"Mark's father was a policeman," Diana said. "He had a badge. When he died, it went to Mark. It was the only thing he kept from his father." She placed her right hand on the stack of books like someone giving sworn testimony. "I found it by the pond."

"When?"

"The day after Jason died," she answered. "It was at night. I went for a walk. That's when I found it."

I had no doubt that this was the same night Mark had found Diana near the "ear of earth."

"Mark used that badge to control Jason," Diana continued. "When he wanted Jason to do something, he'd get the badge and put it right in front of Jason's face. Then he'd tell him what he wanted. It might be for Jason to stay in his seat, or finish his dinner. It could be anything. But Jason would do it if Mark had the badge. He used it like a charm."

"Where's the badge now?"

"Mark has it," Diana answered. "He took it when he came to get the rest of his things."

"Well, why shouldn't he have taken it?" I asked. "It's a keepsake, isn't it? A reminder of his father."

She looked at me stonily. "You don't believe me," she said.

"I believe you found the badge," I said. "I just don't see that it's evidence against Mark."

"Because it's circumstantial?"

"To say the least."

"But isn't most evidence circumstantial?" Diana asked.

"Yes, but—"

"And what is evidence, really?" she demanded.

She was like the Old Man now, peering at me with the same stern eyes, and under her gaze I suddenly felt outmatched, certain that I would stumble, fumble, fall.

"You mean of a crime?" I asked, stalling.

"No, not of a crime," Diana answered as if the question itself were strangely shallow. "Before you have evidence for a crime, what must you have evidence for, Davey?"

I looked at her, unable to answer with any more speed or accuracy than I'd been able to answer the Old Man.

"You must first have evidence for suspicion, isn't that right?" Diana demanded.

I nodded reluctantly.

"So, in any investigation, the evidence for suspicion comes first," Diana said. "Take an apartment in which a woman and two children are found bludgeoned to death. The husband survives and claims to have been attacked by intruders. Chairs are overturned in the dining room. But despite all this evidence for an intruder, a struggle, there is other evidence. It is the Christmas season, and the Christmas cards on the dining room table have not been tipped over. They are standing upright. What is that evidence of, Davey? A crime? Of course not." She looked at me pointedly, then asked in a slow, measured voice, "But it is evidence for suspicion that there was no struggle with intruders that night, isn't it?"

I could find no response to this, at least not one Diana wouldn't immediately tear apart. I could say that evidence for a crime and the suspicion of that crime were in actuality the same, but I knew that in some way they were not, and that Diana would turn that fine distinction into a raging river of caustic argument. For that reason, I also knew that no matter how odd and unconvincing I found her suspicion of Mark, she would make my lack of suspicion yet more so, defend conviction by attacking naïveté. The only tactic I found available was to move the conversation to another place.

"It must hurt," I said, "to feel this kind of suspicion."

Her eyes took on a fathomless sympathy that struck me as very odd, because it could not have been for Mark.

"Yes, it hurts," she said.

"Diana, look. All I want to know is . . ."

She lifted her hand to silence me. "No more for now," she said. "She's here."

For a frozen instant, I went the whole route, assumed this "she" to be nonexistent, without reality of any kind, my sister's dark hallucination. I glanced to where she indicated, and, to my surprise, saw a very real young girl walking toward us through the evening shade, a figure I could see but partially, a bit of skirt, a glint of hair, but still enough for me to know exactly who it was.

"Patty," I whispered.

Diana rose to her feet as Patty neared, and all the stormy aspects of her features dissolved into a wholly sunny smile.

"Hi, Patty," she said, and waved her arm.

Patty reached us a few seconds later.

"Hi, Dad," she said with both surprise and wariness, as if she'd been caught in the midst of a secret mission.

I nodded. "Hi."

She was dressed in a long-sleeved, ivory-colored blouse and long pleated skirt, an attire that reminded me of forties femme fatales, women who had small, pearl-handled pistols in their rhinestone-studded bags.

"Patty and I are going to dinner," Diana announced.

"Mom knows," Patty added.

"Okay," I said.

Diana looked at me pointedly. "So, we'll talk later," she said.

"Yes, fine," I said. "Later."

She took Patty's arm and the two of them turned and walked away, strolling slowly toward my sister's car, alternately caught in lamplight and lost in shadow, until they grew small in the far distance, and at last seemed to fade into the dead of night.

For a moment, Petrie's face is faintly obscured by a vaporous cloud of steam. It rises from the cup of coffee he has just poured, and as you watch it curl sinuously upward, you think, *It was like that, a moment of cloudiness, and then stark clarity.* And when the world flashed back into focus, you saw their bodies in a row, faceup on the embankment, the river of fear flowing past them.

The cloud vanishes as quickly as it appears, and with its vanishing Petrie's features are clear again, though they now seem slightly older and more worn, his eyes just a bit more shrunken, so that you imagine him as he eventually will be, fleshless and unanimated, indistinguishable from Cheddar Man.

Petrie lifts the cup. "Sure you don't want a cup?"

You shake your head.

"Okay," he says softly. His voice is like his features, older, more frazzled, as if it has been dragged over rough ground. He seems oddly weathered by your tale, but determined to go on, see it through to the ending you know he has not guessed.

"At this point, what did you feel about Diana?" he asks.

You see her almost like an apparition, floating in the air, trees beneath her, and a pond glistening far in the distance. The terror of her own imaginings at that awful moment, how like the Old Man's they must have been, leaves you momentarily speechless.

"I'm talking about when you left her that night at the library," Petrie adds.

"Apprehensive," you answer. "I felt apprehensive."

But what could you have done in response to this apprehension? You're not sure that any particular action would have been right or wrong. Death has taught you that we are utterly powerless to see where any given direction will ultimately lead, its consequences, good or bad, small or dire, and that it is this profound inadequacy that delineates the essential tragedy. You know that we all understand this, and yet we don't. Because the darkest things we know remain a storm at sea, its true destructiveness unknown until it finally comes ashore.

"What were you apprehensive about?" Petrie asks.

You consider the question, amazed at how reluctant you are to give a truthful answer.

And so you stall.

"There were lots of things going through my mind," you tell Petrie.

"Like what?"

"What to do about Diana."

"Meaning what?"

"Her suspicion of Mark. What she might do about it."

"Did you think she might do something violent?"

"I didn't know what she might do. I was in a cloud. That's what it felt like. A cloud."

"But it wasn't primarily Mark you were worried about as far as Diana was concerned?" Petrie asks. His gaze grows more intense, like a cat on the prowl, sniffing the ground, closing the distance.

"No, not Mark," you answer. You allow a small part of the cloud that conceals you to dissipate, and thus reveal a tiny corner of the awesome truth. "No, it was Patty."

ELEVEN

Abby was sitting on the front porch, wrapped in a shawl and peering out at the nearly deserted street, when I pulled into the driveway.

"Patty's not home," she said. "She's having dinner with . . ."

"Yes, I know." I sat down in the chair beside her. "I was with Diana at the library when Patty showed up." I recalled the conversation I'd just had, the absurd "evidence" Diana had offered. "I don't want Diana to end up like the Old Man," I said.

The final days of that dreadful end flew past me, dark and swift, as if carried on the wings of a bat. He'd grown more and more desperate, madly plowing through volume after volume, sometimes spouting his own poor verses, sometimes reciting the great ones of others, until he'd finally fallen into a wholly unreachable lunacy, no longer talking directly at all, but through quotations, each duly referenced, which had only made them seem more mad.

"Mark doesn't know what to make of her," I added. "He says I should be careful though."

"Of what?"

"Of getting pulled into whatever Diana's doing. Getting seduced somehow. That's the way he put it, that Diana could be very seductive."

"Does Diana know you talked to Mark?"

"I told her, yes. I don't want to lie to her or keep things from her. It would only feed her . . ." I stopped, briefly unable to say the word. But there was no choice, so I said it. "Paranoia."

My sudden use of that term, so cold and analytical, surprised me. It felt like a dropping away of hope.

Abby clearly saw the dread in my eyes and I saw that it only deepened her own.

"What did Diana say when you told her you'd spoken with Mark?" she asked.

"She guessed it before I could tell her," I answered. "And it turns out that you were right about everything. Diana doesn't think Jason's death was an accident."

"But *why* does she think that?" Abby asked.

"She talked about a badge," I answered. "It was Mark's. His father gave it to him. According to Diana, Mark used it to get Jason to do things. Eat. Be quiet. Used it like a charm, she says."

"A charm?" Abby asked.

"She found it by the pond."

I drew the only possible conclusion. "So not 'an accident' is murder."

It was around midnight when I heard a car pull into the driveway. Abby lay sound asleep beside me. She didn't stir when I got out of the bed, walked to the window, and parted the curtain.

Below, Patty was standing on the driver's side of Diana's car, leaning forward, talking. Diana was behind the wheel, her short blond hair faintly illuminated by the porch light I'd left on for Patty's return. For a time they seemed huddled together, their voices far too low for me to hear, though for some reason I imagined them in whispers, two females in dark conclave.

Then Patty pulled herself erect, stepped away from the car, her pale hand in the air, waving good-bye as the car drifted backward into the street, then drove away, its red lights blinking like small mad eyes in the pitch-black air.

I'd thrown on a robe and gone downstairs by the time Patty came through the front door.

"Out late," I said.

She looked at me as if I'd accused her of bad behavior. "Well, it's not like I was with a boy or something. It was just Diana."

Diana. She'd dropped the "Aunt," and for me that was evidence enough that whatever their relationship had once been, it had altered sufficiently to generate this more familiar form of address.

"Where'd you have dinner?" I asked.

"Some Italian place." She faked a yawn, then turned and headed for the stairs.

"What did you talk about?" I blurted suddenly.

She stopped and faced me. "Private things."

"Private? What does that mean?"

"Private, Dad," Patty answered emphatically.

"Private like . . . secret?"

"Private like private," Patty answered. Her tone was firm, even slightly belligerent, a way of talking to me she'd never used before.

"It's just that I'm worried about her, Patty," I said. "Her mind. What she's thinking. Because I'm not sure it's altogether . . . rational."

Patty looked at me as if I had created a monster in order to attack it. "What are you afraid of, Dad?"

Rather than answering her directly, I said, "If you know something, Patty, I want you to tell me."

Patty's tone now turned exasperated. "Know something about what?"

"About what Diana's doing."

"She's not doing anything, Dad," Patty said. "She goes to the library, then comes back to her apartment."

"I don't mean her routine."

"What then?"

"This stuff about Windeby Girl, for example. What's that all about?"

She laughed dismissively. "Diana's curious about things, Dad," she said. "Did you know that there's a whole field called acoustic archaeology? Diana thinks maybe the first people heard things we can't hear. Their minds might have been different from ours because they couldn't write and so they had to remember everything. Like the Druids. They had to memorize a huge number of rituals. Nothing could be written down, so they must have had these fantastic brains."

She continued in this vein a few seconds longer, and in every word she said I heard my sister's power, the way she infused curiosity with passion.

"Druid means 'oak tree,'" Patty continued, "but it also means 'wisdom.'"

"Patty," I said, stopping her at last. "You have to be careful with Diana. I know she can be . . . very seductive."

Patty stared at me silently.

"I also know that she's convinced herself that Jason's death wasn't an accident," I added. "And that Mark had something to do with it."

Patty didn't answer immediately, but I could see that she was trying to find the words. Finally, she said, "What if she's right, Dad?"

"Patty, listen to me," I said calmly. "Patty, there's not one bit of evidence that Jason's death was anything but accidental."

Patty's expression was pure challenge. "Then prove that to Diana."

She'd thrown down a gauntlet I had to pick up. "All right," I said. "I will."

But how?

I still hadn't fallen asleep when dawn broke the next

morning, and so, at first light, I went walking among the houses of my slumbering neighbors.

Early morning, more than any other time of day, gives a false sense of harmony. The quiet only adds to the fabrication. Closed doors give the appearance of never having been slammed, and the general lack of movement suggests a similar lack of agitation.

For a long time, I walked in this fantastical quiet, all the while trying to plot a course that would bring everyone to safety.

I replayed the most recent events, first Jason's death, then the court's determination that it had been an accident, then Diana's subsequent rejection of that finding.

If reason had played any part in Diana's rejection of the court's decision, then it seemed to me that reason might also play a part in her acceptance of it.

This thought brought me to the question of evidence, what it was and what it wasn't. Diana might fog the air with talk of "evidence for suspicion," but it was clear that such evidence only mattered if it could actually be used as evidence for a crime. Mark's badge, whether found on the banks of Dolphin Pond or not, had no such incriminating potential.

The good news, it seemed to me, was that Diana was still operating in the realm of evidence, however flimsy the evidence she'd found. In that way, I decided, she was not "like Dad," a distinction I found heartening, and whose slender tendrils I grasped with all my might.

By the time I returned home an hour later, I'd even hit upon a plan.

And so I came to you."

You know what Petrie hears in your voice, the hard-won truth that the only feeling more powerful than hope is lost hope.

"It seemed reasonable at the time," you add.

Petrie has entered the story, and he knows it. You see this knowledge in his face. With his own teeth, he has bitten off a piece of this tale, and it is obvious that, like you, he would prefer to spit it out.

"At the time, yes," Petrie says.

You glance toward the window, note the wide circles of a distant hawk. "It's odd, what can seem reasonable."

Petrie nods silently.

You wonder what he sees, whether he's making a comparison. You were troubled then, but not yet ravaged. Or is it Diana he sees now, running, running. You recall Stewart Grace's words, "like a cat on fire."

Petrie leans forward, runs the tip of his finger around the rim of the now empty Styrofoam cup. "Before we talked, you had no idea?"

"None at all," you tell him.

"She'd kept it from you?"

You are sitting in the Old Man's study, watching as Diana closes his eyes with her thumb and forefinger. *Lets build a pyre, Davey,* she says. It is an absurd notion, homage to the Old Man by means of a pseudo-Viking funeral in small-town Connecticut. But Diana is already gathering up his bathrobe, house shoes, shawl, pajamas, old wool socks, so you decide to go along with the idea, then rise and take the green pillow from behind the Old Man's head.

"One death," you whisper now.

"What?" Petrie asks.

You shake your head. "Nothing."

Petrie flips another page of his notebook. You note that he has used up almost half of them. Pages covered in his neat script flutter briefly, then grow still. At some point he will have to reconstruct this tale, then relate it, answer by answer, from the witness-box. You have been in many courtrooms. You know how it will go:

And you had occasion to interview Mr. Sears, didn't you, Detective Petrie?

Yes.

And did you record that interview?

Yes, I did.

By what means?

By means of a mechanical recording device.

And you took notes, as well?

Yes, I did.

And are these the notes you took on the occasion of that interview?

Yes, they are.

You look at the notes, the unmoving yellow pages. So that's what it is, you tell yourself, evidence.

You glance up from the notes and find yourself staring directly into Petrie's eyes.

"I thought she might respond to evidence," you tell him. "It was as simple as that."

Petrie nods, taking his bite from the story, reluctantly acknowledging the hard but inescapable fact of how thin it is, the line between clarity and confusion, correctness and error, and that it is this cloudy, insubstantial thread that alone supports the weighty illusion of control.

"And so you came to me," he says.

"Yes," you tell him. "I had no place else to go."

TWELVE

Detective Petrie was in his office when I showed up at police headquarters.

"Ah, Mr. Sears, come in," he said.

We shook hands and he indicated a chair. "Please, have a seat."

I did. "Thanks for seeing me on such short notice."

"No problem at all," Petrie said. "I often think of Jason."

Jason passed like a ghost through my mind, an image of him standing at the edge of the water, poised beside that ear-shaped stone, the air around him electric with voices. But even as he remained at his lonely station, he seemed to fade, so that in my last vision he was eerily translucent, his body undulating with softly lapping waves, already turning into water.

"I remember your sister, too," Petrie added. "She took it very hard."

"Yes, she did."

"I hope she's been able to go on."

"I'm afraid she hasn't," I told him.

"Really," Petrie said. "I'm sorry to hear that."

I said nothing, but merely stared at him, amazed that it had actually reached this point, that I was here, in a police detective's office because Diana would not accept Jason's death, and that this refusal had worked like a suddenly shifted gear within her mind, edging out reason and replacing it with something whose exact nature I was still unable to determine.

"I don't know if you can help me," I said. "But I couldn't think of anyone else I could go to."

Petrie nodded, but said nothing, and I saw that he was a man used to waiting for tales to unfold, knew that they did so in fits and starts, that some things were too fearful to face head-on.

"I'll help in any way I can," he said. He waited for me to begin. When I didn't, he said, "On the phone you mentioned that you had questions about Jason's death."

"Yes."

"What questions?"

"I was wondering if you ever found any reason to suspect . . ." I stopped, because the final two words struck me as both formal and ludicrously theatrical. "Foul play."

Petrie didn't look at all surprised by the question, though I couldn't tell if it was because he'd earlier suspected foul play himself or was simply accustomed to other people suspecting it.

"Foul play?" he asked.

"I know the court declared Jason's death an accident, but I was wondering if you had any other thoughts about it."

"Thoughts?" Petrie asked tentatively.

"Well, you carried out an investigation, didn't you?"

"We always do in a case like this. A child. Drowned. At the very least, we have an untimely death. So, of course, we look into it."

"So, you looked for evidence that maybe Jason's death wasn't an accident?"

Petrie leaned forward. "Why these particular questions, Mr. Sears?"

"I think my sister believes that Jason was murdered," I told him flatly.

"By whom?"

"Her husband, Mark."

Petrie's eyes darkened just a shade. "That's a very serious charge."

"I know."

For the first time Petrie appeared actually to address the issue seriously. "Murder," he said. "If we suspected that, or even if we didn't, we'd still be aware of red flags."

"Evidence for suspicion," I said, quoting my sister. "Like what?"

"Like signs of prior abuse," Petrie answered. "If we saw a child with scars or burn marks, we'd check the medical records, look into the past." He offered a professional smile, a stage gesture, nothing more, utterly neutral, and which he withdrew almost instantly. "But of course, we look at the present situation, too," he added. His tone now sounded more like a recitation, so that I knew he'd gone over all these things before, laid it out for the many suspicious relatives or friends who'd come to him as I had, with dreadful possibilities in their minds. I could almost hear the conclusion upon which he was closing in. *And so, you see, there is no evidence of . . . foul play.*

"In a case of drowning, for example, we look for any sign of force," Petrie went on. "Bruises, of course. And ligature marks. In this business you learn that some people just aren't very smart. They assume that death by strangulation resembles death by drowning, for example, and so they try to make it look like a drowning. They take a dead body to a river or a pond and toss it in. It's crazy, but they do it. But when people drown, they have water in their lungs. If they're dead before they go into the water, there won't be much water in their lungs because they weren't breathing when they were put into the water. It's as simple as that." He considered what he'd just said, then amended it. "There is such a thing as 'dry drowning,' of course. It happens when people panic and simply stop breathing. The lungs shut down. They drown, but there's very little water in their lungs."

"Was there water in Jason's lungs?" I asked.

"Jason's lungs were full of water," Petrie answered.

"So there's no doubt that he was alive when he went into the water?"

"No doubt at all," Petrie said. "And there were no signs of anything unusual. None of the things I mentioned. Bruises. Ligature marks. His body was perfect. You saw that yourself."

"I only saw his face," I said.

Petrie nodded. "Yes, of course," he said. "But your sister saw it."

"What?"

"She wanted to see Jason," Petrie told me. "She called just before the autopsy. She said she wanted to see him before it was done. And of course, we permitted her to do that."

"Just her? She came alone?"

"Yes."

"When did she come?"

Petrie's eyes rolled up slightly, held a moment, then returned to me. "That would have been Saturday. The day after Jason died. The body was already on the table, ready for autopsy. It was covered, of course, but she pulled back the sheet." He hesitated, as if unsure whether he should say more. Then he added, "All the way down. From head to foot."

I could feel myself hovering over the scene, a motionless presence, bodiless as a miasma, an invisible eye, peering down to where Diana stood beside the stainless steel table, Jason's naked body bathed in the bright light of the autopsy room.

"It seemed strange to me," Petrie said. "The way she studied him."

"Studied?"

"I was just off to the side, but I could see that she was looking up and down the full length of his body." He stopped, the import of that earlier insight only now sinking in. "I got the feeling she was looking for something."

"Why did you think that?"

"Because of how methodical it all was," Petrie answered.

"She didn't hold him in her arms or anything like that. But she took his hands, one at a time, and looked at them very closely. Especially the palms."

"Why would she do that?" I asked.

"It was like she'd read a bit about forensic pathology," Petrie answered. "Knew the way it was done, what the pathologist looked for. Defensive wounds, for example. Or puncture marks from a needle. She asked us to turn Jason over, so we did. On his stomach. She bent down the way she had before and looked at him very closely."

"Did she find anything?"

"No," Petrie answered. "At least nothing she mentioned. When she was done, she took the sheet and covered the body. Then she turned and walked out of the room." He shrugged. "I followed her out to her car. I was afraid she might break down. You know, the way she did after you told her that we'd found Jason in the pond."

It rang through my head again, raw, brutal, primitive, an animal wail.

"At the car, I asked if there was anything else I could do for her," Petrie went on. "She said no." He gazed at me intently. "You didn't know about any of this?"

"No."

"I have to tell you, it made me a little uneasy, the way she was asking about the investigation."

Petrie's expression gave only the tiniest hint that he saw just how forcefully his words had hit me. In the following silence, he said nothing, but only watched my face as the words sank deeper and deeper into me. And yet I knew he could see that I wanted to vanish, abruptly and without a trace, simply erase both myself and Diana from his mind. I'd come to find out if he'd ever been suspicious of Mark, and discovered that he'd been suspicious of Diana instead.

Petrie sat back and folded his arms over his chest. "It's in the official playbook, Mr. Sears, the rules of investigation. When a wife disappears, you take a good look at the husband. Scott Peterson, you know? And when a child dies, you take a close look at the mother. Andrea Yates, for example."

"But Diana wasn't even at home when Jason drowned."

"So she said."

"And Mark backed her up."

"Husbands defend wives."

"You had no reason to suspect Diana," I said.

"We had knowledge of her past," Petrie said. "Or at least I did."

I had no idea what he was talking about, so I waited.

Petrie leaned forward. "Diana took your father back home and cared for him there, isn't that right?"

"Yes."

"She left school," he added. "Her senior year."

"How do you know all that?" I asked.

"She cared for him until he died." Petrie's tone suggested facts gathered by investigation, as if he'd gone through my sister's private papers, looked among them for an incriminating receipt or letter. "Like Jason."

"She devoted herself to Jason, yes," I said. "In the same way, I mean."

"That's a lot of work, caring for a boy like that," Petrie

said. "Or caring for an old man. Same thing, really. A person can become clinically depressed in a situation like that. I've seen it happen a few times. Depressed and desperate."

"You thought Diana was depressed?" I asked.

Petrie appeared genuinely surprised by the question. "Your sister never told you that we talked to her?"

"Talked to her about what?"

A shadow passed over Petrie's face. "Your father, how he died."

"I was there when he died," I said.

"Not exactly."

"What do you mean?"

"You weren't in the room," Petrie said. "Not when he died. Diana told me that."

I recalled the long walk I'd taken in the cold drizzle of that morning. It had lasted perhaps twenty minutes, no more. But in that interval, the Old Man had passed away, his eyes still open when I returned to his room.

"No, I wasn't with him," I said.

"Diana told me that you were upset," Petrie added. "That your last meeting with your father hadn't gone well."

"It sounds like you questioned Diana pretty thoroughly," I said. "Why? My father was an old man. He'd been sick a long time."

"Mentally sick."

"That's right."

"But otherwise, quite healthy."

"People his age die suddenly all the time," I said.

"Yes, they do."

"So you must have had other reasons," I said. "For suspicion."

Petrie nodded. "There were ligature marks on your father's wrists and ankles. That's why the coroner called me that day."

I stared at him, shocked. "Ligature marks?" I repeated.

"They were very faint," Petrie said. "And so the coroner didn't necessarily suspect anything. He just had a few questions, more or less mandatory. So we checked a few things out, looked into the past, talked to a few people."

"About Diana?"

"And about you," Petrie answered. "We learned that you weren't close to your father. In fact, you'd been estranged for quite some time."

"He was disappointed in me," I said. "He had some vision of me being a great intellect." I shrugged. "But I'm not." I stared at him evenly. "If you thought there was something suspicious about my father's death, why didn't you talk to me about it?"

"As a matter of fact, I intended to," Petrie said. "I came over to your father's house to do just that. You weren't there, but Diana was. So I talked to her, and she explained everything."

And so he'd never questioned me about my father's death. He'd questioned only Diana, and in all her answers, she'd been quite convincing, he told me. As for the ligature marks, they were from the straps the hospital had used to restrain the Old Man while at Brigham, she'd told Petrie, restrained because he could not control himself, no longer knew what he was doing.

"We checked with Brigham, and it was true," Petrie said. "They'd strapped him down several times before your sister checked him out of the hospital and took him home."

"And that was enough for you to decide that you didn't need to talk to me?"

"Yes, it was," Petrie said. "There was no reason to look any further. We knew that there was no insurance to speak of. No big inheritance. And by all accounts your sister was devoted to your father. So we filed a report, and that was the end of it." He smiled quietly. "No evidence for suspicion, I mean."

"That my father had been murdered?"

Petrie nodded. "Murdered," he said. "Yes."

Without willing it, I returned to my father's room, saw him again with his eyes open, mouth agape, Diana collecting things for the pyre, a robe, old shoes, my decision to go along with it, helping her do it now, reaching, as I had at that moment, for a dark green pillow, and finding a touch of unexpected moisture so that I'd looked up to see my father's watery lips, and at that moment heard his voice on the phone, rousing me from sleep the night before, murmuring, *Help me, help me,* before Diana had taken the receiver from him, her voice typically persuasive, *Go back to sleep, Davey, all is well.*

P etrie's gaze drifts down toward the cup.

"Suspicion is a shifting shade," you tell him.

He lowers the cup to the table and slides it to the right. "Your father's death, the things I told you about it when you came to my office, is that where it began?"

He means my journey, one you now imagine as a winding road through a green cemetery. One stone. Two. Three. Four? The first death returns to you, the Old Man's midnight plea, *Help me.*

"He called me," you tell Petrie. "The night before he died."

"What did he want?"

"He wanted me to help him. Diana took the receiver. She said everything was fine, that I should go back to sleep. So that's what I did."

"And that was the last of it?"

"No, that wasn't the last of it."

You see the papers in Diana's hand, pages and pages stapled to-gether. You are standing with her in the Old Man's study, clearing out his things. She lifts the papers toward you. *This is why he called you that night, Davey.* You take the papers from her, the horrible paranoid enemies list the Old Man has compiled through the years. Diana speaks again, *Look at the last page.* You flip to it obediently, Diana watching you closely. *Look at the last name, Davey.* Your eyes drift down the list: Jacob Stern, professor, plagiarist; Margaret Picard, reviewer, dilettante; Laslo Kapowski, editor, sycophant, until you reach the final name the Old Man had written in his familiar tortured scrawl. Diana Sears, daughter, cunt.

"He broke her heart," you say quietly. "He called her terrible names."

You are with her again, both of you in the study. You feel her draw the list from your fingers. Her voice sounds in your mind. *It's all right, Davey, he didn't know what he was doing.*

"Those last days must have been terrible for her," you say now. "And I wasn't there to help her. I stayed away until the very end."

A phone rings in memory. You are at home, watching *Gaslight*, the original version. How easy it is, you are thinking, to convince a woman that she is insane.

"Diana called me," you tell Petrie. "She said my father was very weak. She wanted me to come over. She was hoping we could reconcile before it was too late."

You remember her words distinctly now, how emphatic and strangely certain Diana had seemed that there would be no later opportunity.

"And so I went over that morning," you tell Petrie. "To the old house on Victor Hugo Street."

You describe Diana leading you past the stairs and down the corridor, to where the Old Man sat in the high-backed chair.

"He was typing a letter when I came into the room," you tell Petrie. "He didn't look up when Diana told him I was there."

You stop because it is difficult to tell the rest. You compose yourself, regain control. "Finally he lifted his head and gazed at me directly. He said, 'You are dust to me.'"

You recall Diana's touch on your arm, directing you out of the room and back down the corridor.

"Diana told me to go for a walk, to come back later. So I did."

Petrie nods softly. "Yes, a couple of neighbors saw you walking," he tells you.

You feel a cold rain spitting in your face as you trudge up and down Victor Hugo Street, counting the minutes until ten have past.

"When I got back to the house, she was reciting to him," you tell Petrie.

Her voice is a whisper in your mind.

In Xanadu did Kubla Khan

A stately pleasure-dome decree

Where Alph the sacred river ran

Through caverns measureless to man

Down to a crystal sea.

"Coleridge," you murmur quietly now, your gaze on the window, where a shower of autumn leaves floats toward the ground, shifting as they fall, dipping left and right as if trying to take wing, or at least slow their inevitable descent.

"He was already dead," you add softly.

Then, to your surprise, there in the stripped-down interrogation room, you begin to recite. It isn't Coleridge, or anyone remotely like him.

Memory is stigma,

Stain,

Enigma.

You smile joylessly, ironically, then, a boy still under the Old Man's stern, oppressive sway, obediently give the required citation. "Kinsetta Tabu. 'Cheddar Man.'"

Petrie looks at you oddly, as if you have slipped behind some invisible curtain, into a separate world from which he must draw you back or into which he must follow.

"Dave," he says, his voice clearly strained, like someone reaching for a drowning man, offering his hand, yet fearful of being pulled in. "Dave."

His voice jerks you back to the room, the fading light beyond the window, the dire present. "Yes?"

"What were you thinking?"

"About Diana."

"What about her?"

"That there is no net," you tell him, "and that we are always falling."

"Yes," Petrie says very softly.

You see that he believes it, and that this dark recognition has chipped away at his stony professionalism. Still, you know that he has no choice but follow the descent until it reaches rock bottom.

There is more to tell.

And so you do.

THIRTEEN

During the next few days, I thought of nothing but Diana, though only of her recent past, her talks with Bill Carnegie, and her trip to the morgue, along with the maze of bizarre associations that seemed equally part of her investigation, Cheddar Man, Yde Girl, even the eerie lyrics of Kinsetta Tabu. It seemed to me that her inquiry into Jason's death had become a pseudoscientific enterprise, a concoction made up of scraps from anthropology, forensics, mysticism, a badge. Together, these elements composed a mad witch's brew that was no more based on real evidence than some cauldron swill of pig's snout and bat's wing.

The question was what to do about all this. I'd already talked to Mark, Bill Carnegie, Detective Petrie. I'd even talked to Patty, a conversation that chilled me as I replayed it, the challenge she'd presented to me.

And so it seemed to me there were no further "witnesses" to question, not a single person who might shed light on what Diana was thinking or might do next. Not a single living witness.

Then I thought, *Save one.*

Douglas Price wasn't difficult to find. A quick people search brought his name and address onto the screen, though without an accompanying phone number. I wrote down the address, then called Abby and told her that I'd be late for dinner.

The tone of her voice was clearly apprehensive, like someone who no longer felt safe in her own house. "Where will you be?" she asked.

"There's this man I need to see," I told her. "Diana spoke to him. I want to know what she said."

"When will you be home?"

"I don't know for sure."

To my surprise, she said, "I'll wait up." Another silence, then she added, "Be careful, Dave."

For the next few hours, I worked at my profession, the one the Old Man thought "common as a fly." Diana had had a different opinion. *You deal in dissolutions,* she'd once said to me. Which was an altogether accurate appraisal, since my law practice primarily dealt with marriages and businesses that had to be dissolved. Perhaps, at least in that way, I had always been a student of crack-up and collapse, the still smoldering ashes of bad deals and relationships. Like Mephistopheles, as Diana had gone on to point out, the air is always smoky where I am.

Nor was there any doubt that this air had grown more acrid in recent days, I thought, as I made my way to my car after work that afternoon.

"Going home to kith and kin," Charlie said when he saw me at the door.

"Not right away," I told him.

He eyed me with mock suspicion. "You don't have something on the side, do you, Dave?" He grinned. "Some dangerous woman?"

I recalled my dead father's wide-open mouth, felt again the unexpected moisture, then saw Diana and Patty as I'd last glimpsed them together, strolling into the darkness. *Only my sister*, I thought.

The drive to Price's house took a short fifteen minutes. The road meandered among rolling hills and over scenic wooden bridges, and I let myself enjoy the small pleasures of the countryside, its soft curves and simple planes. The farmhouses I passed along the way were neat and orderly, and in their uncomplicated contours the surrounding fields seemed to take life on its own terms and in that way reveal the saving balance of acceptance.

Price's house turned out to be quite the opposite of the farmhouses that surrounded it. The grounds were overgrown, with large untended shrubs standing raggedly alongside the house. The yard was bordered by a low wooden fence that had long ago been given over to patches of flaked paint. The house itself was no better, with sloping drains and loosely hung wooden shutters that hadn't been painted in years. An old Chevy sat in a garage that was little more than a tin roof held up by wrought-iron posts. Sagging gray screens covered the windows, and beyond them, thick brown shades were tightly pulled down, as if light were an enemy against which Price had fortified his dilapidated castle.

A narrow footpath led to the front door, though even this path appeared more or less unused, a fact that indicated that Price rarely left the house and that few if anyone ever visited it.

The door opened before I had a chance to knock, and behind a rusty screen I saw a face that appeared infinitely old.

"Douglas Price?" I asked.

"Yes."

His voice was weak and rather wheezy, so it didn't surprise me when I glanced down and saw a plastic yellow oxygen mask dangling from Price's neck. A tube connected the mask to a red tank strapped to a chrome dolly he grasped with his other free hand.

"I'm David Sears," I told him.

He looked at me blankly, through watery blue eyes. His skin had a tallow shade to it and his hair was more or less uncombed so that overall he seemed like his house and yard, ruinously abandoned.

"I think my sister may have contacted you recently," I added. "Diana Sears?"

"Ah, yes," Price said. A bony hand stretched into the evening light and flipped up the four primitive eyebolt latches that secured the screen door. "The door bangs in the wind," he explained. "I don't like the noise." He eased himself out farther into the light, and I saw white, shoulder-length hair that on a professor might have given off a sense of aged wisdom, but only made Price look more neglected. "Come in," he said.

I stepped inside the house and followed Price down the dimly lighted hallway and into an unexpectedly tidy room, lined with bookshelves, and furnished with a large wooden table and a few wildly unmatched chairs, some heavily padded, some bare wood, and which included both a rocker and badly worn recliner.

"I shift around a lot," Price explained. "Restless legs syndrome." He shrugged. "I don't know if it's mental or physical," he added. He chose the recliner for himself and indicated that the rocker was for me. "Make yourself comfortable."

The rocker emitted a high, painful cry as I sat down. I leaned back in the chair and the crying stopped.

Price eyed me closely for a moment and I knew that he'd noticed that I was somewhat anxious.

"She's a woman on a mission," Price said. "Your sister."

The word "mission" struck me as decidedly romanticized in its description of Diana's current effort, but I let it stand without comment.

"I was quite impressed with her," Price added.

I leaned forward and cupped one hand in another. "Diana read me what you wrote about what happened at Dover Gorge," I said.

Price lifted the mask to his face and took a quick inhalation, then withdrew it. "She had it with her, my little pamphlet," he said. "She asked if I'd really heard those things I'd claimed to hear, and I told her that I had."

I offered no argument to this because I knew that Price had "heard" something, though I also knew that it had come from inside him, as all things of that sort must.

"I told her that the things I'd heard had seemed real to me at the time," Price continued. "I'm not a whole person, you see. I wasn't then, and I never have been. What I wrote about Dover Gorge was written by a shattered man." He smiled. "I said the same thing to Diana. Her response was very sweet. She said, 'Light passes best through shattered things.'"

"That's a quote," I told him. "From our father."

Price smiled. "Is it? I'm not surprised. She said her father was a poet."

And as if summoned like Hamlet's ghost, the Old Man suddenly appeared before me, spouting four lines of his own poor doggerel, lines I'd unknowingly memorized and buried all these years:

> *Through life's dim light*
> *This much I see:*
> *If Sorrow bettered us,*
> *We would better be*

"Not much of one, I'm afraid," I said. "Did she mention her son?"

"Yes," Price answered. "Jason, I believe?"

"That's right. What did she tell you about him?"

"That he'd drowned," Price answered. "She said she took it very hard. She didn't believe in anything. God. Heaven. So there was no comfort or solace for her, no place to go."

"She had a brother she could go to," I said quietly. "She still does."

Price looked at me intently. "There is such a thing as metaphysical loneliness," he said. "It's a place where there is no one else, and never can be." Something in his gaze was almost tangible. "You've been there, too, I think."

I waved my hand, cutting off what I expected to be a warm tide of psychobabble.

"I don't mean to be rude," I told him. "But I came to find out about Diana."

"What about her?"

"What she said to you."

"She didn't say much at all," Price informed me. "She's more of a listener, your sister. She struck me as passionately curious. I told her that, and she said she'd gotten it from her father."

I thought of the Old Man's crazed searching, desperate, panicked, forever in mad pursuit of some elusive truth.

"Did Diana tell you her father was crazy as well?" I asked.

"Yes, she did," Price said.

"It scares me," I added. "What she might have 'gotten' from him."

I suddenly saw the Old Man as a figure of terrible malevolence, giving Diana orders from the grave, directing her research into ancient murders, feeding an appetite for posing unanswerable questions, an appetite he'd quickened and nurtured by his own mad search, Diana now as much the fruit of that deranged garden as the poisoned daughter in the Hawthorne story he'd so often read and discussed with her.

"Which is why I came here," I added. "I need to know what you talked about."

"My little pamphlet," Price said with an idle shrug. "Not the whole thing. Just something I wrote about a man I met at Brigham. Pendergast was his name. Ray Pendergast. He wasn't a patient. He worked as an orderly. Very nice man, gentle."

"What did you write about him?"

"I wrote about the voice he heard," Price answered.

Diana had not mentioned any part of Price's pamphlet other than the one she'd read-recited that evening at Dover Gorge.

"What voice?"

"The one that spoke to him the day his brother died." Price paused and took another long inhalation from the mask. "Ray lived with his father on a small farm outside New Haven. He had a brother who was, well, not gifted, shall we say. His name was Dennis, and he had to be watched because he sometimes wandered off and Ray and his father would have to go looking for him. One day, the father sent Ray into town to get supplies. He'd already started down the road when he heard it. The voice. It said, 'Don't go.' According to Ray, it was so clear he thought his father might have called him, so he went back to the house. Dennis was in the father's workroom. Ray didn't see his father, but he heard him walking around upstairs. So he ignored the voice, and went on to town. When he got back, Dennis was missing. They found him in the well."

"Drowned?" I asked.

"It looked like an accident," Price said. "But Ray didn't think it was."

"Why?"

"Because Dennis had always been afraid of the well, wouldn't go near it." Price returned the mask to his mouth and took in a long, ragged breath. "He thought the boy had been murdered."

I thought of the morning Jason disappeared, how Diana had gone shopping, left her son with Mark.

"Diana asked lots of questions about Pendergast," Price said. "What I knew about his childhood, what happened to him later, if he'd ever heard that voice again." He shrugged. "I didn't know the answer to any of her questions."

"Did she tell you why she was asking them?"

"No," Price answered. He smiled. "So I only know one thing about your sister. She's a seeker."

A wave of irritation swept over me at the vast speculative literature these "seekers" both produced and devoured, books about pyramids, crystals, pentagrams, the whole sorry archive of their crazed and fruitless searching.

"What, exactly, do you think she's seeking?" I asked.

"I don't know," Price said. He held me in suspense a moment, no doubt trying to gauge what my reaction might be. "I told her about Gaia," he said finally. "Do you know what that is?"

"No."

"It comes from the Greek," Price told me. "It's the belief that the world is a living organism, that it sees and hears. I have always been interested in its auditory aspects. Particularly in stones."

"Stones," I said dryly. "Because you heard something in those stones in Dover Gorge?"

"Yes," Price said.

I shook my head, and in that gesture Price correctly saw how baseless and nonsensical I believed such ideas to be.

"Don't be so sure," Price said. "After all, many people rely far more on what they hear than what they see. The Umeda people, for example . . ."

As Price continued to speak, relating the various practices of the Umeda, I realized exactly why Diana had come to him.

"The Umeda have certain ritual sites that—" Price went on.

"Diana's looking for a partner," I interrupted. It had come to me in a series of images, my father dead, a moist pillow, a funeral pyre, all of these visions spiraling through my mind to the accompaniment of Mark's chanting voice, *She enlists aid. She can be very seductive.*

"That's why she came to you," I added. "She's looking for an . . ." I stopped because the word that came to me was so dire. ". . . an accomplice."

"An accomplice?" Price asked. He shook his head. "No, no. She already has someone like that."

"Who?"

"Her daughter," Price answered casually.

"Diana doesn't have a daughter," I told him.

"Oh," Price said. "I just assumed she was her daughter. The girl who was with her."

"Patty?" I asked.

Price nodded. "That might be her nickname, yes."

"What do you mean, nickname?"

"It wasn't the name the girl used when she introduced herself."

"What name did she use?"

Price seemed to see the apprehension and urgency with which I waited for his answer, both of which spiked upward when he gave the name.

"Hypatia," he said.

You think the words, but do not say them. *Two deaths.*

Petrie rolls up the sleeves of his shirt, his gaze focused on you intently as he does so. "Patty," he says. "You had no doubt it was Patty?"

You recall the image that came to you at that moment, two faces melting into each other, becoming one in thought and purpose. "No doubt," you tell Petrie. "I had no doubt that Patty was part of it now. That she was being seduced."

"But into what?" Petrie asks.

"Diana's 'research.'"

"But you still didn't know what that was, did you?"

"No," you admit. "But there were clues."

"Clues?"

"What she'd talked to Price about. That stuff in his book. Pendergast's story. A father who kills his son. All of that was somehow poisoning Diana's mind, and she was pouring that same poison into Patty's mind." You hear the beat of your voice accelerate, the rapid fire of your words, something frantic in them. "Diana was making nutty connections, I knew that much. She was going in the wrong direction."

"What direction was that?"

The word that occurs to you is "downward," but you know that if you say it, it will lead your story in the wrong direction, too.

"What direction?" Petrie repeats.

His tone is neither threatening nor insistent. He is deep in the mystery now, its murky water rising around him as it rises around you. He holds to the form of the interrogation like a floating log, speaks to you coaxingly, so that you think of a careful surgeon, one who uses his probe cautiously, easing the cold gray bullet from the brightly glistening flesh.

"Toward death," you answer, and with those words you come to a full stop.

In the following interval of silence, you recognize the long fall you have made in that direction, from death to death, the terrible slant of things. You wonder how many of these deaths you might have prevented.

"Things weren't clear to me," you tell Petrie.

You hear Abby's voice, urgent, frightening. *You have to do something, Dave.*

"I didn't know what to do."

You have to do something.

"I needed help. I needed advice. But I'd spoken to everyone I could about Diana. My wife. Patty. Bill Carnegie. Mark. You. Even Douglas Price. I didn't think there was anyone else I could go to. I was desperate. I would have talked to anybody." You see her not as she really appeared, but as some phantom version of herself, eerily transparent. "In fact, I did."

"Talked to someone?"

"Yes."

Petrie leans forward. "Who?"

In remembrance, she turns toward you, a child locked in inexpressible oddity.

"Nina," you tell him, and feel the old order of your mind explode, fall back to earth in smoldering bits, a lethal disarray. "I talked to Nina."

FOURTEEN

Night had fallen by the time I got back to town. It was a cool, autumn evening, and on the way through the village I noted the little shops hawking clothes and postcards and felt the awesome stability of uncomplicated things, of people questing after nothing more elusive than what they needed to sustain themselves at whatever level they'd sought that sustenance. The Old Man had found such a life disreputable because, according to him, it existed only on the surface of things. And yet it seemed to me that the surface was where life thrived, the surface that provided the only stability we had. We skated upon this thin layer of ice, and yet it was just thick enough to keep us from the cold and fathomless depths into which we would otherwise inevitably plunge.

Most of the shops were already closed on the town's main street, the lights out in its shoe stores and bakeries, a darkness that made a single luminous square all the more prominent, so that I glanced toward it as I passed, glimpsed the poster in the window, Kinsetta Tabu nakedly sprawled beneath grotesque little piles of beheaded Barbie dolls.

I recalled the weird lyric Diana had played for me, *World of whirl is whorl of world.* It struck me as nonsense, of course, but it had clearly spoken to Diana, and evidently she had passed whatever bizarre meaning it had for her on to Patty.

I had already purchased Kinsetta Tabu's CD and was on my way out of the shop when Nina came through the door. She didn't see me, and so, invisible, I watched as she turned to the left, walked to a far aisle, her back to me as she began to finger through a group of CDs.

She was a very slender girl, and very pale, dressed in black head to foot. Silver chains of various size and length hung from every available button and belt loop, and her shimmering blue hair was sprinkled with a fine, bloodred angel dust that sparkled eerily in the shop's bright light.

I had never felt the slightest need to engage Nina, and to the degree I'd ever thought of her, it was in blessed contrast to Patty. But the distance between them had closed, Patty now under an influence that seemed to me as weird and unpredictable as whatever it was that caused Nina to array herself in chains and sprinkle her hair with flecks of glistening red.

"Nina," I said.

She turned and looked at me warily, as if I were some creature who'd wandered unexpectedly out of the jungle depths.

"Hi," she said.

I stared at her silently, with no place to go, now wondering what it was I'd hoped to learn from her, what insight into Patty.

"I was just buying a CD," I continued awkwardly. I drew it from the bag. "Kinsetta Tabu."

I'd expected her to be surprised by the unexpectedly contemporary nature of my choice, but she seemed to regard it with the same silent disdain she no doubt had for Bob Dylan or Frank Sinatra or any other relic from the indistinguishable bygone eras of the distant past.

"Patty likes her," I added.

Nina nodded. "Yeah, I know. She mentioned it. It's like some new craze with her."

"Craze?"

"You know, always listening to it."

"But she's not your thing, I guess," I said. "Kinsetta Tabu."

Nina shrugged. "She went to the Grammys. She's a fake."

"I really haven't listened to her very much," I continued. "Like I said, it's Patty who . . ." I stopped, and a terrible wave of anxiety swept over me, a vision of my daughter adrift, becoming Hypatia, Diana's accomplice. "Patty," I sputtered. "She . . ."

Nina looked at me as if I'd suddenly become ill, an older man having a heart attack. Then, quite suddenly, she appeared to grasp the nature of my distress.

"You're worried about her," she said.

I nodded, still unable to regain my voice.

Nina smiled delicately. "That's nice," she said. "That's a nice thing." Her eyes miraculously glistened. "A father."

In an instant, everything changed, identities reversed, along with expectations, life in its full cataclysmic surprise. And in that bright, unclouded flash, I saw Nina not as weirdly adrift, but as rooted in her weirdness, the bizarre dress and flecked hair not as signs of floating character, but as proof of character itself, the weighted hand of her moral compass steady at true north.

"Does Patty talk to you?" I asked quietly.

Nina nodded. "She used to . . . a little."

"But not now?"

"Now she doesn't really talk to anybody." She seemed unsure of what my ancient, cracking heart could bear, hesitant to add anything to its burden. "She reads books all the time," she added. "She gets them from . . ."

"Her aunt," I said. "Diana."

"Diana," Nina repeated. She smiled. "The Huntress, right?" She seemed pleased to have stored this small mythological reference.

"The Huntress, yes," I told her, though in regard to my sister, I still had no idea of the nature of her prey.

The lights were on in the library, but as I turned into the parking lot beside it, I noticed that Diana's car wasn't there. I glanced at my watch. It was only six o'clock, well within her working hours. I recalled that once before she'd mentioned having gotten a ride. Perhaps she'd done that again, and was expecting a ride home.

I got out of the car, walked to the front door of the library, and went inside. There were a few people scattered about, mostly older, along with a smattering of young people in the room's computer section.

"Dave?"

I turned to see Adele Connors, a girl I'd dated for a time during my last year of high school. She'd been very smart and very curious, and I'd been powerfully drawn to her. But it was an attraction I'd avoided, though not because I'd wanted more. More would have been sealike, seething, boundless, and there would have been no foothold in the swell. And so I had wanted less.

"Dave," she said, clearly surprised to see me. "How long has it been?"

"I'm not sure," I answered.

"Since I married and moved away," Adele said. "I only came back last year. I guess you're not a regular patron of the library."

"No," I said. "I'm more of a movie fan." I noticed the small tag that hung on her blouse. It read, HEAD LIBRARIAN. "So you work here," I said.

"A widow has to do something." Her smile was delicate, wistful, like someone gazing at an old photograph, and it struck me how often we see our lives through the prism of other possibilities, a husband who lived, a different place, a different job, and that to do more, look deeper than into the simple, shallow pool in which we swim, is to stare bare-eyed into the unfathomable abyss.

"It seems like a thousand years ago, Dave," Adele added. Her smile widened. "So, fill me in."

I shrugged. "Married. One child. A daughter."

"I have two boys. Twins. Both in college now."

"I came back here after college," I told her, a mere after-thought to the family matter that now bore so heavily upon me. "I'm a lawyer."

"I knew that much at least," Adele said. "I've seen your shingle. Attorney-at-law." She smiled again, her schoolgirl smile. "It goes so fast, doesn't it? Life."

The years of my own small life passed like prisoners before the bar, but the lockstep of time was not a movement I could slow, so I saw no reason to address it. I glanced about. "Where's Diana?" I asked. "I dropped by to talk to her. But if she's busy, I can wait until she gets off."

Adele looked puzzled. "Gets off?"

"Yes," I said. "Eight o'clock. Isn't that when the library closes?"

Adele nodded softly. "Yes, that's when it closes, but . . ." She stopped, and I saw a strange uneasiness stirring in her eyes.

"What is it?" I asked.

"Diana doesn't work here, Dave," Adele said. "She comes here. She stays for hours. But she doesn't work here. Have an actual job, I mean."

I felt that little grip of terror that accompanies a sudden bump in midflight, all the steady motion of the plane in an instant undermined. "But Diana, she . . ."

Adele pressed a single finger to her lips, then motioned for me to follow along and led me to the rear of the library and into a small cramped office.

"It's a small town," she explained once she'd closed the

door. "I didn't want people to hear." She walked behind her desk and sat down. I took the only other chair in the room.

"So Diana just comes here to read?" I asked.

"Yes," Adele answered. "She goes from section to section, picking books off the shelves. She'll gather up eight or nine books. Then she'll take them over to one of the little study carrels we have near the window. She stays there all day."

It was the way Diana had studied as a child, and it was the way the Old Man had studied, piling books on his desk or spreading them across the floor, flipping from one to the other, amassing a vast store of information.

"And she takes notes," Adele added. "But not in a notebook, like you'd think. She brings in a bag full of little paper squares. Yellow. Like Post-its. That's what she writes on."

"Have you ever read any of these notes?"

Adele suddenly looked hesitant to reveal more, like a woman reluctant to tell someone else's secret. "Yes," she said quietly. "Just this afternoon I found a few of them on the floor beneath her desk. I picked them up. I was going to give them to her when she came in tomorrow."

"May I see them?"

She gave me a long, evaluating look. "I really shouldn't, Dave," she said.

I leaned forward. "Adele, please. I have to know what Diana's doing."

"Is she in trouble?"

"Not yet," I answered. "But she could be in the future."

Adele still made no move toward the notes.

"You know our history, Adele," I said. "My father. You know what he was like."

"Is that the kind of trouble you think Diana may be in?" Adele asked.

"Yes."

With no further protest, Adele opened the drawer of her desk, drew out a small white envelope. "You can't keep them," she said. "You can just look at them."

I opened the envelope, took out the few yellow squares of paper inside and read them, though not without difficulty, because the writing was so tiny I had to squint very hard to bring the words into focus.

The first read: *Acoustic affects have been registered in Scandinavian standing stones.*

The second bore no connection I could see to the first: *Musicogenic epileptics—brain discharges—at 6 Hz.*

The third read: *Stone tombs resonate at 95 Hz and 112 Hz, a frequency range comparable to the human voice.*

I returned Diana's notes to the envelope and handed it back to Adele. "You said she was here today?"

"Yes. She came in when we opened and didn't leave until about an hour ago."

"Was she alone?"

"For a while," Adele said. "Then I saw someone else sitting with her. A teenage girl. They were studying together."

"A teenage girl," I repeated. "With blond hair?"

Adele nodded. "I know Diana's gone through a terrible tragedy," she said.

"Losing her son."

But I was thinking only of Patty now, how vulnerable she was, how few defenses she had against my sister.

"Terrible," Adele said, "to lose a son."

I nodded. Or a daughter, I thought.

I drove directly to Diana's apartment, but her car wasn't parked on the street or in the parking area at the rear of her building. Nor could I detect any hint of light beneath the tightly drawn curtains of her apartment. I waited for a long time, checking my watch occasionally, but there was still no sign of Diana, and so I decided to visit various places of interest, locations where I thought she might go on a night of "searching."

It was a trail that led through her recent past, first down the hill where she'd been seen walking during the wee hours of the morning, then along the main street of the village, past the library, and farther down, past my office, and then out of town. Next I drove to the house on Old Farmhouse Road, where I got out briefly and looked around. The night was clear and the moon was full, so that I could see all the way to where Dolphin Pond glimmered brightly. The ear-shaped stone seemed to erupt from the ground at the water's edge, and I tried to imagine it as I thought Price might, not simply as a stone obelisk, but as part of an eerily living earth, though exactly how he envisioned so vast an organism was well beyond the powers of my own quite limited imagination. I hoped it was also beyond Diana's, a volatile element she had not added to the mix already boiling in her mind.

There was no sign of Diana at the house or the pond, and so I continued on, this time to the house where we'd lived as children. I parked there and waited, half expecting the door to open and Diana to step out and wave me in as she had that final rain-drenched day. But the door never opened, and even if it had, someone else would have come through it, some member of a different family, with different problems.

After a while, I headed back toward town, but not before a brief tour of the campus near our house. I drifted by the deserted quadrangle where Diana and I had frolicked as children, the old bell tower where she'd pointed out and named the stars, the little park where we'd sat, Jason only a few yards away, staring blankly at the other children.

Mark wants to put him away, I thought suddenly, the voice in my head almost as clear as Diana's.

Mark.

I suddenly felt a little bite of fear, and imagined Diana crouched behind a row of bushes, waiting for Mark to leave work.

I pressed down on the accelerator and made my way to where the old campus with its stately Federalist architecture gave way to the modern glass-and-steel facade of the Hamilton Research Institute.

The nearly deserted parking lot was large and well lighted, so it was easy for me to find the spot reserved for "Dr. Mark Regan."

It didn't surprise me that Mark's car was there. He'd rarely returned home until late in the evening, and during all those long nights, Diana had played and talked with Jason, ceaselessly working to connect with him, enter his world as if in hope of chasing away the demonic voices that, like invisible piranha, were eating him alive.

I pulled into the empty spot in front of Mark's car, got out, looked over the deserted moonlit parking lot, then into the shadowy interior of the car itself.

But what was I looking for?

The answer to that question stunned me.

I was looking for something that might corroborate Diana's groundless suspicion, glancing into Mark's car as if I might find a murder weapon lying openly in the backseat. It was an absurd act based upon an absurd notion, but I'd done it anyway. And I thought just how right Mark was, even heard him repeat his warning, *She can be very seductive.*

Oh, yes, I thought, she can be. I'd almost been seduced myself. And so how much easier it would be for her to overpower someone far less able to resist her, someone whose trust she could win, her own voice now in that person's head, feeding her unreal notions of evidence, filling her mind with suspicion, shaping a new identity, bestowing a new name.

The voice I heard was my own dark whisper. *Hypatia.*

I whirled around and headed back to my car, now feeling less like a movie detective than the hapless victim of my sister's enigmatic sorcery. I pulled myself behind the wheel and hit the lights. The twin beams shot straight ahead, and in their bright rays I suddenly glimpsed a glint of yellow paper tucked like a tiny parking ticket beneath one of Mark's windshield wipers.

I stopped, but left the engine running as I got out and retrieved the now familiar square of yellow paper. Diana had not bothered to fold it, and so I knew that she had no intention of keeping secret what she'd written.

The script was Diana's but the words were French, a quote from Émile Zola, the renowned line he'd penned as the opening salvo of one of history's great cries for justice, and which the Old Man had shouted again and again as he thundered from room to room, waving his list of enemies in the smoldering air.

It read simply, *J'accuse.*

etrie turns, reaches into the pocket of the jacket that hangs from the back of his chair, draws out a small plastic bag, and slides it toward you. The yellow slip is secured inside. You have little doubt as to who supplied it. It could only be Stewart Grace.

"Physical evidence," you say.

Petrie slides the bag toward you. "The only kind of evidence there is."

You are standing in the middle of a room, the walls alive with yellow slips. "Unless there is a reality to what we imagine," you tell him.

Petrie looks at you questioningly.

You stare at the small square of yellow paper, and for an instant it strikes you as oddly magical. "Blue smoke and mirrors," you add quietly. "False bottoms." You touch the paper with the tip of your finger, let its terrible import sink into you. "Have you ever been to Brigham?"

Petrie nods reluctantly, unsure of where you're taking him.

"The rooms where they sit in corners, holding their knees to their chests, silent, rocking."

Petrie's wariness intensifies. "I've seen that, yes."

"Why don't we do the same?"

"Because we're sane," Petrie answers.

You shake your head. "No," you tell him. "Because we're evasive. Evasion is the only thing that makes sanity possible."

Petrie looks at you sternly. "Back to the here and now," he says in a tone of stern instruction.

You know that Petrie still cannot fathom what you must have thought, let alone what you actually did. Following your story is like moving through a house with windows in the floor, doors in the ceiling, staircases that rise toward flat walls. It can be navigated only by means of your own off-kilter stars, an unfixed sun, the moon in jagged orbit.

The words weave like a genie in the air between you. *Three deaths? Four?*

You have no answer, save that reason was no longer a major player in the game. In that way, you were like the Old Man in his ravings, focused on the enemy, the true carrier of your blood's derangement.

You are in Diana's room now, the one on Victor Hugo Street, gazing at the words she festooned in block letters across her wall:

WE ARE ALL, ALL SPECTACULARLY FLAWED. True to her training, she supplies the citation: *Jean-Paul Sartre.*

A bland insight, you decide, but fatally true.

"Let's continue," Petrie urges quietly.

You glance about the room, unable to meet Petrie's eyes. The coffee urn rests on its now tepid base. Above it, the wall calendar features the plain brick facade of the local insurance company that supplied it. The mirror beside it could use a quick swipe. You move on to the window. The hawk no longer circles, and you wonder if, before the evening shade, it found its prey, or didn't.

You find the strength to look again at Petrie. You know that he must press on, though he seems tired now, like the coffee urn, somewhat stained and not as full as before.

He reaches into the plastic bag and withdraws the yellow square of paper. He squints slightly, then holds it up for you to see the two words written upon it.

"Do you know what this means?" he asks.

FIFTEEN

It means 'I accuse,'" I said a few minutes later as I handed the small yellow square of paper to Abby. "It was meant for Mark. I found it tucked beneath his windshield wiper."

Abby stared at the paper as if it were a blood-stained knife.

"There's no doubt that Diana put it there," I added. "It's her handwriting. She uses the same kind of paper to make notes in the library. She doesn't work there, by the way."

For a moment, Abby remained silent but I could see a terrible ferment behind her eyes, burning fuses, thousands of them. Then she said, "I saw those same yellow slips in Patty's room. On her desk. Tucked in books. I thought it was schoolwork. Research for some paper."

"Is she in her room now?" I asked.

"Yes."

I turned and headed for the stairs, but Abby's voice stopped me.

"What are you going to do, Dave?" she asked.

"I'm going to find out what she's 'researching,'" I said firmly.

Seconds later, I knocked at Patty's door, then waited until it opened.

"Hi," Patty said softly.

I held up the yellow paper.

Her eyes went oddly dark, but also curiously steady, as if she had been expecting my visit.

"Did you know about this?"

She gave no answer, but only stepped back, drawing the door open, so that even before I entered the room, I noticed the large poster she'd added to her wall, the same one I'd seen at the shop in town, Kinsetta Tabu sprawled across what I now saw to be a blood-spattered carpet.

"Where'd you get that?" I asked.

"Diana gave it to me," Patty said.

I stepped into the room. A drawing had been taped to the wall just to the right of the poster. It was very crude, and though it appeared to be somewhat representational, it was impossible to tell exactly what the figures represented.

"It's Diana's test," Patty explained.

"A test for what?"

"Imagination," Patty answered. She stepped over to my side. "Tell me what you see," she said.

"Nothing," I answered. "Lines and squiggles, a little color."

She laughed. "You don't have much imagination, Dad."

"What do you see then?"

"That was the test," Patty said. She looked at the drawing with a subdued but unmistakable pride, as one might look at some framed certificate of achievement. "I saw a fence."

"A fence?"

"Diana thought that was great," Patty told me. "Very imaginative, she said. Because I made it a human thing."

"A human thing? What does that mean?"

"Human action," Patty answered. "I saw insecurity, the way we're always threatened, and so we draw protective walls around ourselves. Particularly around our minds."

I knew that every word of this had come from Diana, but I avoided saying it.

"In a painting like this, anyone can see anything," I told her.

"Yes," Patty said. "It's the voice that tells you what to see. That's what imagination is, Dad. A voice. Only sometimes it's even more than that."

"In what way is it more?"

Rather than answer directly, she asked a question of her own.

"Did you know that Dostoyevsky said he didn't write *The Brothers Karamazov*?"

"Then he shouldn't have put his name on it," I said dryly.

"He said the brothers themselves wrote it."

"Yeah, but they didn't," I replied evenly. "Because they were characters, Patty. They were characters in a book. They didn't write anything because they didn't exist."

"But they did exist," Patty argued. "They were voices. Others have heard them, too. Lots of great writers have heard them."

Patty's own voice was less lifted in challenge now than in steadfast conviction.

"Like Harriet Beecher Stowe," she added. "Poets, too. William Blake, for example, and—"

"I'm not talking about poetry," I broke in. I waved the yellow slip before her unmoving gaze. "I want to talk about this note," I said in a voice I labored to keep calm. "I found it on the windshield of Mark's car." I pressed it toward her. "Read it, Patty."

She didn't take it from me. "I know what it says," she told me.

"You do?"

"Yes," she said lightly, as if she were acknowledging nothing more than the current state of the weather.

"Then maybe you can tell me why Diana would do something like this," I said.

Patty lifted her head like someone before the judge's bench, convinced that what she'd done was not a crime despite what the statutes read. "Because she's doesn't want Mark to get away with it, Dad."

"Get away with what?"

A look of absolute disbelief swam into Patty's face. "Don't act like you don't know what Mark did," she said as if she were correcting the worldview of a child. "I know you know."

"I don't know what you're talking about," I protested.

"I'm talking about Mark," Patty said. "That he's evil."

In my hand, the small square of yellow paper suddenly took on the full weight of the world, the great pull of the earth pressing down with the accumulated burden of all our vast misguidedness.

I shook my head. "Patty, there is not one tiny piece of evidence that Mark is . . . 'evil,' as you put it."

Patty watched me from the high aerie of her certainty, a god looking down on a poor, benighted mortal. "There's more than one kind of evidence, Dad." She walked to her desk, drew a thin book from the disordered pile she had there, and handed it to me.

"What's this?" I asked irritably.

"Just read it," Patty replied.

I glanced at the title. "I already have," I told her. "As a matter of fact, I've also spoken with the author." I tossed Douglas Price's pamphlet back onto her desk. "As you have, too, evidently."

She picked up the pamphlet and with a reverence I'd never seen her display toward books of any kind, returned it to its place with the other books on her desk. Then she turned back toward me, and had I not known better, I'd have sworn that her eyes were made of cold blue ice. "You're spying on us," she said.

"I'm trying to figure out what you're doing, Patty," I said. "What Diana is doing . . . to you."

"Doing to me?" Patty asked sharply.

"Yes," I answered. "Drawing you into this . . . I don't even know what to call it."

"Drawing me in because she can, right?" Patty asked. "Because I'd believe anything she told me. Like some kid believing in Santa Claus."

It was precisely at that moment I saw just how deep the danger was, the dark, toxic water that was rising around my daughter.

"Patty," I said softly. "I want you to understand something. There is a difference between sense and nonsense, and that difference is very large."

Patty peered at me from what seemed a planetary distance. "Diana knows things, Dad."

I could see the pure admiration Patty felt for Diana, which, it seemed to me, only deepened the danger.

"Patty . . ." I began.

Patty lifted her hand in a gesture borrowed from her mother. "I don't want to hear any bad things about Diana." She placed her hands over her ears. "No more, Dad."

I knew that even had I more to say, not a word of it would actually have been heard. My voice had been banished from her head, and at that moment, I could find no way to make it audible again.

And yet I tried.

"Patty, listen to me," I said. I reached for her hands, tried to pry them from her ears. "Patty, Diana is . . ."

She jerked away from me, strode to the CD player on the shelf beneath her window, and turned up the volume.

"Patty," I said, "listen . . ."

But the volume was too loud, drowning out all other sound, so that neither of us could hear anything but the macabre, malevolent hiss of Kinsetta Tabu's coldly threatening voice:

Father/Sister
Twister.
Father/Daughter
Slaughter.

Abby was sitting tensely at the kitchen table when I came back into the kitchen.

"What happened?" she asked.

"Patty's convinced that Diana's right about Mark," I said wearily. "That he's 'evil.' That was the word she used."

I vainly hoped that Abby might downplay this dread idea, recapture the lost lightness of her being, but she only took a quick sip of coffee, then said, "So what were those yellow pieces of paper in Patty's room?"

"Bookmarks," I answered. "At least that's what they looked like. She's studying the same stuff as Diana." I recalled the three notes Adele had shown me in the library, the only evidence I had. "Stuff about stones. Sound." I drew in a long, troubled breath. "But whatever it is, Patty's studying it with her. They meet at the library."

"How do you know that?"

"I went to the library after that meeting in New Braddock.

I was going to talk to Diana, but she wasn't there. When I asked where she was, I found out that she doesn't have a job at the library at all. She just spends all her time there." There was no point in holding anything back, and so I didn't. "Patty also went with Diana to meet this guy who wrote a little essay about Dover Gorge. He thought she was Diana's daughter, and that her name was Hypatia."

"Hypatia," Abby repeated darkly. She shook her head, and with that gesture seemed to shake away the last of those little particles of sunlight she'd so carefully stored in her brain. "I was always afraid of this." She added nothing else for a moment, then she looked at me and I saw the depth of her fear. "You have to do something, Dave," she said in a tone of stern command. "Before it's too late."

I thought of the stack of books I'd seen on Patty's desk and imagined my hand resting upon them like a man taking an oath. "I will, Abby," I said. "I swear."

That night, as I lay sleeplessly in bed, I wondered if perhaps in every life a moment comes when you realize just how little you have actually escaped from whatever it was you'd fled. Before then, I thought I had escaped the Old Man's terrible legacy, and that Diana had as well, that his long derangement had died with him and been buried in the ground.

Mark thinks it is in us, I heard my sister say.

And he was right to think it, I decided now, though I could only guess with what terrible fatality he'd watched this same illness settle over Jason, found his own paternal voice drowned out by the other voices in his son's head, drowned out as mine was now drowned out by Diana's, drowned out as fully as it had been silenced by Kinsetta Tabu's mad chant only a short time before, the voice of my fatherhood now merely a weak, ineffective murmur against my sister's wall of sound.

Petrie's eyes widen somewhat, like one who has just found a shimmering nugget in a pile of dark earth.

"So you were afraid?" he asks. "You were afraid of Diana?"

Was that the dark engine that propelled you, you wonder now. Fear. You feel the plot materialize, recall the grim joy of its implementation.

"No, not fear," you answer.

"Anger?" Petrie asks.

A bitter truth breaks the surface of your mind with all the fearful clarity of a shark's fin. "I think I've always been angry," you tell him.

"Why?"

"Because I never live up to expectations," you answer.

"Who does?" Petrie asks.

You note the sudden, oddly broken tone of your interrogator's voice, and in his eyes you glimpse a world of recognized but still festering inadequacies—the times and ways he has let down people, late arrivals, dinners grown cold on the family table, the school plays he didn't attend, the softball games he missed, the flowers he didn't buy, or even think of buying, the long gray line of little things that mattered only in the grim accumulation of them.

"We are all spectacularly flawed," you tell him.

Petrie rises, and in that gesture you sense a man who does not wish to have this conversation.

But you press the issue anyway. "Everyone," you add emphatically.

You watch as Petrie silently crosses the room, and in the slump of his body you recall something the Old Man once said: *Self-esteem is only possible for a man who is lost in illusions, or who has none of them at all.* How starkly lucid he was, your father, when he was lucid at all.

Petrie walks to the coffee machine, examines the urn, then slowly turns, walks back to the table, and resumes his seat across from you.

"Okay," he says, determined to regain the surety and balance you know he briefly lost. He picks up the blue pen, holds it above the paper of his notepad. "What then?"

Fear, you think. You are a river of fear.

"I was afraid," you answer.

"What were you afraid of?"

You give the true answer. "That I was right in everything I feared. That Diana had to be stopped. And that I couldn't stop her."

Petrie stares at you evenly. "But someone else could?"

"Yes."

Petrie's pen doesn't move, and so you know that he is after dates, names.

You give him both.

"October 14. Robert K. Santori."

SIXTEEN

The next morning I looked through my files and found his name. Dr. Robert K. Santori. I'd handled his divorce some years before. The negotiations had gone well, and so there'd been no need to go before the court. Santori had behaved very sanely, given the fact that he'd actually discovered his wife in the arms of another man. "Quite a nice fellow," he'd quipped at one point, "but then my wife always had good taste in men."

The case file was brief. It took me only a few minutes to refresh my memory. Santori had worked at Brigham for nearly fifteen years before setting up his own practice in an office in the Chandler Building, a squat professional structure that was practically on the grounds of the county hospital.

I hadn't actually talked with Santori since the divorce, but I could still remember certain stories he'd told me about the time he'd worked at Brigham, the grave madness he'd treated there, sometimes with some success, as he'd said. He'd readily admitted though that a great many of his patients had remained beyond his reach, and so had simply been "tranquilized," so that they lived, as Santori said, "a mothlike existence," fluttering but unaware. I'd never asked about the Old Man, whether he'd treated him at Brigham, helped to strap him down, injected him with tranquilizers or perhaps simply glanced into his room to see Diana at his bedside, quietly reciting to him.

I'd called Santori just after lunch, told his receptionist who I was, and asked her to please have the doctor call me. He'd done exactly that within an hour, and without giving much away, I'd asked for a "consultation."

"Let's just call it a 'conversation' for now," Santori said. "We'll get to the billable part later on."

His office in the Chandler Building was small and neat, with the usual bookshelves and framed licenses and diplomas. The fabled couch was made of brown leather and sat off to the side, like an afterthought. Santori, dark, portly, with black bushy eyebrows, greeted me with a hearty handshake, then took his place behind a large wooden desk.

"So, I understand this has to do with your sister," he said.

Two plain chairs rested in front of Santori's desk. They looked vaguely as if they'd been scavenged from some public institution, and I couldn't help but wonder if the Old Man had been strapped down in one of them at some dire point.

"My sister, yes," I said, then lowered myself into the nearest chair.

Santori had iron gray hair, parted in the middle and combed very flat so that a perfect line ran backward from his brow to the back of his head.

"When we spoke earlier, you mentioned that she'd recently lost her son," Santori said.

I thought of that death, and began to see it as it may or may not have happened, a boy moving through high grass toward a glimmering pond, voices growing louder and more insistent as he closed upon the water.

"That's right," I answered.

Now Jason had broken through the grass, the unfeeling stone before him, insensate, as it had to have been, and yet, in my imagination, oddly waiting.

"His name was Jason," I added. "He drowned a few months ago."

Time blinked, and Jason was in the water now, motionless, already dead, his legs together, but his arms spread out, birdlike, as his body curled forward then drifted down and down, to the bottom of the pond.

"An accident," I said. I heard Diana's wail, deafening yet silent, as if silence itself served to magnify sound, made audible what would otherwise have remained forever unheard things.

Santori leaned back slightly. "I take it her behavior has changed since her son's death?"

"Her whole life has changed."

"In what way?"

"She ordered her husband out of the house," I said. "They got a divorce not long after."

"That's not unusual, of course," Santori said. "Marriages often don't weather the death of a child."

Weather.

I don't know why the word struck me as peculiar, or at least as a word Diana would have noticed had she been sitting in the other chair. I could almost see her there, listening intently. She would have noticed "weather," noticed that Santori had applied a meteorological term to the buffeting we take in life, the thermals that drag us down or lift us to grand but perilous heights. Or was it a geological reference, Diana would have wondered, the work of wind and water, the wearing down of stone.

"Did Diana appear upset by the divorce?" Santori asked.

"No," I answered.

In fact, I thought, she had tossed her marriage away as casually as a candy wrapper, forgotten as soon as it had been discarded.

"Diana isn't a woman scorned," I added.

"Let me be clear why I asked," Santori said. "Sometimes behavior, even behavior that can appear, for lack of a better word, crazy, may have a perfectly rational basis. It may seem crazy, but the reason for it may not be. A person might set a fire in order to get attention." He smiled. "Or kill a rock star or a politician."

"Diana has always gotten plenty of attention," I told him. "Especially when she was a child. From my father."

"Why so much attention from him?"

"Because she was so smart," I answered. "A reader and a

memorizer. She could quote huge passages. She was very gifted in that way."

"And it served her well, this giftedness?"

To my own surprise, I answered, "No."

No, because at that moment it seemed to me that Diana's high-voltage brainpower was the very force that had blown her into playground corners and walled her up in libraries. It was almost classically tragic, I thought, a gift that was simultaneously a curse.

Abby's voice sounded in my mind. *She got it from him.*

"She got it from our father," I said. "He was very gifted, too."

I recalled the day we'd brought him home from Brigham, how desperately he'd clung to Diana as she'd led him from the hospital to my waiting car, reciting for him softly all the way:

> *Go and catch a falling star,*
> *Get with child a mandrake root,*
> *Tell me where all past years are,*
> *Or who cleft the Devil's foot*

I'd walked behind them, my mind fiercely recording every word she spoke as they flowed down the walk together, smoothly in tune, two parallel streams, Diana murmuring softly in his ear as she eased him into the backseat, then climbed in behind him. All the way home, she'd continued her recitation, though no longer of whole poems, as I'd noticed, but stringing together verses from different poems and different poets, shifting meters slightly on occasion, yet seamlessly sewing the disparate lines into a perfect fabric of meaning:

> *Then you have done a braver thing*
> *Than all the Worthies did,*
> *And a braver thence will spring,*
> *Which is to keep that hid.*

It was to me a demonstration of towering skill, and she had done it as easily and with as little note as I might have spun out "Humpty Dumpty."

"Dave?"

I came back to the present, the modest room where Santori sat behind his desk. "Yes?"

"Did you hear my question?"

"I guess I didn't," I said.

"I asked what first alerted you that Diana might have a problem?"

"I suppose in one way or another, I've always been on the alert."

"Why?"

"We have a family history," I told him. "My father was paranoid."

"Institutionalized?"

"Twice," I said.

I remembered the first instance, how the proverbial "men in white coats" had arrived, seemingly out of nowhere, on the day after my father had stared at me in his mad ire, *It's you,* then rushed up the stairs to run his bath.

"The first time was when I was five," I told Santori. "Diana was nine."

"How long was your father in the hospital?"

"About a month, I think. Diana and I were placed in foster care. A nice old couple. They had a farm."

"And then you were both returned to your father?"

"Yes."

"Any other mental illness in your family?"

"Not that I know of," I said.

"On your mother's side?"

"My mother left us," I said. "I never knew her or anything about her."

Santori nodded. "When was your father institutionalized the second time?"

"When Diana and I were in college," I said. "I was a freshman. Diana was a senior at Yale. She was on full scholarship. She gave that up to take care of my father. She did that until he died."

"And after that?"

"She lived alone for a while, then got married. A few months later Jason was born." I shrugged. "That's about it, her history."

Santori nodded. "Okay, let's move forward then," he said casually. "What's been happening lately? With Diana, I mean."

I told him what Leonora Gault had told Abby, that Diana walked about in the early morning hours, and that she seemed unwilling to let people into her apartment.

"So you've never been in her apartment?" he asked.

"No, I haven't," I answered.

He picked up a pad and pen, leaned back in his chair, and placed the pad on his upthrust knee. "What else have you found troubling about Diana?"

I told him about the e-mails and faxes, my sense that Diana was doing research of some kind.

"Is this a new behavior?" Santori asked. "Delving into research?"

"No," I answered. "She's always had a great deal of curiosity."

I thought of all her many passions, the collections she'd maintained as a child, everything from seashells to the souvenirs she'd gathered on the modest trips we'd taken with the Old Man, a little piece of cobblestone from New York City, a bit of ground from Gettysburg. How many times had I seen her take out one of these small tokens of our travels, peer at it intently or press it to her ear, always with that little crinkling in her brow.

Santori wrote a brief note then looked back up at me. "Please continue." He smiled warmly. "The devil is in the details."

I told him about the trip to Dover Gorge, the passage from Price's book that Diana had recited. He asked me to tell him what was in the passage, and listened quietly as I described it. When I finished, he laughed softly. "Well, it's certainly not an alarming piece of work, is it?"

"No," I said.

"Why do you think that passage appealed to her?" Santori asked.

"I don't know," I said. "But it interested her enough to look up the guy who wrote it. She found out that he was still alive, and she went to his house."

Santori took another note. Then he said, "What do you know about this visit?"

I told him about Ray Pendergast, the voice he'd claim to hear, the murder he suspected, a little brother down the well.

"I don't know what's in Diana's mind," I added. "But I do know she spends hours and hours at the library."

"She's never told you what she's reading there?"

"No, but I saw some of her notes, stuff about sound, mostly."

"Do you think that she's somehow covering something up?"

"Yes, I do."

A pause, then, "Dave, what was your relationship with Diana before Jason died? Were you close?"

"Yes."

"And after he died?"

"I guess we're not as close now."

"How do you feel about that?"

This sounded like a question from *Spellbound*. I could almost hear Gregory Peck asking it of Ingrid Bergman, but I answered it anyway. "I miss her," I admitted.

Santori leaned forward in his chair and eyed me closely. "Has she gotten close to anyone else? I mean, since Jason's death?"

"My daughter."

"Really? In what way?"

"Patty's gotten taken in by all this stuff Diana believes."

"But you don't quite know what Diana believes," Santori reminded me.

"I know she thinks her husband is 'evil,'" I said. As if it were Exhibit A in a case against my sister, I took out the single square of yellow paper I'd found on Mark's windshield, and handed it to Santori.

"Diana put this on her husband's car," I told him.

"Ex-husband," Santori corrected. He read the note then passed it back to me. "What do you think she's accusing him of?"

The word fell from my mouth like a drop of blood. "Murder."

He regarded me intently for a moment, then asked the one question that surprised me. "Do you believe that, too?"

"No," I answered instantly. "If I did, I'd help her find the evidence."

Santori hesitated briefly, then said, "What options have you considered?"

I shrugged. "What options do I have?"

"Well, I take it Diana's never hurt herself, right? Or hurt anyone else, for that matter?"

"No."

"Would she talk to me?" Santori asked.

"Probably not," I said.

"Would she submit to any kind of evaluation?"

"I don't think so."

"Which means, of course, that she wouldn't voluntarily

seek treatment," Santori said. "That's not unusual, of course. Part of mental illness is not to perceive mental illness."

"So what can be done?"

"Not very much, I'm afraid," Santori said. "Because she hasn't done anything. Evidently she feels that her husband is a murderer. Okay. Fine. But other than that little note, she hasn't done anything about it."

"So we just wait until she does?"

"Yes, of course, we do," Santori answered. He nodded toward the small yellow slip I still held in my hand. "Clearly Mark's her target." He looked at me pointedly. "I mean, no one else is in the line of fire, right?"

"No one else," I said, then thought, *But Patty.*

S o you were no longer focused on Diana?" Petrie asks.

"No," you admit.

"Or Mark?"

"Only as a means," you answer, though you cannot be sure at what point the plot actually began to form. For a moment, you see yourself in images of Shakespearean villainy. Richard. Iago. You have not thought of these figures since you left Victor Hugo Street. How much, how very much, you have buried, half a lifetime of pure learning.

Petrie draws a long breath, and you hear his mortality in the slight wheeze at the end. Another death approaching. Far off still, perhaps, but gaining ground.

You recall a saying of Cocteau's, that Death is not really the issue, only the me . . . me . . . me . . . who is dying.

Me. Me. Me.

Three deaths.

How odd now, the little firings of your mind.

Petrie taps his pen against the notepad, and you wonder if he does this in order to return you to this room, his questions. Are you drifting away now, drifting into your own imagined world . . . like Dad?

"Coffee." You blurt the word so suddenly, perhaps even vehemently, that Petrie is clearly startled.

"You want coffee?" he asks.

"Yes," you answer, though what you really want is something grounded in reality, a taste, or perhaps nothing more than the feel of a warm cup in your hand. "Please."

Petrie rises, walks to the urn, pours the last of the coffee into a Styrofoam cup.

"Thank you," you say politely when he hands it to you.

He sits down, picks up the pen. "Okay, where were we?" He looks at his notes. "Oh yes," he says. "Mark."

You see his face, but it is not his face. It is the face you think Diana saw when she thought of him, a hideous mask.

"Santori called him the 'target'?" Petrie asks.

"Which he was."

"An innocent man."

"No one is that," you say grimly.

"Wrongly accused."

You take a sip from the cup, feel the tepid fluid in your mouth, wonder what it would taste like, truly innocent blood.

SEVENTEEN

Mark was clearly surprised to see me, but the grave look on my face as he came into the foyer of Hamilton Research must have alerted him to the fact that something had changed, that the clouds were darkening now and quickly rolling in.

"What is it, Dave?" he asked.

"Not here," I told him.

He turned to the receptionist. "Tell Dr. Stephens I'll be a little late for the meeting."

With that we walked out of the building, then along the edge of the parking lot to where a couple of wooden benches rested under a large oak tree.

I took out the paper I'd found on his windshield the night before and handed it to him.

"Diana left this for you," I said.

He took the paper, read what he saw there, then looked up at me quizzically.

"It means, 'I accuse,'" I told him.

"I gathered that," Mark said. "But of what?"

"I think she means murder," I told him bluntly.

A dry cackle broke from him. "And who exactly did I murder?"

"Jason."

"Christ." He shook his head wearily, not so much like a man unexpectedly accused as one suddenly and annoyingly distracted. "That's all I need right now. Diana off her nut."

Off her nut. The words hit me like metal pellets, but I couldn't argue that they were wholly misapplied to Diana's scattershot state of mind.

"Where did you find this . . . accusation?" Mark asked.

"She tucked it behind a windshield wiper on your car," I answered.

"Where was my car?"

"Here," I answered. "In your parking spot."

"So she came to the center?" Mark asked. "She physically came to my workplace?"

The question had an oddly legalistic ring to it, but that didn't change the answer I had to give.

"Yes, she did," I said.

I watched as a pained question formed in his mind. "She's this far gone, Dave? Murder?" He waved the yellow square in the air between us. "Accusing me of murder?"

Rather than answer, I leaned forward and asked a question of my own. "Do you have any idea why she'd come up with something like this?"

"None at all," Mark said. "I thought she blamed herself for what happened to Jason. That was crazy, too, but not as crazy as this. I had no idea she'd snapped this way." He looked at me sharply. "It's in her blood, of course, this craziness." He shook his head like a man lost in metaphysical confusion, the whole universe one big enigma. "All that debris in her blood. Like her father."

Mark's fearful vision of the Old Man materialized before me, with bristling hair and wild, erratic eyes, madly pawing his way through book after book, searching for the answer to a question he'd never revealed.

"Then Jason," Mark added. "Passed down to Jason."

"You didn't have to marry her," I said.

"I know," Mark said. "But she was so brilliant, Dave. You know that. The talk of the campus." He shrugged. "Besides, I thought it was the right time."

"The right time to what?"

"Marry. Have a family."

"There's a 'right' time for that?"

"You know, get settled." He glanced down at the note Diana had left him. "I can't believe she came here. To my workplace. Anyone could have seen this, Dave." He waved the yellow slip again. "An accusation. Based on nothing."

"Not exactly nothing," I said cautiously. "At least in Diana's mind."

Mark's eyes went cool. "What are you talking about?"

"The badge," I told him.

"What badge?"

"Your father's badge," I answered. "She says you used it to get Jason to do things."

"That's right," Mark said. "Little things like sit down, stop rocking back and forth. What about it?"

"She found it near the pond."

"So what?"

Before I could answer, he guessed what the answer would be. "You've got to be kidding, Dave. She thinks I used that badge to lure Jason to the pond?"

"I think so, yes."

"Jesus," Mark muttered. "Jesus Christ."

"It might help if she knew how the badge got there," I said.

Mark abruptly stepped back and looked at me as if I were now his accuser. "I can't believe you're interrogating me, Dave," he said.

"Look, Mark," I explained. "I'm just trying to find out what set Diana off, what made her suspicious."

"What made her suspicious?" The question clearly struck him as ludicrous because the answer was so obvious. "She has a suspicious mind, Dave. She doesn't need anything at all to set her off, as you put it." He released a dry laugh. "Hell, she could even become suspicious of you."

"Me. Suspicious of what?"

"Well, why not murder?"

"What? Who?"

"Your father," Mark said casually. "You were there, weren't you, the day he died?"

"Yes, but I didn't kill him."

"But you were in the house, weren't you?"

I recalled the moment I'd returned from my walk, my father's last words still ringing in my ears. "No, I wasn't," I answered. "I went for a walk. He was dead when I got back. Diana was with him when he died."

"But you're not accusing Diana of murdering him, are you?" Mark asked. "Which is exactly my point, Dave. You have as much reason to suspect that Diana killed your father as she has for suspecting me of killing Jason." He looked extraordinarily satisfied by his own reasoning. "So, quite obviously, Diana's suspicions are absurd. In your line of work, I believe the phrase is 'without foundation.'" He let this sink in, then asked, "Is she still reading about these prehistoric murders?"

"As far as I know," I said.

"Where does she get this stuff?"

"The library, at least some of it. And from the Internet."

"The Internet, of course," Mark scoffed. "The universal nuthouse. You can find anything there. She was always on the Internet, you know. While I was at work. And sometimes late at night after Jason had gone to bed. Either on the Internet or that old typewriter of her father's. Hours and hours. Tap, tap, tap."

As if the repetition of that word were a strange, occult summons, I once again remembered the Old Man at the same clanking machine, used and overused, with cracked keys and broken letters. The vision of Diana hunched over the same dark mechanism pierced me with an icy blade of dread.

Mark pocketed the small yellow note I'd given him. "Evidence," he explained. "If I ever need any."

"Evidence of what?" I asked.

"Harassment," Mark said flatly. "Because it's harassment, you know, what Diana's doing to me. I could file a complaint. I'd be within my rights. You should know that better than anyone, Dave."

"I don't want it to go that far, Mark," I told him.

"I don't either," Mark said. He drew in a tense, frustrated breath. "But you need to understand the kind of pressure I'm under. I've been at work on this project for four years. I'm getting close to something really big." He seemed almost to explode. "I don't have time for this shit, Dave!" Anger and frustration shot from him in a wave of heat. He let it run its course, drew in a long, composing breath, then looked at his watch. "I have a meeting. I'm sorry, but I just have no more time for this."

"I understand," I told him.

We walked back to the entrance of the center. Mark's car was parked in its designated spot. He glanced toward it as we went past. "I guess I'm looking for another note," he said. His tone was now irritated and impatient, a man on a mission, one who simply could not afford my sister's discomfiting intrusions. "It distracts me from my work, Dave, this nutty business with Diana."

"Me, too," I told him. "I'm way behind."

He said nothing in response to this, but I knew that he found my work of little consequence in the broader scheme of things. I would write no great book, solve no scientific mystery.

I would leave humankind where I'd found it, add nothing but a few trivial legal papers to its accumulated store.

"So," Mark said when we reached the short flight of concrete stairs that led to the center's main entrance. "Keep me posted."

"Yeah," I said.

We shook hands, and I noticed that Mark's skin was moist, clammy, as if his time with me had readjusted some small thermostat within his body, stoked a million molecular fires.

"Okay, well, take it easy," he said, almost gruffly.

He headed up the stairs, then stopped and looked back at me. "I wish I could tell you that this crazy stuff with Diana doesn't bother me," he said. "But it does, Dave. And I can't permit it to go on."

The threat was clear. Diana was in his sights.

"I'm working on it, Mark," I assured him.

He did not look reassured. "There'll come a point when I'll have to step in," he said. "You know that, don't you?"

"Yes, of course."

He turned and moved briskly up the stairs. I thought he might stop at the top of them, look back again, wave, assure himself that we were on the same page in regard to Diana. But he was off to his great work, and I knew that nothing would be allowed to turn him round again.

On the drive back into town, Mark disappeared from my mind altogether. Instead, my thoughts drifted back to the past, to the shattered family that had occupied the old house on Victor Hugo Street.

But rather than the turmoil and disarray that had continually rocked my youth, I recalled a rare and peaceful interlude, no longer than a few, precious minutes, but, in remembrance, oddly powerful.

The Old Man had raged on for most of the day, furiously adding names to his ever-expanding enemies list. Diana had come home from school at the usual time and begun her recitations, so that by late afternoon the Old Man was calm, very nearly sedate.

After a quiet dinner, he'd risen from the table, and with a look of surprising tenderness motioned us into his study, where, to our amazement, he'd set up a screen and carousel projector.

"I want you to see me," he said softly, his voice barely above a whisper. He nodded toward the old sofa and so we went to it and sat down.

Then, with no further word, he began the show.

Click: A boyhood photograph, the Old Man no more than four or five, frolicking on an ocean beach, his hair wet and glistening.

Click: Now he was at boarding school, perhaps seven or eight, standing a few yards in front of an ivy-draped, brick building.

Click: He was in his late teens or early twenties now, a college man, tall and handsome, books beneath both arms.

Click: Midtwenties, dressed in black pleated slacks and a light blue, short-sleeved shirt, with a blond-haired girl at his side.

Click: My mother and father nestled together beside a sleek new sedan, a JUST MARRIED banner hanging from the door.

Click: All four of us now, posed in the front yard of the house on Victor Hugo Street, my father and mother no longer touching shoulders as couples usually do in such photographs, but instead standing separately, like two stony obelisks, a fissure visible between them, I an infant in my mother's arms, Diana, a little girl, clinging to my father's hand.

Click: My father alone now, standing limply on the portico of a large brick building, alone but with others around him, people rocking softly in white chairs, here and there a nurse, all in white, with a neat, peaked cap.

"So be it," my father whispered as the screen went dark.

I looked over and saw that Diana was crying, and for the first time, I drew her beneath my arm, became her comforter. "Okay," I said softly. "It's going to be okay."

Okay, I thought again, as I made my way through town to my office. *It's going to be okay.*

And half believed that it might yet be so.

O kay," you say now. "Okay."

For a moment, you feel unmoored, your mind afloat in a littered sea clogged with strangely recognizable debris. You bobble in the gray water, curiously buoyant, watching things drift by, a red rubber ball, a green pillow, a slip of yellow paper, a fallen branch.

"From then on the die was cast," you add softly.

Petrie's flesh seems moist, soft, and for the first time, you notice a battered tenderness in his face.

"The design was in place," you tell him.

You think of this design as a badge in the form of a five-pointed star, each point represented by a name, the Old Man, Diana, Jason, Patty, you. The dots are aligned, waiting only to be connected.

"What design?" Petrie asks quietly.

"Like in that poem by Hardy," you tell him, no longer surprised that you remember it. So much has surfaced, after all. "The iceberg grows while the ship is built. A piece of the iceberg breaks away as the ship sets sail. Each floats toward the other until . . ."

"Life is not a poem," Petrie says softly.

"No, it isn't."

"What happened is not a poem."

"No," you confess. "Poems don't bleed. Poems don't die." The fingers of your right hand curl into a fist. "Or kill."

"Or kill," Petrie repeats.

You see how wearisome it is to live as he does, always in the aftermath of some act he couldn't stop. You know that he will live that way forever. And that you will, too.

Petrie lowers his head and rubs his eyes.

You want to speed up the process, send him home to his family, let him regain whatever has been drained from him, replenish the store of his illusion.

"Stewart Grace," you say. "He called me about two days later."

Petrie takes the cue and immediately returns to the story. "Did it scare you?" he asks. "Because you must have thought he was calling about Diana."

"No, it didn't scare me." What you say next is a sheet you draw back to reveal a still bleeding wound. "I felt . . . important. Because he was a big lawyer. Rich. Famous." You pull the sheet back farther, reveal the depth of the damage. "And I was nothing."

EIGHTEEN

Stewart Grace called," Lily said as I walked into the office. "He wants you to call him back right away."

"Stewart Grace?"

"It sounded urgent."

And so I returned the call immediately, then waited for Grace's secretary to put me through to him.

"Hello, Dave," Grace said. "I just got a call from Mark Regan."

I said nothing.

"I understand you and Mark had a conversation a few days ago," Grace went on.

"Yes, we did."

"Mark found that conversation very troubling," Grace said. "So I was hoping you and I might have a conversation, too. About your sister. Her state of mind."

I knew no way to refuse such a conversation, nor any reason to. I'd watched Grace in court often enough to know his style and approach, and that both were coolly analytical. I'd even noticed that he was particularly adept at using various medical metaphors to win the jury over to his side. Because of that I knew that Stewart Grace would lead me through a careful analysis of the current situation. He would measure the tumor Mark felt growing on his life, keeping him from work, the grim distraction of my sister. He would stage this malignancy, postulate its future growth, present his views on reducing or excising it.

I would listen to all this, then offer a response. Crisis management would no doubt be my model. I would run a table-top exercise in containment, posit worst-case scenarios, plan for the moment if and when the building fell, the levee broke, the earth split, the fire roared up the canyon's arid funnel.

"Diana's state of mind may not be that easy to determine," I said.

"Which makes it all the more necessary to discuss it, don't you think?" Grace asked.

"I suppose."

"Good," Grace said, almost cheerily. "Shall we say, my office at 5:30 this afternoon?"

What could be the harm, I thought.

Stewart Grace was everything I was not, the son of a real estate tycoon, educated first at Choate, then at Harvard, member of every exclusive club in the county, with a slender wife who was every inch his equal in style and good looks. He had a large house on Pendleton Lake, one set so far back from the road that it could only be glimpsed dreamily through a forest of stately trees. I'd never been invited there, even to one of the benefits Grace periodically hosted for local charities and to which almost anyone with a checkbook might be expected to be summoned. We'd never had occasion to speak other than casually, and even then, it had been a hasty affair, with Grace, as always, on the run, reaching for his cell phone, then easing away to speak in confidential undertones to one of his high-profile, sometimes celebrity, clients. Both his sons were in college now, one at Columbia, the other at Stanford, and his daughter, or so I'd heard, was studying cello in the privileged, and no doubt rarefied, atmosphere of Juilliard. My father's words returned to me, *You are dust to me.* But not to you alone, I thought.

And so I knew where I stood with Stewart Grace as I made my way to his office later that day. I was a small-town lawyer with an undistinguished practice, a guy whose house was on a quarter-acre lot, whose daughter went to public school, a guy who spent his evenings watching movies in his little den, on a little screen, stringing out the days of his little, little life, the only claim upon his time a sister who had obviously spooked the brilliant scientist who was his friend. Given all this, it didn't surprise me that Grace kept me waiting for almost half an hour.

When the moment to receive me finally arrived, one of Grace's perfectly tailored female assistants ushered me into an office that looked like one of the big-time corporate boardrooms I'd seen in movies. Not one desk, but two. Along with an impressively grand conference table decked out with several crystal bowls of fresh fruit.

Grace was dressed in a dark blue, three-piece suit. He was tall, almost towering, with a great shock of gleaming white hair, a high, soaring eagle of a man. He was standing by the conference table as I entered.

"Would you like anything, Dave?" he asked. "Something to drink?"

"No, thank you," I said.

He made a dancer's turn and strode not to his desk, but to a small, leather sofa a few feet away. "Please," he said, indicating one of the three matching chairs that surrounded it.

I chose the one in the middle.

"We've never had much time to talk, have we, Dave?" Grace asked.

"We've never actually talked," I said.

Grace laughed. "Met, but not talked," he said. "That's an apt distinction." He leaned forward and adjusted the right leg of his perfectly tailored trousers. "Your father died in a mental hospital, I understand."

The remark shocked me, coming out of the blue as it had, and in doing so shifted the burden to me, as if I had to prove myself, demonstrate that I wasn't in the least "like Dad."

"No," I told him, the reflexive instinct of a small animal defending his tiny burrow against the intrusion of a big one. "My father died at home."

"But he'd only been home a little while," Grace said with the full confidence of a man who already assumed that he knew more about my life than I did.

"He left the hospital in January," I said, brandishing this simple fact like a rapier. "He was admitted a month before."

"So he was only in the hospital a month?" Grace asked doubtfully, as if he'd already decided that I couldn't be trusted to remember details.

"One month and six days," I said. I leaned forward. "What does this have to do with—"

"If you could indulge me for just a moment longer, Dave," Grace said smoothly. "I'd just like to establish the ground-work, you might say, for our future discussion."

I settled back into my chair, a gesture he rightly took as my permission to continue.

"Now, that was the last hospitalization," Grace said. "But not the first, I believe."

"Not the first," I admitted.

"When was the first time?"

I immediately recalled the day before he'd been taken to Brigham, his explosive rage, the sound of water running in a bath upstairs while I sat, bouncing a red rubber ball, then Diana bursting, breathless, through the front door, a fearful gleam in her eyes, *Where's Dad?*

"I was five."

"Do you remember why he was committed?"

"No."

"He wasn't behaving in a bizarre fashion?"

"Not any more than usual," I said.

"What do you remember about that first . . . intervention?"

"Diana came home from school," I said. "We hung around together all day. Then . . ." I stopped.

"Then?"

I saw it as if on film, a series of frozen movie frames. Diana sleeping in the chair beside my bed that same night, jerking awake each time she heard the Old Man's footsteps in the hall. The arrival of two officials the next morning, one of them an older woman whose gray hair peeped out from beneath her cap. The Old Man led down the stairs and into a waiting car that had large white letters printed on its side. Diana and I hustled into a completely different car and taken to a ward of some sort, where there were other children.

"Then they came and got him," I said. "The next day." I shrugged. "He may have done something that night."

"Gone out and done something," Grace said.

"Yes," I said. "Something we never learned about. Maybe gone into town, done something. Who knows what? Like he did at the university. Screaming. Throwing rocks. Something threatening, so that someone called the authorities and they came and got him and took him to Brigham."

"How long was your father in Brigham?"

"That first time? Three weeks."

Grace smiled softly. "Interesting to hear your family history."

"I get the feeling Mark has already given you my family history," I said.

"Yes," Grace said. "But only in very general terms." He reached for a leather-bound pad, opened it, then plucked a pen from his jacket pocket, a rosewood Montblanc. "What was your father's diagnosis?" he asked.

"Paranoid schizophrenia," I said.

Grace jotted the words in his pad. "And I understand the child was mentally ill as well?"

So this was the line of dark causality Mark had drawn, and which I had already affirmed. It was in us, yes. It always would be.

"Schizophrenia," I answered. "Early onset."

Grace wrote this down, too, then looked up at me with an expression that struck me as genuinely sympathetic, even tender, the regard of the blessed for the cursed. "I'm glad you escaped it, Dave," he said.

"Thank you," I said, because nothing else seemed appropriate.

"I think we all want to help your sister," Grace said. "It's really a matter of how best to do that."

"What does Mark think best?" I asked.

"Is it up to Mark?" Grace asked. He looked at me pointedly. "Mark is a divorced man. He has no actual connection to Diana. You're her brother. What do you propose?"

He could not have asked a more paralyzing question, and he knew it. For what did I propose really, save to watch and wait? Which was exactly the proposition I offered, though less directly.

"There's no indication that Diana's dangerous," I said.

"Really, Dave? Are you sure?"

I knew Grace was getting at something, but I couldn't tell what it was until he reached into his desk. "Mark was quite distracted after he spoke to you a few days ago. But that's not why he called me, and that's not why we're having this conversation." He handed me several sheets of paper. "It's these," he said. "He received these e-mails this morning. Each came separately over a period of five or six minutes. As you can see, they are quite disturbing."

One by one, I read the quotations Diana had sent him.

> *How easily murder is discovered!*
>
> SHAKESPEARE, TITUS ANDRONICUS, ACT II, SCENE III

> *Murder most foul, as in the best it is,*
> *But this most foul, strange, and unnatural.*
>
> SHAKESPEARE, HAMLET, ACT I, SCENE V

> *For murder, though it have no tongue, will speak*
> *With most miraculous organ.*
>
> SHAKESPEARE, HAMLET, ACT II, SCENE II

> *One sin I know another doth provoke.*
>
> SHAKESPEARE, PERICLES, ACT I, SCENE I

I handed the papers back to Grace and labored to conceal how shaken I was by what Diana had done, how, in the final stages, the Old Man had done the same, spoken almost exclusively in quotations, as if he were but a helpless, wooden dummy, Shakespeare the ventriloquist, and if not him, then some other figure from the canon.

"Murder. Foul. Unnatural." Grace leveled his steady gaze upon me. "These are not pleasant words."

I nodded, but said nothing.

"As you can imagine," he added, "Mark finds such words very disturbing. They're accusations, really. And threats. Particularly the last one."

"But only words," I offered quietly.

"Yes, only words," Grace added. "For now. And so the question for Mark is, what next? But really, that question is not for Mark. It's for you, Dave."

I was out of my league with Grace, and I knew it, and in his august presence I felt again as I had when I was a little boy, sitting at the dinner table, waiting for the Old Man's question, certain I would not be able to answer it to his satisfaction.

"I think you should be aware that this matter comes at a particularly difficult time for Mark," Grace added. "He is near a breakthrough, and so his efforts at the moment are highly focused." He looked at me sternly. "It would be a shame—in fact, Dave, it would be unacceptable—for him to be distracted."

Under Grace's commanding gaze, I withered in the same way I'd withered beneath the Old Man's intimidating glare. I dried up, became dust.

"So, we have a dilemma," Grace continued. "And really, Dave, the dilemma is for you. I'll pose it as a question: What if Diana committed some act of actual aggression against Mark?"

I had no answer to this question, so I simply waited for him to complete the circle.

"You would come to her aid, would you not?" Grace asked. "You would act to help her. You would intervene."

He was asking for a pledge, my word that if Diana committed "some act of actual aggression," I would join forces with him and Mark, do whatever had to be done to restrain her.

"Yes," I said. "I would."

Grace appeared satisfied with my answer. "She's not currently under care, I understand."

"No, but I spoke to a psychiatrist about her."

"Really?" The pen perked up. "Who?"

"Robert Santori."

Grace smiled broadly. "Ah, Robert. I know him. Good man." The pen briefly skirted across the page then abruptly stopped. "What did Robert advise you to do?"

"He wanted Diana to come in for a visit."

"Did you tell her that?"

"Not yet, but I will."

Grace nodded softly, then closed the notebook. "Well, I don't think there's any need to belabor this matter any further, Dave," he said. "We're prepared to wait before taking any additional action." He smiled. "I have no doubt that you'll keep your part of the bargain."

"I'll keep it," I told him.

Grace looked at me gravely. "I'm also sure you'll do all you can to prevent Diana from endangering herself further."

"Yes," I promised. "I will."

"Good," Grace said. "Let's hope Diana stays out of harm's way."

Then, as if I were a schoolboy and he the beneficent headmaster, Grace walked me to the door, opened it, and with a soft nudge returned me to the dusty little playground of my life.

Charlie was in his office when I arrived. He looked up from his desk as I walked by.

"Dave, talk to you a minute?" he asked.

I slumped at the door. "What is it?"

"Ed Leary called," Charlie said. "He wanted to know if you'd heard from Ethel about that latest offer."

"Actually, I haven't made the offer yet."

Charlie looked as if he'd expected this answer, and that it confirmed other suspicions. "Why not, Dave?" he asked.

My excuse was utterly empty. "I've had some problems, Charlie," I said. "I've been . . ."

"Distracted, yes, I know," Charlie said. He leaned back in his chair. "Do you want to take off a few days?"

I shook my head.

"Do you want me to take over some of your cases?"

"No, please, I'm sorry, Charlie," I told him. "I'll speak to Bill Carnegie right away, tell him what Ed's decided."

"Actually, I think you should talk this whole thing over with Ed first," Charlie said. "When he called, he told me about this blank-check-type deal he wanted to give Ethel. I don't think it's a very good idea."

"I know and—"

"We are supposed to keep clients on the right track. That's why they call us 'counselors.'"

"I know that, Charlie."

Charlie didn't look entirely convinced, but at the same time he clearly didn't want to pursue the point. He'd never been one to show his muscle, so I knew he had more concerns, and probably deeper ones, than just whether or not I'd sufficiently advised Ed Leary.

"Okay, Dave," he said.

"I'm on it," I assured him. "Ed Leary. Right away."

He was at his shop, leaning over a slab of granite, running his large hands over its polished surface.

"People don't like seams," he said as I came over to him. "They think it's disrespectful. So that means—"

"Listen, Ed, I want to talk to you about that offer to Ethel," I interrupted.

"What about it?"

"I don't think you should give her a blank check like that," I said.

"Why not?" Ed asked. "You know how I feel."

"Maybe you shouldn't act on feeling," I told him. "It can be dangerous."

He looked at me warily. "Dangerous?"

"I think you should reconsider, that's what I'm saying."

"And do what?"

"Make another offer. A little more generous, if that's what you prefer, but not a blank check."

Ed didn't look convinced.

"Step by step, Ed," I added. "That's the way to go."

Ed shook his head. "I don't know," he said hesitantly. "When I had that talk with Diana—"

"Diana should keep her mouth shut," I blurted sharply.

Ed looked at me, stunned. "What?"

"Diana's not a lawyer," I said hotly. "She shouldn't be giving legal advice."

Now Ed looked genuinely hostile. "It wasn't legal advice she was giving me, Dave," he said. "It was advice about life, and she said that—"

"Why do people listen to her?" I interrupted, now thinking how I'd listened to her, too, and that Patty had, and that there might be many, many more out there, rootless people, uncritical, easily undone . . . her victims. "She can be very seductive," I added. "Especially with people who aren't very . . ." I stopped abruptly, but Ed heard the word I didn't speak.

"Smart?" he asked. "People who aren't very smart?"

"I didn't mean it like that," I told him. "I just meant people who . . ."

Ed's gaze was pure steel, and it stopped me in my tracks.

"I think you better go, Dave," he said.

I stared at him silently.

"I don't want you handling my case anymore," he added.

"Look, Ed, I didn't mean . . ."

"No," Ed said firmly. "I don't want you as my lawyer anymore."

I could see that his mind was made up. "All right," I said. "Let me know who takes over the case. Your new lawyer, I mean. I'll send your papers over to him."

Ed nodded coolly, but said nothing as I turned away.

Nor did he say anything as I headed for the door, though I knew something must be building in him. I could feel it like a dark surge rising behind me. I'd reached the door and already opened it when it broke over me in a loud, accusatory call.

"Diana deserves a better brother," Ed yelled.

But I could barely hear him over the roar of my own anger, soaked as I was in the flammable liquid of the day's humiliations, a mere flicker, as it seemed to me, from explosion.

You lift the forefinger of your right hand. "Fear." Then you lift the forefinger of your left hand. "Anger." You bring the two fingers together and entwine them. "It works like that in me."

You cannot discern the way in which those two foul streams at last flowed together. Their merging has been too long and too subtle, and so the backup eluded you, as did the annihilating torrent it was bound to release, like great falls shrouded in fog, all that violent churning beyond view, lost in a cloud of unknowing.

"And Ed Leary brought this out?" Petrie asks.

"Ed. Stewart Grace. All of it because of . . . her."

You recall the utter rage that swept over you, Diana in your face, interfering with your life, a dreadful intervention that dropped like a stone into the even flow of things, chaotic, disruptive, humiliating.

"I was tired of it all," you say. "Tired of having to . . ."

"To what?"

"Deal with her."

Petrie nods softly. "I see."

"So I decided to do something," you tell him.

"And that's when you confronted her?" Petrie asks.

You see it all again, the whole desperate scene, the two of you no longer seeing or hearing each other, both reduced to primitive bits of psychic flint, good for nothing but producing sparks, setting lives on fire.

NINETEEN

On the way back to the office, I glimpsed Diana's car in the lot beside the library. She was no doubt inside, holed up in the little cubicle Adele had described, hunched over her books, using her own strange sorcery to build her case against Mark.

I hurtled past, a little meteor determined to avoid the destructive gravity of her madness, now feeling no less threatened by it than Mark, and thus in league with him against her.

Charlie was in court that afternoon, and so, with the exception of Dorothy and Lily, the office was empty. I took advantage of the lull to dive into the mass of paper that weighed down my in-box. I held my focus entirely on that purpose, reading letters and dictating responses.

"This one is to Bill Carnegie," I told Lily when I finally arrived at Ed's file. "Dear Bill: Please be advised that my representation of Edward J. Leary in the matter of—"

Dorothy appeared at the door. "This just came for you," she said. "From your sister."

She stepped into my office and placed the package on my desk.

I stared at it like a ticking bomb. "We'll finish this later," I told my secretary. I waited until she'd safely left the room then opened the package Diana had sent me.

The stack of pages was almost a foot thick, and all written, as I noticed, on the Old Man's battered Royal, though they were not his ravings. Instead, every word on these hundreds of pages had been written by Diana, essays on scores of famous writers, from the Greek dramatists, through Shakespeare and the Elizabethans, then to the poetry of Milton and Donne, and further on through the Romantics. She'd written on novelists, as well, Trollope and George Sand, Dickens and Melville, Hawthorne and George Eliot.

I had no doubt it had taken Diana years to write these essays, years of rereading the texts and searching references on the Internet, doing all this scholarly work in the little snatches of time she allowed herself while the Old Man, and later Jason and Mark, slept in their separate rooms.

She'd placed a white sheet of paper at the top of the stack, and there typed out her single sentence message: *Offered in evidence that I'm not like Dad. These are not the disjointed, paranoid writings of a crazy person. Conclusion? I know what I'm doing, Davey.*

I knew that this was Diana's way of explaining the dreadful quotations she'd e-mailed to Mark. She was saying that she wasn't "like Dad" because she was perfectly aware of what she'd done, which was to let literature speak for her, and by that means assert the truth, though at a slant. In effect, she'd placed Shakespeare in the witness-box, let him lift his arm, point toward Mark, mouth a timeless truth, *For murder, though it have no tongue, will speak / With most miraculous organ,* using the Great Bard as her voice, voicing what she knew.

But what did she know? I asked myself as I returned Diana's writings to the box. Nothing. What real evidence did she have? None.

And yet she'd taken a dangerously crazy step down the accusatory road she'd been following since Jason's death. I had no doubt that she'd take another one as well, and another and another, maliciously and obsessively focused on the one name she'd placed on her enemies list. For now, only one. But the list would grow, I decided. Like Dad, she would add other names to it, people in league with Mark, people bent upon concealing what he'd done, protecting him from the consequences of it. In my mind I saw her tap, tap, tapping at the Old Man's Royal, adding name after name, Bill Carnegie, Stewart Grace. It would not take long, I knew, until she added mine.

I knocked at the door of Diana's apartment a little past eight. There was a rustle behind it, a shuffle of papers, the screech of a chair across bare floor, footsteps. Then the door opened, but cautiously, a single eye staring at me from a narrow slant of light.

"I have to talk to you," I told her.

Rather than invite me in, she closed the door, turned off the light, then opened the door again, and stepped out into the narrow corridor.

"Did you get my package?" she asked.

"Yes."

"And?"

"Like I said, we need to talk," I told her.

She said nothing. Her gaze was utterly still.

"About Mark," I added. "And about Jason."

She remained silent, her eyes motionless.

"Did you hear me, Diana?" I asked.

"Yes," she answered quietly.

"Mark has hired a lawyer," I added. "That little piece of paper you put under his windshield. *J'accuse.* That would have been enough, but then you sent him those quotations with the loaded words. Murder. Unnatural. 'One sin I know another doth provoke.' What's that particular quotation supposed to mean?"

Diana didn't answer.

"That one murder provokes another murder, right?" I asked. "Isn't that what you're saying?"

Diana didn't answer, and her silence whipped the horses in me.

"How else could Mark interpret that, Diana?" I demanded. "Except as a threat. And he'd be right. It's very threatening.

More than an accusation. A threat. Do you know how serious that is, to threaten someone like that?"

Still, she said nothing.

"Well let me tell you—as a lawyer, okay?—let me tell you, it's very, very serious."

Diana's lips parted slightly, but she didn't speak.

I glared at her sternly. "I want you to stay away from Mark, his e-mail, his fax machine, his car, his work, his house, or anything that has to do with him," I told her firmly. "But I want more than that. I want you to stop this research you're doing. It's not healthy, Diana, staying at the library all day. And don't tell me you have a job there, because I know you don't."

She looked surprised by my accusation. "I never told you I had a job at the library," she said. "I told you I worked there. I do."

"That's a very fine distinction, Diana," I said. "The kind Dad used to make, remember?"

"So I'm like Dad?"

"Not yet."

"But getting there?"

We had reached the dark heart of the matter much faster than I'd hoped, but there was no way to step around it, come at it from a different slant.

"I want you to see someone," I told her. "A doctor."

"So it's true," Diana said with a curious sadness. "You think I'm crazy. Patty told me you'd reached that conclusion."

"Patty?" I asked significantly, "Isn't her name Hypatia now?"

"By her own choosing."

"And how did she happen to come up with it?"

"I told her that it was the name her grandfather had wanted for her."

"Did you add that her grandfather was insane?"

"But he wasn't," Diana fired back defensively. "Not all the time."

"He was a paranoid schizophrenic," I said determinedly. "He thought he was being persecuted. He had an enemies list. Even you were on it, remember?"

Her eyes probed me in some oblique and indefinable way. I could almost feel the heat of her mental interrogation on my skin. "I remember," she said softly.

"Hypatia was persecuted," I continued. "But our father was never persecuted. And for the record, you're not being persecuted, either."

"I've never said I was."

"It's Mark who's being persecuted," I told her hotly. "By you, Diana."

She faced me silently.

"But I'm not here to help Mark," I added. "I'm here to help you."

"By sending me to Brigham?" she asked.

"I'm not sending you anywhere."

"This doctor, you've already met this person," Diana said.

It was not a question. Typically, she had seen it all in my eyes, or in some element of my body language, or perhaps simply by the invisible mental probing that was as much a part of her as the flashing eyes and shining hair.

"What's his name?" she asked.

"Santori."

"As in 'sanitori-um'?" she asked rhetorically. "As in sanitary? Is he to clean my mind? Am I to be 'sanitized' by this Santori?"

"This is no time for cute wordplay, Diana."

"Wordplay?" Diana shot back. "Cute?"

"Diana, you're accusing Mark of murder without the slightest evidence. You're threatening him."

"And he's distracted?"

"Of course, he is."

"And so he wants you to help him send me to the asylum." She shook her head determinedly, and a kind of purified anger leaped into her eyes, one that blazed so hotly I could almost feel the heat on my face. "To be strapped down, walled up. Treated like mad Queen Margaret." Then her voice rose in an unmistakable grandeur, like a madwoman on the stage: "'If ancient sorrow be most reverent' . . ."

"No more quotes, Diana."

"'Give mine the benefit of seniory.'"

"Enough!" I said sharply.

"'And let my griefs frown on the upper hand.'"

"Stop it!"

She looked at me as I thought she must once have looked at Mark, a gaze that seemed raw and primitive and savage.

"Dad was insane, Davey," she said. "He was insane, but not all the time. Do you know when he was insane, truly insane? When he did things he didn't remember. When he went blank, and did things, and then came back to reality. It's when you leave reality and don't know it that you're genuinely mad, Davey. And I've never done that."

"I didn't say you'd—"

"You're not insane merely because you look for the truth," Diana declared. "Even when you look for it in unorthodox ways."

"Yes, but—"

"So what makes me crazy, according to you?" Diana demanded. "Why do you think I need to 'see someone'? Because I work in the library? Because I read books? Or is it some crazy idea I have? And if so, which crazy idea do you find most obviously mad?"

I felt set upon and pinned down, just as I had felt during the agonized dinners of my boyhood, or facing Stewart Grace's manifest grandeur, unable to defend myself or even make my position clear, and in that wriggling weakness, I struck back at Diana in the only way that occurred to me.

"How about voices?" I snapped. "Hearing voices. You mentioned them at Dover Gorge. Do you hear voices, Diana?"

To my surprise, the question appeared to throw her into a strange uncertainty, one I took advantage of like a boxer pounding at an open wound.

"Do you hear voices, Diana?" I demanded. "Do you believe what they tell you?"

She shook her head. "There's more work to be done," she said, then turned toward the door.

I grabbed her arm and jerked her around.

"What work?" I demanded. "Looking for evidence that

Mark murdered Jason? And after you've done all this work, found more evidence, what then? Will you be judge and jury, too? Will you carry out the sentence?"

She pulled her arm free and glared at me silently.

"And if the sentence is death?" I demanded. "What then? Will you be the executioner, Diana?"

Her gaze took on an eerie intensity. "What are you talking about, Davey?"

"Oh, don't look so innocent," I said. "You're not above suspicion, you know."

"Of what?"

"Murder."

She seemed stunned by the word, how easily it had tripped from my mouth.

"Of Dad," I added. "Remember how they came to the house after he died? But they didn't have any evidence. Just some old scars on his wrists and ankles. From Brigham, you told them."

"They were from Brigham," Diana said.

"I'm sure they were," I said. "But I had something else to go on, didn't I. Other evidence the cops never saw. That green pillow, remember?" I looked at her accusingly. "The one we burned before the cops came. It was wet. Which is strange, because you only used it to prop up the back of his head, right? So why was it wet, Diana? Could it be you put that pillow over the Old Man's mouth? Is that why it was wet?"

"You can't possibly believe that," Diana said.

"But how does it feel?" I asked. I stepped back and glared at her mercilessly. "Do you feel like Mark, now? Wrongly accused? Suppose the cops had asked about that pillow. What would you have said?"

She closed her eyes a moment, then opened them slowly, and met my gaze in full. "He spit at me, Davey," she said. "That's why the pillow was wet." Then she turned, opened the door, stepped back into the darkness, and closed it once again, firmly and determinedly, as if to seal us in our separate fates.

You remember something the Old Man said, not something he'd madly raved, but spoken softly, almost to himself, a truth drawn from the well of his occasional acuity: *We are like the earth. The surface temperatures may vary, but at the core, we're all on fire.*

You repeat the Old Man's words to Petrie.

"Were you on fire that night?" Petrie asks. "When you left Diana?"

The question doesn't surprise you. It is your answer that startles.

"I've always been on fire."

You watch as he writes your answer down.

"All right," he says, when he's finished. He looks up from the pad, stares you directly in the eye.

You're no longer sure what he sees. A pitiful man? A wounded man? A violent man? All of the above? Without doubt, a man spectacularly flawed.

"The real mystery is Diana," you tell him.

The statement comes out of nowhere, but you wonder if it sounds planted, like you have something up your sleeve, perhaps laying the groundwork for an insanity defense, or at least one based on diminished capacity, preparing to make the claim that at that terrible instant you were "like Dad," and so had no idea what you were doing.

"I'm not crazy," you tell him.

Petrie does not write this down, but instead lifts the blue pen from the paper and stares at the tip, as if hoping it might come alive, fly from his hand to a blank space on the wall, write out what he needs to know.

" 'There's more work to be done,' " he says.

He is quoting Diana.

"That's what she said, yes."

"In terms of gathering evidence? Is that what she meant?"

"What else?"

He draws his gaze from the blue pen. "Unorthodox."

He is quoting her again, and you imagine him at your side, the two of you together in Diana's apartment, eyes wide in wonder, lips parted in wonder, hearing the rush of feet behind you.

"It was vast," you tell him. "Her effort. What she sought. Her hope."

You are in Diana's apartment again, alone among the spare furniture. You scan the walls and feel yourself drawn into another sphere of knowledge, part of earth, but still unreachable, like an indecipherable script, faintly sacred, the prayer of a vanished people.

"Much more than 'unorthodox,' " you add.

Which makes it all the stranger that you missed it, could not, for all its radiance, see it shining through the cloud.

TWENTY

At the dinner table I was very quiet, but it was a volcanic quiet as I continued to think about my conversation with Diana, silently turning over what we'd said to each other until it all became too much for me and I suddenly blurted, "Diana's getting worse. She's absolutely convinced that Mark killed Jason." I looked at Patty. "But what motive would he have had for doing that?" I asked.

Patty answered immediately, firmly, with no hint of doubt. "Jason was too much of a distraction. Mark needed time for his research. He didn't want to have to think about Jason."

"Is that Diana's theory?" I asked.

"No," Patty answered. "It's mine."

"But you've been discussing it?" I asked. "Mark's motive?"

She looked at me squarely. "Yes."

"And so she's told you about her 'evidence'?" I asked. "The badge she found by the pond. Mark's badge? The one he supposedly used to lure Jason into the water."

"Actually, there's an easier way to do it," Patty said in a tone that struck me as astonishingly offhanded.

"Do what?"

"Drown a person." Her gaze floated toward me slowly, as if carried on a strange, invisible ooze. "If the person is restrained, all you have to do is press down the tongue and drip water into the mouth," she added as if she were informing me about some shortcut in food preparation. "That's the way Waltraud Wagner did it."

Abby shuddered. "Okay, I think we've gone far enough with this," she said like a woman making a final effort to keep back awful news.

"No, wait," I said. "Who is this Wagner character? Somebody in a book?"

"No, she was real," Patty answered. "She confessed to killing forty-nine people in a German hospital. The 'water cure' is what she called dripping water into them. She had other methods, too."

"Where did you learn about this?" I asked.

"From Diana," Patty answered without the slightest sense that I might find this exchange alarming.

"What else did Diana tell you about this woman?" I asked.

"Oh, not much," Patty said. "Except that she got other people to help her. Other nurses."

"She was a nurse?"

"Yes. She killed her patients. I mean, some of them. She and the other nurses she got to do it, too."

"This woman recruited other nurses to kill patients?" I asked unbelievingly.

"Can we please stop this," Abby said before Patty could answer.

But Patty went on undeterred. "Yeah, she recruited them. She trained them, too. Showed them how to do it."

"How to commit murder?"

"Yes," Patty said.

"Waltraud Wagner," I repeated, now forcing myself to doubt the whole story. After all, it had come from Diana. "She still sounds like a character in a book to me."

"No, she's real," Patty insisted. "They called her 'The Angel of Death.'"

I leaned forward. "And Diana is studying this sort of thing, murder methods?"

"Not now," Patty answered. "But back then she did. When she was younger."

"You mean when she was in high school?" I asked. "I never saw her studying this kind of thing."

"It was after she left college."

"When she was living with our father?"

"Yeah," Patty said. "She read all about murders back then. She said it helped her pass the time." She snatched up her napkin and wiped her mouth with a quick swipe. "Gotta go."

"Where are you going?"

"I'm meeting Diana at the library."

I shook my head, and by that movement made the final decision. "No, you're not," I said evenly.

Patty looked at me wonderingly. "What?"

"I said no, Patty."

Abby stared at me, no doubt astonished by the resolution she heard in my voice.

"No, what?" Patty asked.

"You're not meeting Diana."

"Why not?"

What might I dare tell her, I wondered? That her aunt, who had recently taken such an interest in her, carried a dark stain in her blood, one that had flowed down to her from her father, and been passed down to Jason, and was even now blooming darkly within the circle of our family life.

"Why not, Dad?" Patty demanded.

"For all the reasons we've already talked about."

"What reasons?"

"Lots of reasons," I answered. "We've had this discussion before, Patty."

"No, we haven't," Patty said. "Not like this. Not like you telling me I can't see her." She glanced toward Abby, found absolutely no support there, then shot her gaze back to me. "You said Diana had strange ideas, that's all. So what? A lot of people have strange ideas." She sat back and glared at me. "Besides, it isn't really all that strange, what she believes."

"About Mark, you mean?"

"Yes."

"Because you believe it too," I said. "Which is exactly why I don't want you seeing her again until—"

"Until what?" Patty snapped.

"Until you come back to your senses."

"Which means until I agree with you, right?"

"Oh, come on, Patty."

"You're not being fair to Diana," Patty said, suddenly more angry and rebellious than I had ever seen her. "You're not really listening to her."

"This is not about me," I said. "This is about Diana, the fact that she's sick right now." I paused, then added, "And very seductive."

"Seductive?" Patty cried. "You think I'm being seduced?"

I thought of Patty in her full vulnerability. She was inexperienced and more or less uneducated, with not a whit of training in the rudimentary skills of critical thinking. I imagined her mind awash in feelings of inadequacy and disconnection from which she fled into the whorl-of-the-world-awhirl nonsense of Kinsetta Tabu. I had no doubt that by now Diana had added yet other layers of fatuous mumbo jumbo to all this, a circumstance I could do nothing about save prevent her from sinking deeper into the mire.

"Yes, I do, Patty," I said. "I do believe that." I knew that I couldn't reach her with an anger of my own, and so I paused, steadied myself, and calmed my voice. "Patty, listen to me," I said. "This stuff Diana's looking for, this 'evidence' she's trying to find, it won't stand up."

"What do you mean, 'stand up'?"

"In court," I answered. I lifted my hand and, raising one finger at a time, stated the obvious facts of the case. "As far as Mark is concerned, there will be no indictment. There will be no trial. There will be no sentence. Do you know why? Because there is not a shred of evidence against him."

Patty glared at me with a clear sense of confidence that my last points meant nothing. "There are other forms of proof, Dad," she said. "It's not all about law and trials and stuff like that."

I saw the great library of our jurisprudence, all our ancient declarations and honored constitutions, from Magna Carta to the most recent legal brief, all of it catch fire and turn to ash in my daughter's eyes.

"Patty," I said softly. "There is only human justice. It's a flawed thing, I know, imperfect, but . . ."

The laugh that broke from her had the chilling tenor of a witch's cackle. "That's exactly what I expected you to say," she blurted scornfully. "It isn't perfect, but it's all there is." Her smile was pure mockery. "What bullshit."

"Patty!" Abby cried. She looked at me. "I want this to stop, Dave."

But there was no stopping it.

My anger spiked. I leaned forward and planted my elbows on the table. "Then what do you propose?" I snapped. "What justice are you going to carry out?"

Patty rose in a smoking column of righteous ire. "I'm going to my room."

"And you're going to stay there, too," I bawled. "You're

going to go to school, and then you're going to come directly home, and you're going to do that and nothing but that until all of this is over."

She stared at me in angry challenge. "And when will that be, Dad?" she demanded. "When Mark marries again and has another family?"

"What are you talking about, Patty?"

She smiled, but it was a cold smile, like the one I suddenly imagined on the lips of Waltraud Wagner. "You can't stop Diana," she said.

"What are you talking about?" I repeated.

Her eyes blazed. "You can't stop Diana," she cried in a voice filled with seething vehemence. "No one can." Then she whirled around, marched to her room, and slammed the door.

In the echoing void, Abby murmured, "What are you going to do now?"

And I thought, *Something. Something soon.* But I did not know what.

S o I began with research," you tell Petrie. "Just like Diana."

"What did you research?" he asks.

"First, Waltraud Wagner."

Petrie carefully takes down the name.

"That night, I looked her up," you continue.

You tell him the results of your inquiry, that Waltraud Wagner was not a character in a book, but an Austrian woman who'd been convicted of fifteen murders, and who had led three other women to commit at least eight more. She had used the drowning method Patty mentioned. She'd also killed by denying insulin to diabetic patients and by overdosing others with a drug called Rohypnol, which had the very convenient characteristic of being undetectable by the standard tests used in autopsies.

"But it was the function of Rohypnol that captured my attention," you add. "It was an anesthetic whose primary use was in calming down mental patients."

The blue pen halts its flight across the page.

"Like your father?" Petrie asks. "It might have been prescribed for him?"

"I asked myself the same question," you tell him.

You go no farther, because you have no evidence that Diana had ever had access to those tiny tablets, colorless and tasteless, no evidence that they had ever been housed in the medicine chest that hung above the rust-rimmed sink in the Old Man's bathroom. And yet there it was, a grim suspicion, because your mind had become entirely reflexive, a force you could neither will nor control, a collector of disparate facts: the Old Man's madness, Diana's long and no doubt dreary custodianship, the ligature marks found on his wrists and ankles, an Austrian murderess Diana had read about, the powerful drug she'd used for murder fifteen times.

"To entertain a dreadful notion is itself a dreadful thing," you say now. "But I didn't stop there."

Petrie's pen does not move, and you notice that his eyes are no less still.

"I played back the whole conversation I'd had with Diana outside her apartment," you continue. "Then I thought of Waltraud Wagner again, of the way she'd recruited others for murder. That led me back to Hypatia, which led me back to Douglas Price. And from there, I went to Gaia."

"Gaia?" Petrie asks.

"The living earth. Price had told me that Diana found the concept very interesting."

You see that Petrie doesn't need to flip back through his notes to refresh his recollection of what you've previously told him.

"So I looked it up," you tell him now. "Gaia."

Then you tell him what you found. You recall it verbatim, using the very skill you'd buried so long ago, a power of memory, photographic and otherwise.

"Gaia," you begin in a tone of recitation, "known as Earth, was a goddess half risen from the earth, and so unable to separate from it. She was the daughter of Chaos, and bore the burden of his disorder. In time, she took a husband, Uranus, and by him bore Cyclops. Uranus was revolted by the monstrousness of his son, and wished to return him to the bowels of Gaia, wished, that is, that he had never been born, and thus by implication, wished that he were dead. To protect Cyclops, Gaia hid him within herself, and despite the pain did not release him to his father. At last, in agony, Gaia enlisted the aid of Cronus and fashioned the adamantine knife which he used to cut off Uranus's genitals. The blood of that wound fell to earth and from its red drops rose the Erinyes, which we know as The Furies, and from whom sprang justice and retribution."

Petrie stares at you, clearly impressed. "You have quite a memory."

You repeat the line that lingered like an acrid smoke in your mind. "At last, in agony, Gaia enlisted the aid of Cronus."

Petrie watches you edgily, like a man on the front row of an execution gallery.

"Reading that, who could Cronus be but Patty," you tell him.

In a kind of horror-movie scenario, you see a glistening blade rise and fall in Patty's pale hand.

"Not that Diana would do something violent," Petrie says, "but that Patty would."

You remember Patty's angry eyes and see the abyss that yawns before each of us at a certain point, and from which we are saved not by the slow accretion of experience and understanding, but by the mechanics of pure luck, that silent, invisible machine whose tiny gears are always turning, so that missing this bus or catching that one makes all the difference, our long labor to control our lives cancelled in an instant.

"And so?" Petrie asks.

"And so I had to cut Patty off from Diana." You look at Petrie, appeal to the common urge of fatherhood, its most primitive impulse. "I had to," you repeat emphatically. You feel the rain on your face, see it dropping from a length of black wrought iron. "At any cost."

TWENTY-ONE

Charlie noticed the edgy state I was in the next morning, but he said nothing about it. Perhaps by then he'd grown accustomed to the frayed rope I had become. Certainly nothing had happened in the last few days to allay the doubts he had about me, the erratic work, the tense look, the river of fear that carried me along, and which, by then, had merged with the river of anger.

"Hello, Dave," he said cautiously as I swept by his office.

I only nodded and fled into my own.

The phone rang on Lily's desk at precisely 9:13, and I should have known how fateful that call was because an old literary image suddenly returned to me, Satan stepping off the rim of heaven and into the cheerless void.

"Stewart Grace for you," she said.

I picked up the phone. "Good morning, Stewart."

"I think you should come over to my office right away," Grace said.

I heard it in his voice, distant, ominous, the foghorn of the *Titanic*.

"What is it?" I asked.

"Mark's on his way, too," Grace said. There was a brief pause, then he added, "Things have gotten worse, Dave."

I told him I'd be right there, then put down the phone and headed for my car, my mind now entering a fantasy of its own, a vision of Diana leaning against the hood of my car, eating an apple. As I approach she smiles as brightly as when she was a little girl. Then she tosses the apple and it rises in a wide arc, unraveling the dark weave of her groundless suspicion as it soars, so that by the time it touches earth again, she is free of it entirely, all the hellhounds of her mind brought to heel at last.

It was the last image I had of her salvation.

I brushed it easily from my mind.

Grace was seated behind his desk when I came in. He rose immediately and offered his hand. "Thanks for coming right over, Dave," he said. His tone was more grave and solemn than I had ever heard it, so that he no longer seemed entirely confident that he knew his way out of the bramble. "Mark will be here in a few minutes." He sat back down and nodded to one of the two chairs that faced his desk. "Please."

I took my seat and waited, now reviewing all the many steps I'd taken, the decisions I'd made, the observations they'd been based upon, signs glimpsed, signs missed, the whole sorry scheme of things entire.

"As I said, things have gotten worse," Grace told me.

As if on cue, Mark burst through the door. He was dressed in a white shirt and black pants, both neatly pressed, but some part of him, his hair, his eyes, struck me as peculiarly in disarray.

"Dave," he said with a quick nod. "Stewart."

Grace rose from his desk and they shook hands. Then Mark turned to me. "Has Stewart told you?"

I shook my head.

Mark sat down in the chair next to mine but seemed hardly able to stay in his seat, his manner jumpy and alert, as if, at any moment, he expected to be attacked. With a shaky hand he took a thin stack of photographs from his jacket pocket. "She's done it again," he said. "Just what I was afraid of."

"And at his workplace," Grace added grimly.

"She must have come to the center last night," Mark said. There was something frantic in his voice. He looked truly frightened. "I was pretty much alone there. Working late." He thrust the photographs toward me. "Look what she did."

There were four photographs, each of Mark's car, but from different angles, one from each side of the car, one of the front, one of the rear. The car rested in Mark's reserved space at the research center. It was a black sedan and the dark red letters of the word that had been painted the full length of each side and across the hood and trunk were as visible as blood on black velvet: MURDERER.

"Terrible," Mark muttered. "Scary."

Which was true. Because in the photographs the word appeared larger and more grotesque than I would have thought possible, so that the car looked like a huge black animal that had been flayed open, with dripping streams of red flowing down its wounded flanks. In such a state, the translucent headlights appeared pale and lifeless, the dead eyes of a dead thing. I could not imagine the car ever moving again, or making even the slightest sound. Nothing came from it but death.

"It's obvious how serious this is," Grace said.

Mark took the pictures from me and handed them to Stewart, who looked at them only briefly, then placed them on his desk and settled his gaze on me. "Well, Dave?" he said.

I didn't answer, because I didn't know what to say, or what I was expected to say, save that Diana had clearly gone over the edge, that she was now hurtling forward in a wild, white-water madness.

"Surely you see how this is escalating," Stewart said. "Diana's actions, I mean."

I felt that I could do nothing but offer, however briefly, a meek, legalistic defense. "Is it absolutely certain that Diana did this?"

Mark sprang to his feet. "Oh, come on, Dave. Who else could it be?"

Again, I dodged the issue, though by a move I knew to be a feint. "Before . . . when we talked before . . . you mentioned a man at work who—"

"Gillespie?" Mark interrupted. "No way. He wouldn't do something like this. Besides, he's in Toronto." He snapped the pictures from Stewart's desk and thrust them toward me. "This is Diana's work, and you know it."

"Mark," Stewart cautioned. He nodded toward the chair. "Please."

Mark sat down, but again he seemed barely able to remain in place. "I'm a busy man, Dave," he said. "You know that. I can't let this go on. I told you that."

"And we won't let it go on," Grace added calmly. He looked at me for assurance. "Will we, Dave?"

"No," I said quietly, "but—"

"But what?" Mark snapped. "I can't believe you're defending her, Dave."

"I'm not defending her," I said.

He looked at me, thunderstruck. "Surely you don't believe a word of what . . ." He stopped. "Maybe you do," he cried. He began searching through his pockets, one after the other, in a kind of frantic quest. Then he found what he sought and pressed it toward me. "The badge," he said.

It rested in his open hand, made of tin, a five-pointed star with faded letters inscribed in the middle, badly rusted, impossible to identify.

"Go ahead, take it," Mark said. "Give it to the cops. Put it through the lab. See if you can find some kind of evidence on it."

I left the badge in Mark's hand. "It's not evidence, Mark. I know that."

Mark returned the badge to his pocket. "Diana thought I used a badge to murder my son," he told Grace. "Crazy. And now my car. She's ruined my car." His eyes snapped over to me. "I had to drive that car over here, Dave. Through the town. The whole fucking town. With MURDERER written all over it in big red letters."

"Mark," Grace cautioned again. "I'm sure this is as worrisome to Dave as it is to you."

"I wish I could be sure of that, Stewart," Mark said. His gaze bore into me. "Can I be sure of that, Dave?"

Before I could answer, Grace said, "We all have certain options here, and I think we all agree that something has to be done. We know this can't continue, and we know that if it does, it will get worse." He looked at me pointedly. "And certainly no one knows this better than you, Dave, that a condition like this only deepens."

As my father's had, which was precisely what Grace was getting at. He'd started with the mildest of suspicions, with a short enemies list, then descended into a near total paranoia, firing off letters to newspapers, along with various threatening ones to scores of momentarily addled critics, colleagues, even former students. Mark had no doubt told Grace all of this, and now it was to be used as evidence against Diana, proof of her tainted blood.

"Perhaps we should explore this situation clinically for a moment," Grace said.

"Clinically?" Mark asked, clearly somewhat exasperated by the pace of the proceedings.

"She's never received any kind of treatment, isn't that true, Dave?" Grace asked.

I nodded.

"But you mentioned it to her, didn't you? The possibility of her getting help? You told me that you would, and I assume you did?"

"Yes. I told her she needed to see someone."

"What was her reaction?"

"Not good."

"I see." Grace nodded toward the photographs Mark still held. "This is destruction of property, Dave, a clear escalation in Diana's behavior. I'm sure you remember our last conversation. About having to act if things appear to get worse. Well, things have gotten worse, don't you agree?"

"Yes."

Grace leaned forward and folded his arms on his desk. "So, Dave, what do you want us to do? Do you think a restraining order would have any effect on Diana's behavior?"

"No," I said.

"A talk with you? Or with me?"

"She wouldn't listen to either one of us."

"What then can we do?" Grace asked.

I thought only of Patty, how, step by step, Diana had stolen her from me. I reviewed all I'd done in the last few weeks, all the conversations I'd had with Diana and others, the treatment I'd offered for her steadily increasing derangement, a failure that stoked a fire in me that seemed even more fierce than the one I'd felt the night before.

"Diana has to be stopped," I said, my voice suddenly as hard as a hammer on a nail.

Grace looked relieved by the bluntness and determination.

"For her own good," I added.

Grace and Mark nodded. Then Grace said, "How can that be done, Dave?"

"The police can do it," I answered. "They can arrest her."

Grace appeared surprised by the extremity of the action I'd just proposed.

"You mean have Mark file a complaint with the police?" he asked.

"Yes."

Grace didn't seem convinced that such was the proper action. "But we don't really have any actual evidence that Diana did it."

"No," I agreed, "but we have plenty of evidence for suspicion." Then I made the case against my sister, her puny evidence, the weird faxes and e-mails, her freakish "research," the accusation she'd left on Mark's car, followed by a series of threatening quotations. I nodded toward the photographs Mark still held in his right hand, the butchered car, dripping with bloodred paint. "Now this."

It was a convincing argument. I could see how successful it was; perhaps, in all my life, my first success.

"So we have to take this step," Grace said. "You see no less . . . dramatic . . . way of intervening with Diana?"

"No," I answered crisply. "Diana won't listen to me. She won't listen to anyone. She needs help. It has to be imposed upon her." I drew in a long breath. "Like Dad."

Grace nodded slowly, like a man accepting a course of action to which he could lend only tepid support. "Of course, it'll take a little pressure to get it done immediately."

But I knew he could get it done, and so did he.

"Are you in agreement, Mark?" Grace asked.

Mark's eyes brightened. "I think it's a good idea. Get a criminal complaint, get a cop to serve it." He looked at me. "Show Diana that she's crossed the line."

I nodded. "For her own good," I repeated.

Mark could barely conceal his eagerness. "A shock," he said. "A shock to her system."

Grace leveled his gaze on me. "Final call, Dave."

"Do it," I said, and added nothing else.

You smile, though you realize how coldly inappropriate it is, how it may seem to make light of all that has happened. But you can't remove this arctic smile from your lips. It holds there, like an accusation.

Petrie stares at you distantly. "What?"

"An old Irish saying just occurred to me," you tell him.

"Which is?"

"That if you want to make God laugh, tell him your plans."

Petrie notes this comment in his notepad.

You watch the slender shaft of his blue pen flit left and right, quick as a dragonfly.

"All right," Petrie says when he looks up again. He starts to ask another question, but glances at his watch instead.

"How long?" you ask.

"Three hours so far."

"How much longer?"

"Until we know." He drops his head slightly, then stretches his arms outward, briefly assumes the hallowed Christlike position.

"I never believed in anything," you tell him. "Neither did Diana."

You see her in her awful panic, running, running, and know that at that moment she had felt no metaphysical protection, no staying hand, that it was all a snake pit she was desperate to escape.

"No God. No afterlife."

Now you are at the Old Man's grave. Diana tosses in the rose, then strolls at your side down the hill to the waiting car, speaking quietly as she walks, reminding you of the good days you'd all had together, the little trips, the sudden sparks of wisdom that had come from the Old Man. *Madness,* she says, *must be forgiven.* But you cannot forgive the Old Man, though you don't admit this. But more than anything, you know now, you could not forgive her either. Dust is not capable of forgiveness.

You feel suddenly helpless before your own ground-down aridity. "Nothingness is dangerous," you tell Petrie.

Petrie stares at you silently.

"Nothing good fills a void," you add.

You see that Petrie understands the truth you have just stated, as well as how starkly it plays upon the matter at hand.

"We'll know soon enough," he tells you.

Three deaths, the Wicker Man mutters. And you think, *So far.*

"Until then," Petrie adds, "we go on."

In your mind, a phone rings, and you feel your body jerk involuntarily, as if each cell is wired to the bell's jarring clangor.

Ring, ring.

Suddenly, you recall three phrases you had no idea you'd memorized, the final words of excommunication. *Ring the bell; close the book; quench the candle.*

Ring, ring.

As you must, you answer.

TWENTY-TWO

I was in my office when the phone rang.

"It's Stewart Grace."

His voice sounded grave.

I felt something empty, a small chamber of my soul. "Tell me."

With no effort to soften the blow, Grace described the horrific scene that had occurred at the library an hour before. The officer had approached Adele at the main desk, asked for Diana, then had been escorted to the rear of the building where she sat at the small, dark carrel that had become her second home. She'd seen him coming, Grace told me, risen to her feet and begun "in a panic" to gather up her books. But the terror that seized her had made her clumsy, too, and as quickly as she snatched up some books, others tumbled from her arms. And yet, despite the falling books, how they gathered in a pile at her feet, she'd not abandoned them. "It was as if they were her children," Grace told me, and so she'd still been desperately gathering them into her arms when the officer reached her.

"Then all hell broke loose," Grace said.

It began with a wail, and Grace didn't need to describe it for me to know what it sounded like. It had been so anguished that for a moment the officer had stopped in his tracks.

"By then the whole place was in an uproar," Grace said.

I could see it in my mind, men, women, children, all so quiet before, heads down, reading to themselves, hardly aware that there was anything beyond their own minds. Then it had come pealing over them, wrenching and fearful, reminding them that for all their thought and studied decorum, for all their deep immersion in written fact or fiction, they were still irredeemably mired in a random and unscripted world.

"The thing is, Dave," Grace said, "she put up a fight."

The battle he described was almost unbearable to consider, and yet I couldn't keep my mind from spooling it out, as in a movie, one whizzing frame at a time. As the officer closed in upon her, Diana had swung at him hard and fast, with a fist, rather than an open hand, while still clutching as many books as possible in the one arm she had left. Then that arm, too, had broken free and she'd thrust and punched as the officer struggled to subdue her. At one point, she'd broken away and begun to run, her eyes wild with terror, as she hurtled down aisle after aisle of bookshelves, spinning right or left, then running in the opposite direction, until at last she'd slammed directly into the officer and both of them had tumbled to the floor.

"Then she stopped," Grace said.

Stopped entirely, without the slightest sign of any further struggle, stopped and lay on the floor, staring off into the distance, motionless, silent, with hardly a hint of breath.

"Where is she now?" I asked softly.

"They didn't arrest her, of course," Grace answered. "An ambulance was called."

"They took her to the county hospital?" I asked.

"No," Grace answered. He paused, and I knew it was his decent sympathy for my family's blighted history that delayed him from delivering this last bit of dreadful news. "She's at Brigham," he said.

The old brick facade still gave off a stiff Edwardian air, and as I went up the short flight of cement stairs, I recalled the photograph of my father as he'd stood here, leaning against one of the columns, a cigarette dangling from his lips, his black hair in tangled disarray across his brow.

"She's much calmer now," the doctor said as he led me down the long corridor. "We had to sedate her, of course." He paused at her door. "It's always something of a shock," he warned. "Seeing someone in an . . . artificial state."

He meant the deadly lull of whatever antipsychotic drug she'd been given, the sense it gave of someone being held beneath water. "I've seen it before," I told him.

"Really?"

"My father."

He smiled softly. "Sorry," he said, then opened the door.

She was not in the same room as the Old Man's, but when I came into it, the bland, institutional whiteness struck me as entirely the same. It was in the pallor of the walls, the ghostly translucence of the curtains, the pale blinds, and when I saw her sitting in a chair by the window, facing out, I felt the iron circle of our fate grip me in its awesome vise.

"Diana?" I said quietly.

She didn't turn, but continued to stare out the window, her eyes capable of vision, but not insight, as if her mind and heart were both in a state of rigor mortis.

I came over and sat down on the bed, her face now in profile.

"I came as soon as I could," I told her.

Her eyes held to the view outside the window with a terrible fixedness, as if once locked upon an object they couldn't move again.

"They're going to help you, Diana," I said.

She continued to face the window, and in profile her features seemed oddly small, a pale, ivory cameo of herself.

"You're going to be all right," I assured her.

In the following stillness she appeared suspended in a strange, sad trance, her face no longer neutral, but bathed in a darkness that came from within her, slowly seeping outward, like a stain. Then her eyes drifted over to me, and her face seemed to absorb the eerie, unreal light of the room. "'This whiteness keeps her ruins for ever new,'" she whispered.

I looked at her quizzically.

"*Moby-Dick*," she cited as if she were a little girl again, laboring, against tremendous odds to calm her mad and murderous father. "On the whiteness of the whale."

I left Brigham a few minutes later and drove directly to Stewart Grace's office. Mark was already seated in one of the sleek leather chairs when I arrived. He rose immediately and vigorously pumped my hand.

"I'm sorry, Dave," he said. "The way things happened. The way Diana acted."

Grace shook his head. "Very regrettable, that scene in the library. And entirely unforeseen, of course."

"Like everything else," I said.

"Of course, I hope we can all continue to address your sister's situation in a reasonable manner," Grace said with a hint of sudden wariness.

Clearly reason was the goal here, and with Mark and Grace calmly looking on, it struck me just how good men are at agreeing upon exactly what "reason" is, how it should be pursued, and at what cost achieved.

"How is she?" Mark asked, now resuming his seat.

I answered with the only accurate description. "Drugged," I told him. "But still herself."

It was obvious that this was not a description in which Mark took comfort.

"And her mental state?" Grace asked.

As if she had suddenly materialized in the room, I saw

Diana sitting beside me, still beneath a harsh light, bathed in white ruin. "She quoted *Moby-Dick*," I told him. "There's something indestructible about her."

Grace eased himself into a chair. We were all in somber business suits and appropriately shined shoes, three reasonable men about the business of a woman's fate.

"So," Grace began. "I know that none of us expected that terrible scene at the library, but I also think it confirmed just how serious the situation had become with Diana." He was looking at me, soliciting agreement.

I nodded, then glanced to my left and noticed Mark peeking at his watch.

"And because of that I think we can draw certain conclusions that might have seemed extreme prior to the attack," Grace went on.

The word "attack" struck me as somewhat extreme in itself, but not as incontestably bizarre and jarring as Mark's sudden need to know the hour.

"Wouldn't you agree, Dave?" Grace asked in his familiarly solicitous tone.

As if roused by a trumpet whose distant call had all but faded, I suddenly found it in me to assume the role of Diana's attorney. "She was defending herself," I said.

"Defending herself?" Mark barked like a man whose drifting attention had just been called to a bloody scene. "You call what Diana did, 'defending' herself?"

His tone gave off a dismissive mockery, and in response my manner hardened.

"Yes, I do," I said.

Mark looked at me wonderingly. "She punched a cop, Dave."

"Maybe she didn't know he was a cop," I offered with a lawyerly shrug.

"What Diana knows or doesn't know is pretty much up for grabs, wouldn't you say?" Mark asked.

Able lawyer that he was, Grace immediately grasped that the discussion had taken a perilous turn, all of us in a ship that was clearly heading for the rocks.

"A moment, gentlemen," he said gently. He made a subtle calming gesture that Mark instantly heeded, like a dog told to sit.

"We have reached a juncture," Grace said. "I'm sure that's clear to all present. So the issue is, what is to be done with Diana?"

I looked at Mark and decided to test the waters.

"You filed the complaint," I said. "What now?"

Mark glanced at Grace, and by that gesture clearly asked for guidance.

"I'm sure Mark doesn't want to be unreasonable," Grace said. "We're only concerned with what's best for everyone involved, including Diana." He waited a beat, then asked, "So, what do you propose, Dave?"

In the following silence, I heard Diana's voice in recitation and suddenly remembered with unexpected vividness and accuracy the lines she'd quoted to the Old Man as he sat, already dead, by the window:

I have come to the borders of sleep,
The unfathomable deep
Forest where all must lose
Their way, however straight,
Or winding, soon or late;
They cannot choose.

Then she'd kissed the Old Man's brow, and added the citation she knew he would have required of her. "Edward Thomas," she said. "'Lights Out.'"

"Diana never abandoned anyone," I said quietly. "Not her father. Not Jason. She never found someone else's suffering . . ." I stopped and looked at Mark. ". . . distracting."

The proposal I then made seemed based on some ancient formula that was itself derived from the inescapable evidence of all human life, the ills and torments we cannot foresee, the rash acts and dreadful consequences, the plans that shake God with derisive laughter, all our knowledge hardly knowledge at all, with no dependable route through the cloud of unknowing.

"I'll take care of her," I said. "Like she took care of Jason and my father." Then, as if suddenly swept clear of all my old resentments, I felt, for the first time in my life, the strange luxury of selflessness, how, by it alone, we gauge success.

Mark looked at me warily, then turned to Grace. "Those pictures of my car, do you still have them?"

Grace nodded.

"Give them to Dave," Mark said.

Grace opened a drawer of his desk, retrieved the photographs and offered them to me.

I didn't take them from him. "What do I want with those?" I asked.

Mark snatched the pictures from Grace's hand and thrust them toward me. "To remind you of what Diana did," he said. "And that it's up to you to make sure she doesn't do anything like it again."

I took the pictures as if he'd challenged me to do so. "Fair enough," I told him.

Grace seemed relieved that it was over, another shaky vessel stirred into safe harbor. "Fine, then," he said to me pleasantly. "Let's consider the matter settled."

Which we did," you tell Petrie. "But it wasn't settled."

The play of fate, its blind workings, are briefly visible in his face. You see the times it has handed down some arbitrary judgment, swerving cars and ricocheting bullets, that little shadow in the X-ray that sets everything aside, turns unencumbered future into guarded aftermath.

For the first time, he asks a vaguely philosophical question. "Do you think it ever could have been settled?"

You imagine the outcome you'd had in mind when you'd imagined it all settled. You enjoy family outings, anniversaries with Abby. You watch Patty grow into adulthood and Diana grow old in study and achievement. Then you are in Diana's apartment, glancing, awestruck, from wall to wall.

"No," you answer.

The scene abruptly changes and you are in your car, driving away, everything settled. Stewart Grace's office building fills the rearview mirror. Its windows reflect a score of suns, and all of them are bright and full of promise. You are captured by the air's radiance. You are happy. You have never been so happy. Even now, you smile as you remember it.

"I thought I was like Diana, at last," you tell Petrie. "That I had succeeded at something. Saved Patty from Diana. Saved Diana from herself. Now I could bring Diana home. We could all help take care of her. Patty wouldn't see her as some kind of god, but just as someone who needed help. Because it had worked, you see, my idea. My idea. Not Diana's. Mine. It had worked like a charm." The suns dim in the windows of Grace's office building as you move away, and in the distance, you glimpse a gathering of clouds, but their dark, approaching line gives no hint of warning. "I even thought my father might be proud."

TWENTY-THREE

The drive to Brigham took only a few minutes. At the desk I explained that the complaint against Diana had been voluntarily withdrawn and that the aggrieved party, namely Mark, had agreed to have her released into my custody.

I already knew what the rather kindly administrator told me, that Stewart Grace had phoned ahead to confirm everything I'd just said, and that the police had done the same, so that no official charges had been pressed against my sister.

She was sitting on her bed when I came into the room, and at the first flash of her eyes, I saw that the earlier sedation had worn off somewhat, though she remained subdued and oddly weakened, like someone at the end of a long journey.

"Davey," she said.

"We're leaving now," I told her. "I'm going to take you home."

She remained in place, made no effort to rise from the bed. "*The House of Mirth*," she said, almost to herself.

It was the book my father had cradled in his arms the day we'd driven him back to Victor Hugo Street, a cold winter day, with snow covering the lawn and the walkway and outlining the bare trees in white.

"I remember how terrified he was," I said.

In memory I followed behind as Diana and the Old Man made their slow way down the snow-covered walkway.

Diana seemed to return to that same stark moment. "Because he didn't know what he'd done to be put in Brigham," she said.

I walked over to her and drew her to her feet. "I want you to stay with us for a while, okay?"

She nodded.

"Do you need anything from your apartment?"

I saw a sudden, nearly volcanic agitation in her eyes.

"No," she said. "No."

She remained silent during the ride home, and when Abby and Patty came out to meet her, she greeted them with a weary nod and a quiet, broken, "Hi."

"You can stay in the room next to mine," Patty told her, then, with an unforgiving glance toward me, gathered her aunt protectively beneath her arm.

At dinner a few minutes later, Diana remained distinctly subdued. I didn't know whether her general unresponsiveness was due to the drugs she'd been given or whether she was still drifting in the shock waves of what had happened to her during the last few hours.

After dinner we all strolled into the den. I draped my jacket on a small peg by the door, slipped into a pair of loafers, then browsed the wall of videos I'd collected over the years. "Let's make it a comedy," I said as I scanned the titles. "*Monkey Business.* With Cary Grant and Marilyn Monroe," I added brightly. "Is that okay with you, Diana?"

Diana's eyes had never seemed more intensely focused. I could see that she was working through a complicated matter, but it seemed hardly the time to question her.

"Okay with you, Abby?" I asked.

Abby nodded silently, something oddly stricken in her face. "Fine," she said.

We played the movie, but after a time, Diana said that she was tired. Patty rose immediately and escorted her to the guest room Abby had prepared. For a time they talked together. I didn't try to listen, but only made my way down the corridor to my bedroom. Patty's door was slightly open, and I noticed the books strewn about on her bed and across the floor. Her desk was cluttered with them, too, and over the desk, she'd printed out a fragment and taped it to her wall ... *a Web, dark and cold, throughout all the tormented element.*

"Diana's asleep now."

I turned to find Patty standing beside me. "William Blake," she said.

I touched her face. "I know," I told her. Then I went to my bedroom, and, to my surprise, dropped off to sleep almost immediately.

And so I didn't hear Diana when she got up later that

night, didn't hear her pad down the corridor and turn into the den, didn't see her close in upon my hanging jacket, reach into its breast pocket, and draw out the photographs of Mark's car I'd sunk into it, and which she must earlier have glimpsed at some point, but held her fire, and waited until she could see, in solitude and loneliness, exactly what she'd done.

It had begun to rain when I awoke suddenly. Dawn was just breaking, but I made no effort to return to sleep. Instead, I rose and headed for the kitchen. On the way, I noticed that Diana's door was slightly ajar, then peeped into the room to find her bed unruffled.

A terrible jolt went through me, cold and yet electric, and which froze my nerves and set them aflame at the same time. I didn't bother to wake Abby or Patty, but simply dressed as fast as I could and bolted out the door. I didn't know where Diana might have gone, but it was too early for Mark to be at the research center, and so I headed first for Diana's apartment.

I got there a few minutes later, and, like a well-mannered little boy, knocked at the door. When no one answered, I tried the door, found it unlocked, and stepped into the room.

In the shock of what I saw at that instant, I felt as if some invisible lever had been pulled, and I'd plunged through the gallows floor of this world and dropped into a wholly separate and self-contained reality. The walls were festooned with layers of pages printed from the Internet, photographs of fossils, long passages of ancient script, and hundreds of hieroglyphics. Other pictures depicted what appeared to be sites of ancient ritual, stone altars and stone-lined playing fields. The names of scores of ancient peoples had been written in large block letters and connected to one another in a spidery web of interlacing white strings. Still another wall was dotted with musical notations, along with photographs of stone pillars and prehistoric obelisks. Paintings of Gaia, the Earth Mother, hung all about, along with random pages copied from books about forensic science, studies of everything from fingerprinting to ballistics to the rate bodies decay at various levels of temperature and exposure, and everywhere slips of yellow paper were pinned like dead insects to every available surface, doors and window frames, along the edges of her desk, the lifeless hulls of her once living quest.

I knew that somewhere in all that mass were Cheddar Man and Windeby Girl, but all of that seemed long ago, truly ancient history compared to the immediacy of the moment, my need to find Diana.

And so I dashed to the bathroom, knocked at its closed door. There was no answer, so I eased it open, saw nothing there, and closed it again. Then, as if in a movie, I saw Diana skirt by the still-open door of the apartment, then heard the rapid thud of her feet on the stairs as she rushed up them.

"Diana," I called.

But she didn't stop or slow or even glance back to see me in full pursuit. On the fifth floor, I heard the creak of a metal door, then the sound of Diana's feet pounding across the roof of the building. She had already reached the wrought-iron rail at the edge of the roof when I came through that same door seconds later.

"Diana!" I cried.

She stared at me through a veil of rain, unsure, or so she seemed, both of my voice and my physical presence, unable to trust what she heard and saw.

"Diana," I said softly. I stretched my hand out to her. "Diana."

She stared at me brokenly. "I'm like Dad," she said.

"No, you're not," I told her.

"Yes, I am," she said. "I always have been."

"That's not true."

"Voices," she said. "Voices, Davey. Always."

"No," I told her.

She looked at me indulgently, as if I were an innocent. "Why do you think I came home? Why do you think I took you to the closet?"

The memory rose like a hand from the covering soil, the image of a little girl in a blue dress, easing a red rubber ball from my hand, tugging me from where I sat on the front stairs, then down the corridor and into a small closet where I sat in the darkness, as if it were a game of hide-and-seek, all the time listening to the small, child's voice that echoed through me now, echoing just as it had so many years before, down the stairs and along the corridor of the house on Victor Hugo Street, and finally into the closet where I huddled in the darkness, a calming, restorative voice, the one she'd always used to cool my father's crazy ire.

"Over the Mountains
Of the Moon,
Down the Valley of the Shadow,
Ride, boldly ride,"
The shade replied—
"If you seek for El Dorado."

"The closet," I repeated.

I remembered the dry powdery smell of my mother's old clothes still lingering in the air around me, clothes my father, during his various bouts of delirium, would sometimes retrieve and caress. But it was the voice I'd clung to in that darkness, Diana's voice, soft and sweet, drawing the deadly point of my father's paranoid delusion away from me as if it were a knife at my throat.

"Because they told me to," Diana said. "Because he was going to kill you, Davey."

Other memories suddenly returned to me with a jarring immediacy and physicality, so that I felt my hand tucked inside Diana's, her grip firm as she led me out of any room my father entered that afternoon and night, reciting to him as she drew me from his view.

"The voices told me that," Diana said. "And I believed them." She turned, grasped the dripping black railing, and looked out over the edge of the building, far in the distance, to where Dolphin Pond lay behind a shroud of mist. "They told me that day, too," she said. She faced me. "That day with Jason. They said, *Don't go.* But I didn't listen." She stared at me brokenly. "Because I thought that if I listened, it would mean that I was crazy."

She reached into the pocket of her coat and withdrew the photographs of Mark's car she'd taken from my jacket.

"I'm like Dad," she said.

I took a small step and stretched my arms toward her. "No, you're not," I told her.

She drew a tangle of wet hair from her eyes, and eased herself up onto the slippery rail, where she sat, holding on to it with such force her hands seemed like steel claws.

"You didn't do that!" I cried, desperate to stop her. "I did it, Diana. I painted Mark's car."

She looked at me quizzically, and for a moment seemed to believe me. Then something deep within her appeared at once to break and mend.

"Oh, Davey," she said, "you're the best brother in the world."

Then she thrust herself backward at what seemed an impossible speed.

I rushed to the rail and stared down, hoping against all reason that the arms of Gaia might receive her.

But there was only empty air, and so she fell and fell.

Petrie releases a long, weary breath, and you are still enough of a movie fan to recall the priest to whom Salieri confesses in *Amadeus*, how young and hopeful he is when Salieri begins his tale, how worn and shaken when he finishes it.

"But was it you?" he asks in dark astonishment.

You see the brush, the little can of bloodred paint, feel the weight of them in your hands. The black night into which you carried them sweeps in upon you, and you find yourself again crouched beside the car, splashing the word onto its dark surface, MURDERER. But what you remember most is the demonic glee you felt with each swipe of the brush, the bristling, febrile triumph, how at last you had outsmarted her.

"Yes," you answer.

To your surprise, Petrie does not walk you through the steps of your rash act, nor seeks any further explanation of it, and in that choice you sense how far he has waded into the fearful river of yourself, grasps the long vigil of your treasured wrong. You are clear to him now, a crystal stream, Diana the sole remaining mystery.

His question does not surprise you.

"What was she looking for?" Petrie asks.

You are in Diana's apartment now, two days after her death, clearing the walls of the vast array of information she'd gathered around her in a kind of mad cocoon.

"Evidence," you answer.

You see how wild her search was, the hours and hours of tracing linguistic patterns, the history of sound, the viscosity of stone and wood, bicameral theory, linguistics, primitive ritual, studies of "miraculous" intervention, people warned not to get on planes that later crash, ships that later sink, warned by "voices" as she had been.

"But not specifically for Jason's murder," you add.

"For what then?" Petrie asks.

"For trusting what she heard or not trusting it." You pause, try to bring it all together in your mind, grasp the impossible knowledge Diana sought. "How we know things we can't know. The difference between madness and intuition. That was part of it, I think. I'll never know it all."

Petrie turns this over in his mind. There is nowhere to go with any of it, and so he centers himself in the knowable world again, witnesses he can see, words he can take down, voices whose reality he can trust. "When she believed that Mark murdered Jason, was she crazy?" he asks.

You feel the heft of a fallen limb as you grasp it, primitive, apelike, as if it were the first weapon, you the first to wield it.

"No," you answer.

Petrie's eyes draw away from you, as if from the vapors of a witch's brew. "I see," he murmurs.

You know what he sees, but say it only in your mind. *Four deaths.*

He pauses a moment. You know where his imagination has taken him, that he is, in his mind, standing at the gate of Salzburg Garden.

"I didn't plan it," you tell him, then think, *I only heard the voice.*

TWENTY-FOUR

Diana was buried in Salzburg Garden on a day warmer and brighter than usual for the season. In the great trees that dotted the cemetery, autumn was in full riot, and so we stood in a steady rain of flaking red and yellow and gold.

Arrayed like opposing forces on a field of battle, Abby and Patty and I took up our position on one side of the grave while Mark occupied the other, his unchanging lab-work attire of dark pants and white shirt concealed beneath a black wool overcoat. He'd turned the collar up against the wind and sunk his hands deep inside the pockets of his coat. He kept his head bowed as the coffin was lowered into the ground, but when he lifted it again, he didn't look at me directly but with a quick, slanting glance, the way he'd looked at Diana in court the day Jason's death had been declared an accident.

When the coffin came to rest, I nodded briefly to Mark,

turned to leave, then stopped abruptly. Diana had had hundreds of quotations stored in her head, and suddenly it seemed that so did I, for one I'd thought long lost stepped forward abruptly, like a solider called to duty. They were the words Shakespeare had placed in the mouth of a delusional man, but one who, in his madness, had divined the truth. Hamlet's last words whispered in my mind. *The rest is silence.*

And a voice said, *Not yet.*

Abby and Patty had moved on ahead a few paces, but they stopped and turned back when they noticed that I was no longer in their midst.

"Go on to the car," I told them. "I want to talk to Mark."

They'd already walked some distance down the slope by the time Mark came up beside me.

"I'm so sorry, Dave," he said. "The complaint. Taking Diana to Brigham. Now this." He shook his head. "I never meant for anything like this to happen." He placed his hand consolingly on my shoulder. "So sorry, Dave."

I stared evenly into his two glass eyes. "Are you sure about that, Mark?"

"Sure of what?"

"Sure you're sorry."

Mark drew his hand from my shoulder. "Of course, I am. Why would you ask me something like that?"

"I've been thinking about something you said to Diana," I answered. "You told me, yourself. That you thought it was better about Jason. Better that he was dead."

Mark watched me silently, as if I were a dark bird circling overhead.

"You wanted to put him away, didn't you?" I asked.

"Put him away?"

"Some institution. Out of sight."

"I wouldn't put it exactly that way, but yes," Mark admitted. "He wasn't ever going to get any better and so he was . . ."

"Useless."

"That's a harsh word."

"How about this? A hindrance."

"To what?"

"To you." I paused, then added, "A distraction."

"Distraction?" Mark watched me coolly, but I could see an edginess building in him. "Is that what you really think, Dave, that I'm glad Jason's dead?"

I stared at him dead on. "Diana too."

Mark was a tower of self-control. "I don't have to listen to this."

I knew that this was true, that all he had to do was turn on his heel and walk away. Then the rest really would be silence. That was more than I could accept, and so I took a plunge into the dark.

"Did you kill Jason?" I asked.

His eyes widened. "What?"

"Was Diana completely wrong?"

"How can you ask me such a thing, Dave?" He glanced at his watch like a man bored by a tedious subject. "I have to go," he said.

"Did Diana know something, Mark?" I asked. "Hear something? She did with my father, you know."

Mark looked as if he could not imagine the conversation

in which he was involved, but knew no way to extricate himself from it. "What did she hear?"

"That he was going to kill me."

Mark heaved his shoulders in a weary sigh. "I have to go," he repeated.

The voice spoke through me. "Not yet," I said.

Mark tried to step past me, but I'd felt something during the previous exchange, that I'd sunk a dark hook into an even darker water, and there was something on the line.

"How did your badge get to the pond?" I asked.

"Now you're relying on Diana's evidence?" Mark scoffed. He drew in a long exasperated breath. "Dave, let me pass, please."

I shook my head. "Not yet," I said again.

He looked at me sternly. "This is ridiculous, and I won't—"

"How did your badge get to the pond?" I demanded.

He appeared fiercely offended by the question, but the offense struck me as manufactured. I didn't know how his badge had ended up on the bank of Dolphin Pond, or anything else about that morning. I knew only that Mark was a small, shallow man, and that he was glad Diana was dead, because in death she would not be able to distract him.

"Answer the question," I said.

"This is not a courtroom, Dave. This is not a trial."

"Diana said that you—"

"That I murdered my son, yes, I know," Mark snapped, and again tried to step past me.

I blocked his way and fixed him in a steely squint. "But do you know that she had evidence?"

He froze in place. "What evidence?"

"A witness."

"To what?"

"To what happened that day."

"Diana found a witness?" Mark repeated doubtfully, but not without a hint of unease.

And so I went for broke. "Saw and heard everything, this witness. Everything that happened on Dolphin Pond."

The tense laugh that broke from him was utterly false, a stage gesture.

"And so you're not going to get away with it, Mark," I told him.

I saw a tiny fissure split his earlier assurance that with Diana dead it was over now, the twin distractions of his son's imperfection and his wife's search for evidence at last behind him.

"What witness did Diana find?" Mark asked.

His tone held a dismissive challenge, but it was not the dismissiveness of utter innocence in the face of groundless accusation. I didn't know what Mark had done that day, but I knew he had done something. He might simply have sunk into his work and so let Jason wander from the house. Or he might have taken him to the fence, set his gaze on the pond, then left Jason there. Or he might have led him to the gate, or he might have opened the gate, or he might have opened the gate and badge in hand coaxed his son to the water's edge. He might even have tugged him into the pond, beyond the shallow water, and set him adrift to drown.

"Who is this witness?" Mark demanded.

I let a beat go by, then another and another, watching as my silence intensified the strange sense of dire anticipation Mark was trying so hard to conceal.

Another beat, then I said, "The ear of earth."

It was only the subtlest change in the eyes, like a tiny candle suddenly flickering from behind a vast wall of candles, but it was clear exactly what he'd felt at that moment, and that it was . . . relief. Relief because he knew, as I now did, that something really had happened that day, something that lay somewhere on the continuum between wishing Jason dead and murdering him.

"A stone?" Mark yelped. "That's the witness Diana found?" He laughed. "A stone?" he repeated. Then the laughter broke off and he glared at me darkly. "You'd better watch yourself, Dave," he warned, "or you'll end up like your sister."

He seemed grand and self-confident again, certain that in the end I would prove no more distracting than Jason or Diana, creatures that buzzed for a time, but could ultimately be brushed away. He might even have been right, had not the voice spoken again, a voice as clear and distinct as any that had spoken to Diana, and which was no less demanding to be heard and heeded.

The voice said, *Hit him!*

And so I did.

Mark staggered backward with the first blow and covered the lower two-thirds of his face with hands that were instantly bloody. The voice repeated its command, and I hit him again and he stumbled back farther, his eyes filled with horrified amazement that this crazy thing was actually happening, that in a neat little Protestant cemetery on a radiant New England day, he was being attacked, fiercely and repeatedly and without mercy by, of all things, an undistinguished, small-time lawyer.

Hit him.

I hit him again, and this time he fell onto his back, where he rolled left and right, like a confused child in the face of terrible violence from an unexpected source, whimpering and pleading. The voice said, *Like Jason.*

I leaped upon him with all my weight, yanked his hands from his face, pinned his arms beneath my legs, and reached for the fallen limb that lay beside me, and which seemed to have been placed there long ago. I grasped its heavy, rounded bulk and lifted it far, far above my head.

Then two voices split the cloud that covered me, piercing, female. *Dave! Dad! Stop!*

And so I did.

T he rest," you say, "is silence."

Petrie nods heavily.

"Yes," he says.

There is a knock at the door. It opens. You see a plainclothes officer and wonder if it is the same one who came for Diana at the library, chased her, tumbled with her onto the hard, bare floor.

"We got word," he says.

Petrie walks out of the room and closes the door behind him. When he returns, you see an odd surprise in his expression, an ending he did not expect, your twisting story with a final twist.

"Mark's conscious," Petrie tells you. "It looks like he's going to recover."

You think, *So only three deaths. Not four.*

"We're releasing you on your own recognizance," Petrie adds.

"Why?"

"Your lawyer and Stewart Grace have agreed to it."

"Which means that Mark isn't going to press charges."

"That seems to be the case," Petrie says.

Mark's decision does not surprise you. Pressing charges would take time. It would mean a trial, and all a trial entails. He would have to confront your motive in attacking him, and address it. The word you painted on his car would swim again in the air around him. "Murderer." He would not be well served by its repetition. Besides, he has his breakthrough to consider. He does not wish to be distracted.

You look at your hands and marvel that they are intact, that the force of bone on bone has not left your fingers mangled.

"What now?" you ask.

"You're free to go," Petrie tells you. "I'll walk you out."

There is paperwork, as there always is. You go through the routine, sign the various waivers, along with the inventory of what you'd had in your possession at the moment of arrest, your wallet along with everything that was in it, cash and credit cards, your driver's license, the paltry evidence of your life.

"You're lucky, you know," Petrie says as you gather up your things. "You could have killed him. One swing of that limb, and you probably would have."

You say nothing, but only move as Petrie directs you, down yet another corridor to the lobby of the police station, then through it to the front of the building.

Before he releases you, he stops, faces you. "Let this be the end of it," he warns you.

You walk out of the station. Night has fallen. You look up into the cloudless sky, then draw your gaze downward, into the parking lot where, in the distance, Abby waits to take you home.

"Dad?"

Patty steps out from behind one of the building's brick columns. She looks apprehensive, edgy, unsure of what to say or do. You see a dark brilliance sparkling in her eyes, a long-suppressed intelligence, all of it buried beneath the layers of mediocrity your fear imposed upon her. You cannot know where her freed mind will take her. You know only that wherever she goes, throughout all the tormented element, you will go there with her, remain steadfastly at her side.

You draw her protectively into your arms and declare the only truth you know. "I'll always take care of you."

She remains briefly in your embrace, then steps out of it. "Ready to go home?" she asks.

A voice says, *Say you are.*

And so you do.